REBEL WITHOUT A MASK

A Sci-Fi Comedy That Takes No Prisioners

PLANET HY MAN
BOOK 4

KERRIE A NOOR

REBEL WITHOUT A MASK

by

Kerrie A Noor

CONTENTS

GLOSSARY

Voted Ins: Planet Hy Man's politicians. A contradiction in terms as they were never voted in. In the past, they were also known as the "Blue-Rinse Brigade," when they were young enough for hair dye to make a difference.

Whip: also known as a flesh-cracker. In the past used by Man Spies to round up men like cattle during the great coup 1958, now worn like a peacock parading its virility.

Man Spy: women bred to act like men, who captured any free men to be "cared for" and/or "appropriately employed" for the greater benefit of the planet.

Manifesto the Great: the last man to rule Planet Hy Man, he wrote his memoirs while still ruling. In fact, he was so busy writing that he didn't notice the great coup of 1958 until it was too late. His last few years were spent in exile, editing the *Hy Man's Geographic*, a magazine no one had read for years, which is now mainly used for lighting fires when the price of energy goes up. It was also he who developed the early stances of the *incognito pose*.

Incognito Pose: a pose adopted by robots and the masses, helping them to blend into the background, or at least let those of great importance know that they are not worth noticing.

Teflon: a by-product of egg popping, and a material like no other. It is so flexible that a robot made of it will never age and finds yoga as easy as the mere blink of an eye.

Telespray/Telespraying: inspired by Planet Hy Man's first truly scientific woman who had a crush on *Star Trek*'s Captain Kirk. She was an enthusiastic shower-maker who designed a power shower so strong it moved women from inside the shower to outside—she saw the potential.

For a while it was all the rage for the Voted In as they telesprayed from one shop to the next, frightening shop assistants until the shop assistants rebelled and started charging *startle* charges.

Cheese Pizza: a secret passion for many on Planet Hy Man. Once someone discovered how to make hemp pulp *sort of* taste like cheese, the pizza was revived, celebrated, and eaten whenever possible. Hemp pulp never, however, managed to work in cheese sauce.

Caffeine Blast: coffee on Planet Hy Man is for the elite and was introduced mainly to keep the Voted In awake during meetings.

Illegal Beverage: caffeine for the masses is as illegal as bootlegging was on Earth. Keeping the masses alert is greatly discouraged by those in charge; weak decaffeinated tea is all they are allowed.

Egg Popping: a recently accepted profession established by the first retired man spy. Eggs (also known as valuable real-estate) from a successful woman can earn her a tidy commission—which Mex was banking on to provide her with a better robot than the damnable Pete.

Contemplation of the Navel: a practice recognized by the robot-training board as an adequate way of making the passing of time productive, as well as cutting down on minding others' business.

Arts and Stuff: anything gift-wrapped.

Limo Drivers: the last driver retired years ago and now mans the footman's residents' reception. He never remembers any names but he does a good toasted hemp pulp.

The Scent of an Identity: women who have a "longing" or a "something is missing" feeling are more susceptible to the scent than contented women. Men are completely immune.

ESP-ing: the ability to communicate without speaking aloud; a form of mind reading. Outlawed on Planet Hy Man as it made bugging —a truly profitable pastime—pointless.

Messenger: an envelope-like device that usually contained orders of an unpopular nature.

H-Pad: looks like an iPad but has the ability to answer back and is not nearly as much fun.

Sparkly: sparkling water that tastes like champagne, costs a bomb, and can cause great clarity of thought or at least the illusion of it.

Strengtheners: like straighteners, but also work as a bugging device. For years, much was collected from what women said while straightening their hair, until it was discovered that what they talked about while grooming was pretty much the said grooming. Scientists are currently working on a handless set.

The earphone: when Manifesto the Great saw these on a Star Trek repeats he was entranced, "at last a way to block out the chatter from the other half," he exclaimed.

Mind fudging: is the only defense for mind reading. It involves not thinking about what you want to think about but rather creating a thought decoy.

Blow up & blow out: a term used for H-Pads and the like, nobody is sure of the difference except a blow-out is preferable to a blow-up.

Tablet: a homemade sweet Scots claim as their own, sort of in between fudge, and toffee but carries greater mystical qualities.

Last hoorah home: bit like a rest home but with better sandwiches.

The C-Pad, H-pad, H-pad 11 and other pad malarkey: all forerunners of the iPad, which evolved with the *I know better than you* app some would call virus. The iPad metamorphosis from the C-Pad thanks to a liaison with Legless and very smart IT student during Legless's lost in San Francisco years.

A Scrapper: A forgotten element from a forgotten time on planet Hy Man when real animals roamed. A scrapper fed animals scraps from the food chain, it was a dirty job. Now the term is only used when pickle swearing will not do.

Hilda's energy plan: Similar to Beryl's but with more options.

Balancing platform: Hilda dreamed of a balancing platform from the day she was first ask to go out and pick herbs in the compound. She looked at the muddy field and thought there must be a better way.

Jock strap: One of man's best kept secrets on Planet Hy Man. All men on Planet Hy Man looked well-endowed and woman never knew why.

Alice: similar to Amazon's Alexa's with many of *the I know better than you* bugs still intact. No metamorphizes or IT students involved.

MEET THE GANG-PLANET HY MAN

Legless: a man from Planet Hy Man who is past his prime. No one knows why he is called Legless, but he is a man who gave up his pony-tail for the woman he loved.

Beryl: a woman way past her prime. She is the ex-leader of Planet Hy Man and almost resigned to it.

Mex: an ex-Man Spy with little to do but annoy her allies, Woody and Pete.

Woody: Happily employed on Planet Hyman, despite his earth origins.

Vegas: Once Hilda's side kick she now advices H2 the ruler, using logic, common sense and more logic .

Hilda: Has lost everything but is ambitious enough to claw it all back.

Pete: Mex's ex-robot or ex-android as he would call himself, has moved onto bigger things than Mex's laundry.

Don: a cabbie from Glasgow with a soft spot for the character below . . .

Bunnie: a round woman who puts one in mind of Dawn French. She has a way with men, dogs, and lonely women. Except in times of stress, when she throws such "ways" to the wind for a more dominating/shouting approach.

DJ: a young DJ born in Glasgow. He is the same age as Woody and as tall as Woody is short. He is a man frustrated with his mentor, who is also the character below . . .

Archie: an Earthly pensioner who is old enough to know better and old enough not to care. His advice is ignored by many.

DBO: Second in command of Planet Hy Man and happy to stay that way.

H2: Rules Planet Hy Man with as much empathy as possible for a politician.

Pot, Prudence, and Pope: the other three Robot 33. Like Pete, they are clever but, unlike Pete, not shrewd enough to hide it.

Verruca: Is H2's gran a savvy woman who deserves a better name.

Alterationist: Women of hippy origin who can make anything from anything; recycling to them is second nature and what they can do with a potato sack is nothing short of a miracle.

New additions

Mandy: An Identity that pushes everything to the limit, including her gender.

Serenity: A pensioner who refuses to live up to her name.

Dolly: Serenity's pal in crime.

Molly: Don's mother. She does her best to keep Serenity and Dolly in line---not that they listen.

The Cook: Way more than a cook, she rules the hippy colony kitchen with an iron rolling pin.

Minor but still important

Statue workers/builders: Experts at making mountains out of mole hills . They have developed statue making into such an art-form Planet Hy Man can no longer afford them.

Sportswomen: A collection of women who think the statue workers take themselves way too seriously (and don't get them started on the Archeologist).

The Archeologist/Diggers: These women are so sharp they named themselves after earth archeologists, not that anyone on Planet Hy Man has heard of such humans.

PREVIOUSLY ON PLANET HY MAN

Thanks to Verruca's carefully constructed plan, and a carefully constructed vibrator, Hilda is as powerless as an electric toothbrush with no charge.

Vegas, realising that Hilda is mad, has jumped ship and joined forces with DBO, who she will follow to hell and back------ if necessary.

Mex, Woody Pete, and H2 finally find the "wiry thing" or component and "telespray" back to Planet Hy Man to head off the coup, arriving just in time to fight for "truth, justice, and the H2 way".

After an epic Star Wars-like battle that leaves Hilda crying into her not-so-deluxe caffeine, H2 is the new leader with new ideas and a new leadership team.

While Beryl and Legless have made peace, the sort of peace that involves Beryl occasionally staying over, sleeping on Legless's couch and Legless plotting to get her into his bed.

FOREWORD

March 2020—Lockdown is on the horizon.
PM says the UK can
"turn tide of coronavirus" in twelve weeks.

It was a couch like any other, covered in way too many cushions with the worst view in the room of the TV.

Izzie loved it, but then Izzie had a passion for corduroy.

As soon as she entered the living room, Izzie would jump on, bury her head under a cushion, and stay there until dragged out.

One day, she buried her head so far down that she had a panic attack, backing out of the darkness so fast she left her collar behind.

The same collar that had been to Planet Hy Man and back.

Not that anyone noticed. Until, that is, it was too late.

Chapter One

FOR THE LOVE OF BERYL

"One woman's orgasm is another's 'It was OK.'"–Legless after a few whiskies

Legless looked at Beryl: still and cool. She was breathing deeply but silent.

After making love, Beryl had dropped off quicker than a belch, hardly moving from her back—not a snore, a sniff, or even a mutter.

Years of maintaining a beehive hairdo can do that to a woman. Well, that and a childhood spent sleeping in a cabin bed the size of a small trunk.

Beryl always fell asleep before Legless, but tonight was different. They had made love, and now he was watching her.

It had been a long time.

He stared at the stars from their window.

No matter how many planetariums they had been to, he was still confused; he had no idea what stars were which. Sometimes he thought he recognized something, perhaps the Milky Way. He knew Planet Hy Man was somewhere in the same region; he had heard Beryl talk of it.

There were times he had looked at the stars and yearned for home, to go back, wreak havoc on Beryl and her Voted In's, cause a downfall, and have her at her knees.

But not now.

Tonight he looked at the stars through the exhausted eyes of a man after a satisfying shag. It had been a while, and despite Beryl's lack of interest, he had pulled it off, turned her on, pleased her like the good old days when they first "hooked up" on Earth.

He made his way downstairs, heated up yesterday's coffee, and, sipping with an "arrrrh," pulled out his writing implement.

He typed: "The Conquest of Beryl."

This will have them on the edge of their seat. He smiled. *They'll have to let me make a speech now* . . .

When they'd first slept together on Planet Hy Man, Legless had dropped off quicker than a nose dribble, his smooth face as peaceful as a monk.

Legless had taken Beryl by surprise; after a lusty eye exchange and a quick fumble, Legless led her to a cupboard of a room.

"Let's see what we have here," he whispered.

And before she had time to answer, her leathers were off, her corset untied and erect on the floor, and Beryl was gasping on a trolley the size of her childhood cabin bed.

He was a young man enjoying the luscious effects of Planet Hy Man's atmosphere. His nose was a silent hair-free breathing apparatus, while his bladder was strong, capable of holding a keg of beer without a dribble. And as for his apparatus, it was as efficient as a fire hose, quenching pent-up passion that took them both by surprise.

As Beryl's back arched in pleasure, he moaned, sighed, then rolled off, asleep before he hit the floor. Landing on a pile of laundry, he didn't feel a thing, let alone wake up, unaware that he had the legendarily coldhearted Beryl crying with laughter . . .

Years later, when Legless took Beryl for the first time on Earth, it was more a fumble, the eye exchange more wistful than lusty.

There was no comedy fall, more a delicious sigh as they lay, spread-eagled, with surprise. Neither had any idea that their body could pull off past antics with such precision.

Afterward, a sweaty and still-a-little-stunned Legless headed into the kitchen.

"Fancy a cuppa?" he yelled.

"OK," she yelled back with no idea what a cuppa was.

She slid under the sheets and almost giggled.

It had taken a few months for Legless to "conquer," as he liked to call it, despite Beryl visiting almost daily.

The sheltered accommodation Archie had arranged was not exactly what Beryl was looking for. She found the constant wandering of inmates a tad disturbing, the warden's early morning call as inspiring as the mobile hairdresser trying to talk Beryl into a "less dated" look.

She preferred Legless's home, and once she learned to drive, she was never out of the place, despite the mess, derelict cars, and broken hen house. She couldn't stay away.

Beryl had taken to driving like a child to McDonald's.

It had been a year since Beryl and Legless met in Edinburgh. A year since Bunnie, with a toot of her horn, picked Beryl and Legless up from the B&B, since Beryl first pressed the accelerator of a car . . .

Bunnie had been driving Beryl and Legless to their new home in Dunoon when a foot cramp struck like a sledgehammer.

Bunnie, mid steering, let out a shriek, and Beryl, without thinking, grabbed the wheel.

Her ability to maneuver Bunnie's four-wheel onto the Dunoon ferry surprised not only Bunnie but Beryl herself. She had only driven once—on Planet Hy Man—and she'd been so young she could hardly touch the peddles.

Legless, dozing in the back, jumped to attention, and before he could get a word in about gears, she was changing them, sliding Bunnie's four-wheel drive into a parking space like a seasoned taxi driver.

A year on, Beryl still jumped behind the wheel excited as a teenager in a porn shop.

She loved cars; she loved driving, especially to Legless's home and his animals—or his "menagerie," as he liked to call it.

She loved to stroke "Sophia," his scraggy cat, toss leftovers to his moth-eaten dog, Bark Twain, their earthy smells mesmerizing her until she let them inside.

Feeding his hens—or "the girls," as he liked to call them—fascinated her as much as their names: Gina, Lollo, Bridget, and Bardo. She could spend hours watching them, not to mention Charlton Heston the cockle with a strut so majestic even Bark Twain stopped to watch.

But what she loved most was to watch Legless light his fire for her to sleep by on the couch.

He had a nice back, apart from his thin ponytail trailing down it.

She never said anything, but Legless read her mind, and one day the ponytail was gone and Legless was feeling hopeful.

Beryl arrived to find Legless bent over the hearth, cleaning with a grunt.

He lit his standard minuscule fire lighter and waited for the flames to take hold.

The flames flickered, illuminating his perfect round skull. She stopped.

"Shall I get the blankets?" he said without turning around.

"Not tonight," she said.

He looked at her with a grin.

"Let's give that IKEA bed of yours a go," she whispered.

Bark Twain poked his head around the corner, took one look at Legless's naked rump straddled across Beryl, and made for the kitchen, his cushion, and a bowl of water.

Umpteen moans later, Beryl looked out from his IKEA bed with the sort of smile she hadn't cracked since Legless left Planet Hy Man. The sort of smile that would have the Voted Ins and Bunnie choking on their caffeine.

It was a smile that lit up her face; she glowed.

She had really missed Legless: the smell of his warm body, his ability to not only push the right button but do it for the best length of time . . . a knack not even human men knew of.

A couple of minutes under Legless's hands and she was back in that cupboard of a room getting to know her private bits like never before.

She slid further under the sheets, peering at the bedroom they had decorated together as Legless entered the room dribbling tea from two mugs.

She eyed his thin legs poking from his baggy boxers and started to laugh.

"No pickling milk," he muttered.

"Milk? That stuff from cows?" She pulled a face. "I heard it makes men grow breasts."

He looked at her, stuck out his flat chest, and laughed. "Like these?" he said.

She stared at his sprinkling of grey hairs and sighed.

He handed her a mug; she sipped, pulled a face.

"No caffeine?" she said.

"Not what you like," he muttered. "Packet stuff, way worse than that." He gestured to her mug.

She sipped again. The taste grew on her. A bit bitter, but . . . she gulped another mouthful, swallowed it down . . . it warmed her.

"I could get used to this," she finally said.

Soon he had a cupboard full and was trying teas like a true tea jenny. And each time Legless pleasured her, it was he who opened the cupboard and stared at the growing number of packets, shouting . . .

"Herbal? Earl Grey? What is Ma'am's pleasure today?"

Chapter Two

THE DRIVING INSTRUCTOR

"Within months of discovering tea in all its glory, Beryl also discovered a better place to live: a camper van."—Legless's memoir

For months they made love like newlyweds, so many times that Beryl lost count. But still she didn't move in, until he spied the camper van.

They were sauntering through the Barras, a marketplace in Glasgow, Beryl on the hunt for a good old-fashioned Nokia and Legless for something a little different, something to add a bit of spice to their lovemaking.

And there he saw it: a sixties VW camper van, complete with broken roof rack and more rust than paint.

Legless caught sight of the tiny run-down kitchen, the peeling walls, the ripped upholstery, and thought, *How many hours could they spent together sorting the van?*

She might even move in.

Beryl didn't notice it at first, nor the round, dark man under the bonnet; she was too busy rummaging through a box of vintage mobiles.

Legless did. He clocked the stall owner straight away. Feigning disinterest, he turned to catch Beryl lifting a grey Doro 7080.

She casually flipped it open.

"I'd stick to a Nokia," said Legless, "if you really must connect."

The round, dark man's ears pricked up. He turned, caught sight of Beryl's beehive, and assumed the "granny in leather" was a woman of

the sixties: a woman who'd spent her youth on the back of a motorbike, braless, with a reefer in her mouth and probably had her first ride
in a camper van . . .

He went for the hard sell.

"Nokia?" He said with a crisp slam of the bonnet. "I've a bucketful
here in the van."

The round, dark man sipped his 90p instant coffee.

"It's vintage," he said with a cough. "And a steal. Just needs a jump
start . . ."

Silence.

"I'll throw in a set of jump leads."

The round, dark man eyed Legless's skinny legs, skinny arse, skinny
shoulders, and ancient leather jacket. He had the look of someone who
slept with a motorbike . . . spent his days in the shed with a roll-up in
the corner of his mouth and memories of the sixties through the haze
of dope and sex.

He pulled out the bed and, with a "good as new," plonked himself
on it.

The bed squeaked but held his weight.

"This could expand our repertoire," Legless whispered in her ear.

Beryl, with no idea what he meant, ran her fingers along the
cracked bench and creaked open a cupboard. The door flopped to the
ground.

"And I'll throw in a box full of vintage Nokias," said the stall
owner.

They drove home to Dunoon, almost push-starting the van off the
ferry.

Fixing up the van was a bonding experience almost on par with
making love and collecting tea. They spent so much time together that
Beryl finally gave up her sheltered accommodation.

Legless was ecstatic.

They rocked the van with their lovemaking, drank tea as the sun
set, and for a while, Beryl forgot she had been a ruler, a woman in
control. Until, that is, she became a driving instructor.

A year on Earth had changed things, and the tea cupboard hadn't been opened for a while.

They rarely made love, and when they did, Beryl crashed out before he had time to boil a kettle.

Within months of becoming a driving instructor, she was too busy for him, and catching her attention was as hard as asking a football fan mid match what he wanted for tea.

In fact, that is how Legless now felt: forgotten, ignored, like the partner of said football fan mid World Cup.

She couldn't wait to jump in her car and start the day, while Legless —who had "been there, done that, and bought the T-shirt"—was left behind. Beryl had discovered a way to make a living, and she loved it; a pay packet was something new to her, something she ripped open with glee, even though she never bought anything.

She started a taxi service for those in the sheltered accommodation, delivering for Pizza Hut and teaching nervous women drivers well past their eighteen years.

Soon she was so busy she was never in, and Legless began to miss their visits to the planetarium, their weekends away in the camper van. She was even too busy to visit the "Women through the Ages" exhibition, her favorite; it inspired her the most.

He missed pushing a co-op trolley with her, her chuckling at his "buy one get one free" banter with a checkout attendant. He suggested taking a break in her camper van to explore the Highlands, but before he'd even brought home a brochure, she was off, the camper van as redundant as his appendage.

He may as well have been back on Planet Hy Man peddling a stationary . . . at least then she looked at his arse.

He closed his book and smiled. Had they turned a corner? Had he finally conquered her?

He slid his memoir back in its hiding place. *Or is this just a one-off?*

He thought of the look on her face . . . and told himself they had turned a corner, that he had "reclaimed, pulled down the drawbridge, and conquered." Then he slipped back into bed, wrapped his arms around Beryl, and was down for the count in minutes.

Hours later, as the sun rose, Beryl woke to gaze at Legless's wrinkled face contorting with each snore.

He slept like he was an action man in an adventure film, writhing about like a worm on a hook, which Beryl found strangely erotic—not that he was aware. Beryl never told him.

She made her way downstairs, her head full of the day ahead.

She had no idea he wrote about her, that he had been up all night drinking coffee, thinking of her.

She didn't even notice the coffee mess. She just poured herself one and headed out the door.

Chapter Three

THE NEW ROOM WITH A VIEW

"Never question a woman's orgasm, even if you haven't touched her."–Legless after a whisky

Beryl had just moved into the sheltered accommodation when shame struck her like a dose of heartburn. She felt guilty for her past treatment of Legless and, like any good ex-leader, decided the only way to make amends was to commission a statue.

Beryl, now in contact with H2, began a nagging campaign. Persuading H2, however, was another story.

H2, a socialist from her bog-standard haircut to her no-frills H-Pad, ruled with an "every woman's equal" policy.

She created foot rubs for all, public holidays for robots, and a "dress-up day" to celebrate Verruca's saving of the planet (a particularly painful day for Hilda when she rarely ventured out). She scaled down the room with a view, replacing portraits of past leaders with an "ideas board" and the gigantic meeting table with an "everyone has their say" meeting table—a table so small that those around it could smell what the others had for breakfast.

She dismembered the chandeliers of the room with a view; placed one in the updated, extra-large "training for the masses" emporium; and doled out the rest in small pieces like medals to those who "gave their all."

And, with her new, innovative "our policies are an open book" campaign, gave Deidre, Planet Hy Man's top reporter, full access to everything—including what Beryl had been up to.

She was hardly the sort of leader to erect statues, especially on the orders of a past top-heavy regime. Beryl pulled her best bribes, and when that didn't work, she appealed to H2's better nature—and when *that* didn't work, she nag-messaged.

"Legless did discover the spark plug, saved the energy crisis . . ." she messaged a million times.

H2 raised her concerns at the daily meeting with her leadership team: Vegas, DBO, and Alice.

Alice, a ball of a robot, circled the room with a view like an extra-large super-charged snooker ball. "Socialism *is* a bit drab," she said.

"Perhaps something with a splash of color," said Vegas.

H2 skulled her caffeine. She could see the Operators, the hippie colony, and the field-workers swallowing that argument.

The Operators were still a little miffed about H2's "give everyone a second chance, including robots" policy, which the hippie colony embraced until they realized they weren't included.

The Operators felt there were "some who had more chances than an alcoholic."

Deloris's column had included several inflammatory remarks—talk of the field-workers and hippies uniting, breaking away, flying their own flag—until DBO suggested they take over the planet's "dress-up day."

A deal was struck involving the Darth Vader outfits Verruca and Hilda had worn in their much-talked-about fight of the century.

Soon, fields were covered in scarecrows dressed in *Star Wars* outfits . . . and a day off was allocated for dancing around them with sticks covered in burnt tofu and wrestling.

Some would say it was a piss take, but as H2 was a people pleaser to the core, she chose to see it as women having the freedom to express themselves.

The door creaked open, and H2's footman shuffled in sporting his latest recycled-but-cozy leisure suit, now so old he was permanently bent in foot rub mode. He stopped at the caffeine corner, made to fill a cup, and stumbled.

DBO jumped up and, with an "I'll get it" sigh, took him to his seat. "Ignore it," she snapped, thrusting a mug under the footman's nose.

"I'd run a mile from the whole statue thing," said Pete. "It only leads to trouble."

The footman inspected his mug with a sniff. "Unless, of course . . ." He looked up with his best poignant look. "You want to please the statue workers."

"Ruling is not about pleasing," said Vegas.

"They *are* at a loose end," said DBO.

"And there are still plenty of off cuts from the table," said Alice.

The team shifted uncomfortably.

The coffee table project went down like a stink bomb. H2 had recycled the giant meeting table into coffee tables for the field-workers. The field-workers who sat by fires for their tea break took one look at the table perched in the mud and chopped it into kindling.

Vegas looked at H2 with mixed feelings.

Many would have blinged up their outfit once in power; not H2. She, grimly hanging on to her "woman of the women" beliefs, remained in her orange jumpsuit, despite Vegas expressing her doubts . . .

Vegas had seen leaders come and go as quickly as the unrolling of a toilet roll. "It was all about faith," she said, "inspiration," and an orange jumpsuit was hardly going to do that.

"You'll need to do something," said Alice. "That Beryl can nag like there's no tomorrow; she'll never give up."

"That's true," muttered DBO.

"And it won't take long for Hilda to hear," said Alice.

The team looked at each other; the footman tutted. "I told you so," he coughed.

"Yes, so you keep telling me," snapped H2.

"I did warn about all this *open book* malarky—"

"I know."

"—but would you listen?"

"All right," hissed H2. "How was I to know Legless could cook?"

"And that Beryl could drive," said Alice.

The room fell silent.

H2's "open book" theory seemed like a good idea. If the masses knew how shit Beryl's life was, they'd realize how lucky they were . . .

But Deidre's "What's Eating Beryl?" column had the opposite effect. Everyone knew that meat was eaten on Earth, but Deidre's exaggerated stories of Legless's pasta and roasts had many drooling.

H2, in an attempt to "balance things out," did commission a column about Quorn and Japanese tofu claiming that many Earth people didn't eat meat and were "the better for it." But how could she compete with pictures of Beryl wiping her chin after a particularly succulent chicken, or Legless producing his famed cheesy lasagna from the oven?

And Deidre's recent "Driving Earth up the Wall" article didn't help either.

It had the market stall workers so jealous they could spit. Despite Earth being full of men, Beryl seemed to have the sort of luxurious driving-about freedom they could only dream of. And as they trotted through the dry, hard soil every day to work, it grated on them like a pebble in their shoe.

H2 poured another caffeine and stirred.

"Easy on the cream," muttered the footman.

Vegas looked at him. "Cream helps her think." She turned to her hero. "What you need is something to inspire, uplift."

"Thank you, Vegas."

"Something that pulls us all together, and perhaps something more than a jumpsuit?"

"I'm not changing my jumpsuit," snapped H2. "I told you before, utopia *is* equality."

"Vegas has a point, ma'am," said Alice.

"And don't call me *ma'am*."

"The masses need something to look up to, aim for."

"And don't call them *the masses*."

"Perhaps a foot massage?" said the footman.

The others pulled faces.

He slid off his sock to reveal the sort of foot that would shock a podiatrist. He wiggled his toe. "Get the ol' grey matter working."

She sighed and nodded.

He handed her a mask and gloves as the team, apart from Alice, left the room.

Foot-rubbing helped H2 think, and she could go through quite a few.

The elderly footman sighed. "How about a small figurine planted by the gates of the Courtyard of Greatness?"

"Figurine?" H2 muffled through her mask.

"A small statue, ma'am," said Alice. "The size of a thumb."

"I said . . . don't call me *ma'am*."

"Sold as a recycling idea to inspire and uplift . . . that all are equal, including men."

The footman moaned.

"A surprise so intricate no one will see the details," said Alice.

H2 said nothing.

"Perhaps you could press a little more to the right," he said, "near my bunion?"

Chapter Four

THE STATUE WORKERS

"In the realm of happiness, an orgasm can only go so far."– Legless after way too many whiskies

Pete and Woody were in the newly erected state-of-the-art shed when they heard the news.

Mex walked in, tossed her Nokia across the bench, and pulled up a seat with a "figurines—what next?"

Pete and Woody looked up from their plans in mild irritation. Mex had a habit of walking in unannounced.

Once Beryl had made contact with H2, care of Alice, her arse had been left high and dry out the preverbal window—no longer required.

Retired and slightly bored, her sized-down Earth whip ceremonially taken from her, Mex felt as useful as a toothpick with dentures. She had little to do but listen in on H2 and her meetings with her newly acquired pseudo Nokia—the first and only replica of Woody's.

Woody's Nokia flashed red, then beeped several times; then, with an automated "not . . . not . . . not again," it died.

Mex's followed.

"I told you not to bring that in here," said Woody. "Now I'll have to charge them both up again, and God knows how long that will take *this* time."

Mex pulled a face.

The Techno Twins, as she called Woody and Pete, were as close as

Siamese twins—which, as DBO pointed out, was Woody's way of dealing with admiration, women oohing and aahing at him.

"Woody feels safe with Pete," said DBO, which Mex found as understandable as Beryl and Legless's relationship.

Woody got about in hooded cloaks, while Pete—still dressed as a woman—had a stall on the market selling the odd girlie outfit, which for some reason many robots took to, especially the aprons, wigs, and lipstick.

Pete's stall was so busy he employed other robots to help. Some even dressed like him: pointy bra, red lipstick, and a fifties-style wig (color optional).

And it was the running of things that had changed them; just like Beryl, they were full of themselves and way too busy for the likes of a retired man spy.

She huffed.

Give a man a shed, a bit of praise, enough knowledge to hang himself, and the next thing you know, he's acting like he's saving the pickling planet.

"It's not my fault," she said.

"I told you before, they are not compatible."

Mex pulled a face.

"It's the atmosphere," said Woody. "Plays havoc with the Earth bits."

"*Earth bits*," said Mex. "Hardly scientific."

"You have a better name?" said Pete.

Woody set the two Nokias down to charge, his on the bench and, with a pointed look at Mex, the other outside.

Planet Hy Man's atmosphere had turned Woody's Earth Nokia into an all-singing, all-dancing device so advanced it made the H-Pad II seem as impressive as a toilet roll holder.

Everyone wanted one. In fact, so much in demand was a "Woody Nokia" that a project was set up, headed by Woody and Pete. Funded with the "sky's the limit" budget, they rebuilt the charred remains of the Operators' shed and came up with a prototype for Mex to "test run."

They had free rein of any tools they could lay their hands on and access to everything, including firsthand information from the Operators in the Building of Opulence, who watched, recorded, and reported all, including Earth.

Pete, connected by the same "comfortable as an old slipper" earpiece as H2's, was as up-to-date as the BBC news; in fact, that's what he was listening to when Mex walked in.

Woody turned Mex's pseudo Nokia in his hands. "Maybe I should scrap yours and start again."

Mex jumped up to object. "But my Nokia is my only connection . . . with . . . things."

Pete looked up, hand on his earpiece. "There's a virus on Earth."

"Pfff, that place is full of them," said Mex with a soft look at Woody.

Pete stopped, listened, then looked at his comrades . . . . "A pandemic."

"Earth is so dramatic," said Mex.

"In Scotland?" Woody asked.

"Wouldn't worry, just a storm in a whatever," said Mex.

Pete looked at his pal. "They're to wear masks."

Alice and Vegas headed across the market to find a statue worker, which, according to Alice, was as easy as finding a young man. There had been no statues built since the fall of Hilda, and the statue workers had dispersed into various jobs.

They made their way in silence.

The market band was playing an ear-bashing polka, and some of the stall workers were clapping and cheering, others even dancing. In fact, if they were not on the lookout for a statue worker, Vegas would've joined in. She liked a good knees-up, and listening to a polka from the room with a view was hardly the same.

They passed the Voted In's art stall in the middle of a miniature watercolor sale.

"Buy one get one free," shouted Baby, a Voted In with a talent for screeching.

Vegas stopped, looked at the painting. *Not bad for an ex–Voted In,* she thought with a weak smile.

"We're looking for the statue workers," said Alice.

"What did you say?" yelled Baby.

"Statue workers?" shouted Alice.

"Yes, there are plenty more pictures," said Baby.

"Not pictures—statue workers," boomed Alice.

Vegas, rotating Baby's picture for a better angle, said nothing.

The band finished with a robust drumroll and a round of applause. Vegas, sliding the painting back to Baby, cheered with the rest.

A sweeper robot appeared, sporting one of Pete's best-selling aprons and blood red lipstick.

She stopped, her broom inches from Vegas's feet. "You could try the road workers," said the robot.

"You trying to be funny?" snapped Alice.

"I heard three joined last week . . . to help with the floating platforms."

Vegas said nothing.

Mass production of "Hilda's" floating platforms had been a joint decision, agreed to by all but Vegas. It was considered a cheaper, quicker way to sort out the whole potholes-in-the-road situation.

She had her doubts; she still had memories of Hilda on her platform.

The band began a new song.

"It's a subdivision," said the robot with a "don't you know anything?" face.

Vegas looked at Alice. "Subdivision?"

"A division within a division," said Alice she turned to the robot sweeper. "Where?"

"The emporium," the robot said, gesturing with a painted fingernail. "It's full of 'em."

"I wouldn't go in there," said Baby. "That place is heaving with flying platforms, and those things are silent. You have no idea one is behind until *wham*—out for the count."

The robot nodded. "Those workers have as much idea of driving as your team has of roads."

Vegas and Alice headed over to the emporium. Neither had been inside since it had changed to a training center.

They stopped at the front; it still looked like a store, except the doors were shut.

They wandered about, knocking, and when no one answered, they walked in.

The lobby was massive, with a high Victorian ceiling and one of the room with a view's chandeliers in the middle. It was empty apart from a large circular fountain-type stand in the middle—covered, like the walls and floor, with scuff marks and dents.

A floating platform zoomed by Vegas's head.

She ducked.

Alice chuckled, until she was clipped by another and cluttered to the ground.

Three statue workers were assigned to the Legless project.

It hadn't taken much convincing.

Flying platform building was as basic as tying a shoelace. Getting their teeth into something more complex had them as excited as a bride on her wedding day—until they saw the plans.

A scrap of paper with a thumbnail sketch of a figurine. An afternoon's work: hardly inspiring.

"For months we've been in this friggin' place," snapped the ambitious statue worker.

"I thought it was weeks," said the statue worker many called Dozy.

"Assembling on a conveyor belt."

"More design," muttered Dozy.

"Way beneath our artistic talents."

"We did install a brake system that doesn't propel the driver across the room," said the third statue worker.

"Ignored like a traffic sign, and now they want us to build a pickling figurine as big as a salt and pepper shaker," said the ambitious statue worker.

"Bit bigger than a condiment set," muttered Dozy.

"It's an insult."

"We're not even allowed to test-run," said Dozy.

The other two looked at her. "That's just you," said the ambitious statue worker.

"Oh."

"Let's show 'em what we're made of," said the ambitious statue worker.

Dozy, still staring at the plans, nodded.

While the third statue worker, infatuated with the ambitious statue worker, agreed with all her mind, body, and soul.

She, mulling over her morning caffeine, quickly drew up a design fit for a king, queen, and war hero combined, as large as Myanmar's Buddhas and as dominating as Mongolia's Genghis Khan statue.

With more recycling material than a McDonald's bin, they set to hiding their work behind a tent.

Hilda, standing by her vibrator stall nearby, was the first to notice.

Chapter Five

VIBRATORS

"Resolving the seeds of discontent is not an easy thing, even for a seasoned leader."–Beryl

For a month she watched, shivering in her so-called sheltered booth, wondering, *What the pickle is going on behind that tent?*

When Hilda first took over the vibrator stall, she embraced it like a religious convert. She wanted to share her happiness and threw herself into the trading of it.

She sold sleek ones, miniature ones, disposable ones, musical ones, some that vibrated the national anthem, flexible ones, stiff ones, ones that "did the works," budget ones that "did bugger-all," pretty ones, fast ones, slow ones, some with gears.

She even threw a vibrator event—upright vibrators "doing their thing" across the counter like a horse race—until someone complained.

She ran end-of-the-range sales, price-match deals, buy-one-get-one-free days. She made gift vouchers out of scented recycled paper and even had a secondhand sale—a bit off-putting, despite the "ten-ply soft-as-silk" wet wipes giveaway.

She did have her regular customers—*and* her incognito deals: women who wanted to remain nameless, who met in the dark, behind the unnamed covered-up statue in the Courtyard of Greatness.

And despite Hilda's "I'll not tell a soul," they still ignored her in public.

For every customer who enthused over her selection of lubricants, another walked by with a sniff; for every "that was marvelous, let me buy you a caffeine" customer was another who wanted a refund.

Some claimed they were "too noisy," others "not for me," while some even tried to barter her down, ruthlessly—like she was a nobody.

The orgasm business was not all it was cracked up to be. It was as complicated as leading a city with none of the benefits, and being shunned by the other stall owners didn't help. It riled her to no end, making her so angry she wanted to use her vibrators for something other than pleasure . . .

She began to crave control.

—

Hilda waited, watched as the other stall-keepers packed up and left for home.

It had been a grueling day.

But then every day at the marketplace was grueling for her; with no friends and no network, she had to do everything herself, then trot back to the only place that would have her: Verruca's home.

A place many on Earth would call a *cottage*. A place as far from the city as it was possible to be while still connected to the sewage system.

A place that took ages for Hilda to get to—not that she complained. She hardly looked forward to "going home," not with Verruca's personal robot under her feet: a robot with a faulty dictionary app and an annoying habit of being where it shouldn't.

At first, Hilda and the robot moaned about Verruca behind her back, playing tricks, laughing like schoolchildren—until the robot started to "walk in" on Hilda.

Even though she had a lock on her "me time" shed, a Do Not Enter sign on the door, and an alarm system that sounded like a dog mid attack, the robot barged in with no warning, no apology, and a stare that would crumble even the most confident.

The "me time" shed was where Hilda evaluated, appraised and, well, had a good time with her new vibrators. Hilda had taken over the shed when Verruca told her to evaluate and appraise her noisy equipment "somewhere well away from the house." A soundproof place that had low lighting, soft cushions, and a useless lock, but then any lock was useless in *that* robot's hand. Cyborg, as she had taken to calling him, could unpick a ball of tangled wool in minutes. Unlocking a padlock was a piece of piss to him, disarming an alarm system a breeze.

She pointed to the ancient, insignificant old hut at the back of the garden.

No one knew much about it, except that it was pretty ugly and had been dumped there by the hippies back in the days before women ruled.

Cyborg had a fixation for it; there was a soothing hum about it that he liked to retire to. When Hilda took it over, he was confused. He still wanted to sit there . . . and he soon developed a knack for arriving when Hilda was in positions that required decent lighting and soft music for dignity.

In fact, Hilda gave up the idea of "trial runs" the day Cyborg walked in on a particularly intensive assessment involving candlelight, whale music, and Hilda's legs in the sort of position that made her look like she'd fallen down the stairs and wasn't likely to recover.

Cyborg broke into a robotic skip. "Hilda's dead! Hilda's dead!" he shouted, setting off the alarm system.

Verruca rushed in, took one look at Hilda's onesie—tossed aside like an empty crisp packet, her eyes shut mid moan—and just as quickly rushed out with an "Oh."

If anyone could hate a robot, it was Hilda.

She stared at the marquee of a tent. Something told her a change was on the horizon . . . and that change had something to do with the tent.

She tugged on a corner, desperate for a peek, but it was nailed fast.

Cursing under her breath, she headed to the Courtyard of Greatness and waited behind the nameless statue.

A cloaked figure approached.

Hilda shone a light into Vegas's face.

Vegas squinted.

"Who's it for this time?" said Hilda.

"I am not at liberty to say," said Vegas.

Hilda slid her pseudo-leather briefcase onto the foot of the statue. She brushed imaginary dust from the top like she had all the time in the world.

Vegas looked around with impatience.

Hilda clipped it open, then paused.

"Will you just get on with it," snapped Vegas.

Hilda pulled out a recycled customer bag from inside and, with a great amount of ceremony, shook it open.

Flap!

"Easy," said Vegas.

Hilda stopped. "What?"

"Statues have ears," said Vegas.

"Pfff," huffed Hilda. "It's vibrators you're buying, not spy equipment."

"Mex calls them dildos," said Vegas.

"Mex would," said Hilda. She slid a portable vibrator into the bag, then stopped. "So, one of these is for her?"

Vegas blushed.

Hilda laughed. "Thought she'd be too old for that malarky."

"Just hurry," said Vegas. "They're waiting."

Hilda, taking her time, slid a "flat pack" vibrator into the bag, followed by a retractable one.

Vegas made to grab.

Hilda hung on . . .

"Not so fast—I want to know what's behind the tent."

"None of your business," said Vegas.

Hilda tugged. "Then I'll take these back."

"But we've paid you," said Vegas.

Hilda laughed.

"Mex will have me hung by my toenails."

"So one of these *is* for Mex?" said Hilda.

"Just hand them over," said Vegas.

Hilda put on her best soft face. "There's no need to be so ruthless. We used to work together, remember?"

Vegas said nothing.

"The good ol' days?" said Hilda.

"Hardly," muttered Vegas.

"Could we not, you know, do something together—for old times' sake?" Hilda pulled her best smile.

"Just give me the goods," said Vegas.

Hilda's face hardened. "Why do you do this to yourself? Pick up incognito for others like some dogsbody?"

"No one else wants to deal with you," said Vegas.

Hilda's face dropped.

Vegas softened. "It's a figurine, if you must know."

Hilda said nothing.

"To inspire and uplift, OK? Now don't ask me anything else." Vegas made for the bag.

Hilda snatched it away. "A figurine of what?"

Vegas sighed. "Guess."

It didn't take long for Hilda to work it out; she'd been watching that Deidre. It was either that damnable Beryl or worse: Legless.

"But why so big a tent?" said Hilda. "What the pickle are they doing under there?"

"DBO said they're perfectionists. The footman says they're milking it."

Hilda tutted to herself. "Everyone thinks control is so easy."

Vegas took her bag, looked inside. "Any batteries?"

"Rechargeable," said Hilda.

Vegas inspected them with a "Hmm."

"It's all there," said Hilda. "Oh, and I've thrown in my new all-singing, all-dancing vibrator, or *dildo*, as Mex would call it."

She walked away with a chuckle. "Just for you, for old times' sake; let me know what you think."

Vegas lifted up a vibrator, turned it in her hand. *If this is an "all-singing, all-dancing dildo," then I'm a footman's crotch.*

Chapter Six

OL' NELLIE

"A footman's foot is as ugly as a hairless cat. Years of standing can do that to a foot."–H2

Hilda couldn't contain herself. The next morning, while setting up her stall, she started a whispering campaign.

"Don't you think a month is just a pickle too long?" she bellowed into the wind.

"They're just perfectionists," shouted a stall owner.

"Yeah," yelled another.

"It's a figurine," huffed Hilda.

"So?"

"Yeah, so?"

"The size of a hand," said Hilda.

"So?"

"Yeah, so?"

"So what's with the tent the size of a temple?"

"Those workers are just milking it," said a voice from the back.

No one answered, but a few did wonder, sparking off the sort of whispering that breeds discontent.

Hilda smiled to herself. "Everyone thinks it's so easy to rule," she muttered, not that anyone heard.

The statue "went public" by accident when a tornado whipped into the city, tossed a few stalls into the air, and left—taking the tent with it.

Tornadoes had a habit of doing that on Planet Hy Man; up lifting and uprooting like a giant invisible hand from the sky—unlike hurricanes that swirled from beneath, weaving about the legs of things like a weasel on speed.

It was the end of the "Let's hear it for robots" public holiday, and the Courtyard of Greatness was full of sozzled women jigging to the market band medley of polka—a great dance to do when there are no men about to partner with.

Mex, inspired by her Edinburgh adventures, had created a hemp gin, taking toasting to a whole new level. The women couldn't get enough of the stuff and were toasting to anything they could think of.

They toasted to "Pete and his stories of Earth," "Pete and his dedication to yoga," and "Pete for bringing Woody."

The women sighed . . .

Woody blushed, retreating into the back of Mex's cocktail bar.

"Let's hear it for Alice," staggered a market stall owner, "and that *zipping about* thing she does."

"Hear, hear!"

"The H-Pad," shouted an Operator.

"Don't forget the C-Pad," yelled another.

"Hear, hear!"

"The iPad?" said a voice from the back.

"That's on Earth," said a small voice.

"To all the pads," yelled Vegas.

"Hear, hear!"

"T-t-to the Mae West team," stuttered a very old ex-footman.

The women looked at each other. "Who?" The history of robots had never been written down, and not many were old enough to remember the Mae West robot.

"And the turtles," shouted an ancient cleaner.

Silence . . .

The only turtles they knew were the turtle cleaning robots—hardly worth a toast.

"And to all the robots too many to mention!" yelled Vegas.

Everyone was clinking their recycled glasses, losing count of how many they'd had, when Ol' Nellie the tornado whirled in.

As the tent shot into the sky, a gasp fell on the audience.

It took a bit of staring before people started to realize it was merely an askew lap bag protruding from his groin.

Some began to laugh.

Others joked.

Hilda waited. She had spent a month spreading gossip about the cost of the thing; now all she had to do was wait.

A few staggered as their eyes traced the height of the statue.

Others blinked, trying to remember just who this fellow was.

The glasses began to empty.

And when a mechanical bird of prey positioned himself on Legless's nose, it dawned on all of them just how big the statue was.

Hilda pounced with a shout. "Bet that cost an arm and a leg."

Silence . . .

"And the friggin' rest," shouted the voice from the back.

H2 took one look at the apparition looming down on the marketplace and blew a fuse. "What the great pickling hell is that?" she shouted.

She was on her third caffeine at the time, basking in her "triumph of a public holiday" from the room with a view.

"Just look at them," she said to DBO. "Happy as a basketful of pigs."

DBO looked at her. "Pigs?"

"Well, yes. I've seen them on Earth; cuddly pink things."

"Pink things they make bacon out of," muttered the ancient footman, who was about to embellish when "Ol' Nellie" swept in.

The three stared as the tent lifted into the air along with thick red dust.

They waited . . . staring into the cloud as Legless's lap bag protruded through the settling dust.

"That's a trifle large," muttered DBO.

"A trifle?" chuckled the ancient footman. "I wonder what's at the end of it."

H2 charged out of the room and down the stairs three at a time, and before the footman could utter an appendage joke, H2 was in the courtyard.

The statue workers, tanked to the eyeballs, were standing by Mex's hemp gin cocktail bar when she appeared.

DBO and the ancient footman watched from the window as H2 appeared, stopping the crowd quicker than Ol' Nellie herself.

The statue workers, standing at attention with an expectant "well done lads," soon sobered up as H2's grim face loomed closer.

"What did she expect," said the ancient footman, "from a tent so large?"

"I did warn her," said DBO. She shook her head. "But would she listen?"

"Power turns many deaf," muttered the ancient footman.

Chapter Seven

THE MARCH

"A lap bag is too small to hold much but big enough to look silly." —Market stall owner who made a fortune in backpacks (name unknown)

H2 looked up as Legless emerged from the red dust like Australia's Uluru through the early morning mist. She blinked into the sun and stopped.

"Oh! It's a lap bag," she said. "Silly me."

"It's a celebration of the spark plug," said the ambitious statue worker.

"I see," said H2, not really seeing at all.

The crowd stared.

"I thought a spark plug was small, and its smallness was its power," said a market stall owner.

"It is metaphorical," said the ambitious statue worker.

"What's that when it's at home?" yelled a voice from the back.

Woody, a would-be writer who knew a thing or two about metaphors, jumped onto Mex's cocktail bar, preparing to explain and soothe. Not that anyone listened; once Woody appeared, they just wanted to look. He could have said Planet Hy Man was burning and no one would have moved.

"Show us your lap bag!" shouted the voice from the back, and many cheered.

Deidre, Planet Hy Man's top reporter, did a full exposé on the matter, sending many into crazed shouting and those in management arguing.

A no-frills H-Pad was hard enough to work with, but when those who made decisions saw the extra-large statue, they were choking on their caffeine. While they were forced to rule in a room fit for storing cardboard boxes, Beryl was splash*ing P*lanet Hy Man's *funds about, not only on a useless* statue *but* on *a statue of a* pickling man.

DBO tried her best to soothe the complaints. Deidre, however, like a true tabloid journalist, exaggerated, blamed, and inflamed the masses.

"What does Planet Hy Man need with a male statue with a lap bag so long it casts a shadow over the marketplace and a nose so broad that a bird could nest in it?"

By the time Beryl and Legless were tucking into a meaty pasta in their camper van, complaints of the Legless statue were coming thick and fast.

Hilda took advantage, starting a whispering campaign . . .

"A man has no place blocking out the sun," she hissed to many, riling the stall owners to no end.

It didn't take long for the masses to rally.

Within weeks, placards were made and a march held. H2 tried to reassure and inspire, and when that didn't work, she braved the match head-on.

Jumping on a hemp-oil stall, she yelled, "Legless gave us the spark plug!"

They marched on.

DBO jumped on another stall and screamed, "Energy on a shoestring!"

The women continued strutting down the main street, picking up many as they went, until they stood at the toes of Legless's statue.

The three statue workers, poised on Legless's feet, were ready to defend their work.

The women eyeballed each other like caged tigers, not really sure what to do next.

"Don't come any further," hissed Dozy.

The other two statue workers looked at her in surprise.

"I mean it," she said.

Woody sprang from a heel; climbing onto the middle toe, he balanced with a grunt.

A few women sighed, others contained themselves.

He talked of the field-workers working in the sunburnt fields, of their sweaty brows and sun-drenched hair.

"Those hardworking comrades could do with a little shade," he yelled.

The women looked from him to the statue. *Is it movable?*

"That thing is as transportable as the pickling sun," shouted the voice from the back.

"Everything is movable on Planet Hy Man," said Woody.

Some looked convinced.

"And . . ." He looked at the unconvinced. "It would make up for the coffee tables."

H2 blushed.

"I guess we have little to lose," said a quiet voice.

Quicker than a coffee break, a parade to celebrate the removal of Legless was organized.

A team of sportswomen was enlisted to pull the statue down, under the charge of Alice.

Women as beefy as a wrestler on steroids, who filled their sheds with tug-of-war trophies, played rugby for fun, and boxed punchbags to relax. Women so strong they opened jam jars with a laugh, kicked footballs so high they knocked birds of prey to the ground, and push-started transporters with a mere nudge. To them, pulling a statue was like pulling a supermarket trolley.

It was rumored by many that they had volunteered and were determined to show off, insisting on transporting "our Legless," as they had taken to calling the statue.

Ignoring advice from many, including the statue-making team, the sportswomen put together a wheeled device that had many sniggering.

They were old school; they marched. "If you want a pickling parade, then we'll give you one," they shouted, and as they had arm muscles the size of truck tires, no one argued, despite the wheels being of "supermarket trolley" quality.

The statue makers were sent ahead to find the perfect sight that would capture the sun from many angles and ensure daylong shade.

They took protractors, rulers, pencils, a theodolite—which they'd copied from Earth—and any other instrument the ambitious statue worker could think of that would make them look important.

"Let's take a flying platform," said Dozy, "give 'em a test run as well."

The ambitious statue worker glared at Dozy with a "hardly." (Any idea that wasn't hers was never a good one.)

In the end, a site was found, a perfect, brilliant site where the statue would cast a shade all day long for miles.

But getting there would turn tricky.

The route to this spectacular site was via the road to the outlands, the field-workers, and the hippie colony.

A crumbling, potholed track some laughingly called a highway that was a curse to many transporters and on the to-do list for H2 and her leadership team.

"A piece of piss," yelled the head sportswoman. "We've pulled bigger across the mud plains, and for longer."

Which everyone knew was a total lie; the mud plains had dried up years ago.

They pulled the statue through the streets, grunting and groaning for effect, while the statue workers accompanied them on floating platforms.

"Let's cheer 'em on," shouted Alice, zipping over the top of many heads.

The women cheered; some threw flowers. None were aware that

along the route, hidden and unknown, was "the portal"—a portal that, as H2 would later write, "turned things on its head."

Chapter Eight

SOYA-TOMS

"A good friend is like a good bra: close to the heart, uplifting, and supportive without showing."—Pete

Verruca's garden, or *veg-plot*, as she liked to call it, looked straight onto the highway.

She was proud of her garden; the earth had been so dry and unforgiving when she arrived. The cook of the hippie colony warned her against it, claiming that the plot was "as organic as a nuclear reactor."

Verruca didn't listen. She had learned a lot from her time with hippies, enough to know the cook should stick to cooking, and she with her latest state-of-the-art, just-like-a-human personal robot, Cyborg—they were bound to "move mountains."

Besides, the plot did have a magnificent shed.

Over the years, Verruca and Cyborg had built a sort of hedge between the highway and her veg-plot, mainly because Cyborg (who turned out to be anything but state-of-the-art) was more a hindrance than a help and, apart from cleaning the fridge, he was pretty useless. Keeping him busy on the hedge had worked for a while, until the hedge became a home for mechanical birds.

At first, trimming it was a breeze, and cute sparrowlike birds chirped and fluttered about the robot like something out of a Disney cartoon. Cyborg almost skipped as he went about his hedge-pruning duties, making large protruding hand shapes for bird's nests.

The hands were so successful he couldn't help but make them bigger and bigger, filling them with out-of-date tidbits from the fridge cleaning. It was a howling success for all—until a mechanical bird of prey, a great brute of a fellow, caught sight of a tasty bit of tofu and crash-landed on a hand, scaring the family of sparrows in one squawk.

It didn't take long for Cyborg to hang up his clipping shears.

He watched the sparrow family flutter into the distance and turned to the bird of prey. It glared, squawked, and then sunk its beak into the nearest appendage of Cyborg, sending him quickly into Verruca's potting greenhouse.

Verruca, humming to herself, didn't hear a thing. She had become a passionate gardener, nourishing the earth with every trick she could think of.

With Planet Hy Man in a state of peace and her ninja war tactics no longer needed, she retreated to growing veggies from seed, breeding in her greenhouse—soya-toms being her latest, a cross between synthetic tomatoes and soybeans.

The door crashed open; Cyborg appeared, short of breath.

Verruca, mid potting up, continued to hum . . .

"That thing bit me," he panted.

With no idea that a robot could pant, Verruca stuck her head outside the shed and quickly retreated. Aptly naming the bird of prey "Darth Vader," she proceeded to lecture Cyborg on the whole "tidbit issue."

"I did warn you," she said. "Perhaps you'll listen now."

He didn't hear a thing; he was too busy staring at Verruca's soya-tom seedlings.

He turned one in his hand, mesmerized.

"They could do with compost," he said.

"Shit," muttered Verruca. *Why didn't I lock the door?*

Soon she couldn't get rid of him; he was drawn to her soya-toms like wasps to honey.

Every afternoon, he tiptoed across Verruca's veg garden, hell-bent on composting her soya-tom plants; the only thing that stopped him was Verruca's trusty lasso.

Verruca was in her garden when she caught sight of Legless's statue inching by.

Verruca, mid lassoing, looked up from the compost heap when Legless's lap bag edged across the top of her hedge like a suspended submarine.

Even Cyborg stopped, which was no mean feat; he had the focus of a drone.

The lasso dropped to the ground.

"Great pickling manifestation," she said, immediately regretting it.

"Man . . ." automated Cyborg. "A species capable of mass destruction."

"I said *manifestation*."

"Festation . . ." said Cyborg. "An eight-letter word."

"Nine letters."

"What?"

"I said it's nine."

"*Nein*, a German word for no." He looked at her, daring a reply.

Alice zoomed across the top of the hedge. "Make way, make way, our Legless is coming through!"

The statue appeared, casting a shadow across Verruca's potato patch.

"Legless . . ." said the robot. "A statue with a face the size of a spaceship."

"I *can* see," snapped Verruca, picking up her lasso.

"Eagle to the left," shouted Alice.

Hilda appeared, charging across the hemp grass and shouting "Legless is coming!" She stopped, eyed her robot.

Cyborg held her gaze.

If it were possible for a robot to hate, then this one felt it in bucketloads toward Hilda.

"Don't you have a fridge to clean?" she said.

"Get stuffed," said Cyborg.

The parade had not been as easy as expected.

Once they left the city, the cheering stopped, and the sportswomen became disheartened.

The sportswomen assumed the crowd would follow, cheer them on like war heroes; instead, the only follower was a mechanical bird of prey with a menacing look and the memory of a flying football.

As they approached a particularly large pothole on the other side of Verruca's hedge, Dozy, at the front of the march, shouted, "Easy!"

At first, no one listened—until Alice, catching sight of a "canyon of a pothole," zipped along the women's heads, shouting, "Hold fire, hole to the right; hole to the right!"

"What?" shouted the ambitious statue worker from the rear.

"Pothole," shouted someone.

"Pothole, smot-hole—let's keep going!" yelled the ambitious statue worker. *Sportswomen always exaggerated.*

"We've a cannonball of a hole here," shouted Dozy.

"Cannonball, smannon-ball," yelled the ambitious statue worker. "Let's do a little veering to the side."

Dozy, now anything but dozy, looked at the hole looming closer. *Veering?*

"We need to stop," shouted Alice.

The lead sportswoman looked up, then jolted to a halt. "Stop?"

"She said stop!"

"Are we stopping?"

"STOP!" yelled the lead sportswoman.

Hilda and Verruca watched the upper torso of Legless shudder, then still as the eagle circled its head with a menacing cry.

The sportswomen stood about the crater of a hole.

"I wouldn't call that a pothole," one said.

"More a dried-up well."

"Dam, more like it."

"I've seen smaller quarries than that."

The ambitious statue worker pushed through. She stood at the edge of the hole.

"Shall I go get a flying platform?" said Dozy.

The ambitious statue worker threw her a caustic look. "Nothing a plank wouldn't sort."

The woman looked at her. "Plank?"

"A pickling bridge is what you need," said the lead sportswoman.

The eagle settled on Legless's nose.

"The eagle has landed!" shouted Alice, taking what she thought was a wide birth.

The women looked up to see the eagle open a wing the size of an airplane's. Before they could shout "look out," it swatted Alice like a fly.

Alice plummeted to the ground on Verruca's side of the hedge. "Going down!" she screeched—splat into Cyborg.

A few women pushed their heads through the hedge, catching sight of a crumbled heap of a robot rubbing his head with a dazed "what the pickle?" look.

Alice shot out an arm with a comradely "here."

The robot stumbled to his feet and staggered about like he was drunk.

"Throw some water on him," yelled a voice from the back.

Verruca sighed.

"Water is the elixir of life, the fountain of gestation, the urinal with no boundaries."

"He's not thirsty," said Alice.

Verruca sighed again.

"Thirsty-worsty—yes, I can curtsy."

"Get ahold of yourself," snapped Hilda.

"Hold . . . cold . . . told . . . pold . . . I mean, bold . . ." automated Cyborg.

"Told you to clean the fridge," she said.

"Go fly yourself up a friggin' pole," snapped Cyborg before crumbling to the ground with a "going doooooown a . . . a . . . a . . . gain."

Chapter Nine

VERTICAL-SMERTICAL

"The wind of a thousand eagles and many more minions can blow many things off course, including a top-heavy statue made of recycled material."—Lead sportswoman

Bridging the pothole with a vertical Legless was an ingenious plan thought up by the third statue worker. Quickly drawing a diagram, she shoved it under the nose of the ambitious statue worker with a blush.

The ambitious statue worker brushed her aside. Alice's bird's-eye view was not a patch on *her* intuition.

"My gut instincts are never wrong," she said.

"What have your innards to do with measurements?" snapped Alice.

"Well, it built this." She gestured to Legless.

"A figurine the size of a water tower?"

"The figurine was metaphorical," said the ambitious statue worker.

"Actually, I think you'll find it was literal," said Alice.

Hilda and Verruca pushed through the hedge talking of planks, pullies, and "pullers," which riled the sportswomen to no end as they considered themselves *sportswomen* and not *pullers*.

"Girls, girls," shouted Verruca. "Let's work together."

The third statue worker coughed, blushing. "I think I have an idea."

The head sportswoman took one look and nearly knocked her over with a comradely pat on the back. "Let's hear it for the wee one!" she shouted, sparking a round of applause.

The ambitious statue worker, without even a glance at the third statue worker, sniffed. "We'll need to set about levering," she said.

"Well, that's a given," said the lead sportswoman.

"And some pullers."

"We're not pullers, we're sportswomen," yelled a voice from the back.

"Pullers, smull-ers," said the ambitious statue worker.

"You'll need to mind the wind factor," said the third statue worker.

"Don't worry about that, luv," said the lead sportswoman with another powerhouse pat on the back.

The third statue worker stumbled to keep her balance.

"One push should do it," said a voice from the back.

"A piece of effluent," muttered another.

"And the eagle?" said the third statue worker, rubbing her shoulder.

"What eagle?" said a hulk of a shot-putter.

"The one on the nose," Dozy said, pointing. "We'll need to coax it down; perhaps with a bit of tofu?"

"I'm not coaxing any eagle. Just shoo it," said the shot-putter. She tossed a shoe, striking the eagle with perfect aim.

A few women cheered.

It glared.

"There's another here," yelled the shot-putter with a menacing shake of a shoe.

The eagle disappeared into the clouds.

"See, that's all you need . . ."

"But eagles have friends," muttered the third statue worker, not that anyone listened, apart from Dozy.

The sportswomen began their warm-up routine, rolling their shoulders, lunging, squatting, star-jumping, and high-kicking, some tossing rocks about.

It was all show. But even without an audience, they couldn't help themselves. What was the point of killing yourself with training if you couldn't show off?

No one saw the flock of birds or their minions of budgies, apart from the infatuated statue worker.

"Oh, God," she muttered.

"Heave," shouted many. They pulled.

The birds circled, darkening the sky like something out of an Alfred Hitchcock movie.

"Again," shouted the lead sportswoman.

"Heave!"

The budgies dove about the women, circling about, blinding them.

The women began to panic—some yelling and shooing, others roaring, many throwing things.

"Run for cover," shouted the third statue worker.

The women dove under the hedge.

The eagles went mental, thrashing their wings like their lives depended on it.

The statue wavered.

The eagles flapped harder, working up a gust of wind that had many women shielding their eyes.

The statue tipped toward the hedge.

"It's coming this way," shouted the shot-putter.

"Run!" screamed Dozy.

The women scrambled from the hedge like a plague of rabbits.

The statue tumbled over the hedge, flattening it like an egg carton and surprising even the birds.

The women gasped.

It skidded across the veg-plot, the lap bag impaling a large pumpkin that Verruca had high hopes of winning a gold with at the next Great Veg Show.

Verruca raced for her lasso, but nothing could stop the momentum of a recycled statue.

The head crashed into Hilda's "me-time" shed; dog barking filled the air, sparking a crazed circling of birds.

The closed sign exploded into pieces, vibrators rocketed into the sky, and lubricant squirted out like toothpaste as Hilda sprinted so hard she couldn't manage a single curse.

She stopped at the remains of the shed.

There was a puff of smoke.

A muffled "Shit" from Hilda.

Then nothing.

"The portal?" gasped Cyborg, who for once had gotten something right, although no one knew it at the time.

Chapter Ten

THE CLEARING OF SMOKE

"The testing of things requires a mind as open as a barn door."– The third statue worker

When the smoke cleared, the hedge looked like a giant crushed egg carton, and Hilda was gone, her "me-time" shed a mere dark patch under Legless's head, his nose mashed into a screwed-up lubricant tube.

A vibrator receipt flapped past. Verruca grabbed it.

"I always thought there was something weird about that place," said Cyborg, who rarely had the chance to be right.

The third statue worker, not being a "told you so" sort of woman, said nothing.

She, like many, was in a state of shock. Witnessing an all-singing, all-dancing vibrator soaring into the sky and knocking an eagle for six can do that to a woman.

"If only we'd taken a flying platform," said Dozy.

Chapter Eleven

THE F WORD

"You're never too tired for a foot rub."—H2

"What the hell and pickle happened?" yelled H2, glaring at her H-Pad perched against the leg of a chair.

She had watched the whole thing on her knees while administering a foot rub that had the owner of the foot wincing.

In fact, many in the queue ran a mile when the wincing was not only seen but heard, and the rest would have, if they weren't packed into the corridor like a D-cup breast into an A-cup bra.

"Perhaps ma'am should give the H-Pad a rest," said the owner of the foot. "Concentrate on one thing . . . at a time-like."

"Don't call me *ma'am*," snapped H2.

"Yes . . . errr . . . H2."

"Perhaps a more mindful approach," croaked the doorman lounging against the doorframe. "Multitasking is not all it's cracked up to be . . ."

The other footmen nodded.

". . . and watching *Mission: Impossible* proves that is not, well, advisable, especially while seeing to a bunion."

"Or a corn," squeaked a voice from the back.

"Hear, hear!" yelled the next in line: an elderly footman sporting not only the latest leisure suit but an equally up-to-date, microchipped-to-the-max, voice-operated, first-of-its-kind, all-singing, all-dancing wheelchair.

In fact, that was what it was called: the "All-Singing, All-Dancing Wheelchair Mark Two"—although there was never a Mark One.

It was so silent no one heard it coming (until the owner barked an order) and so complicated its manual was not only a book but a magnificent doorstop.

"We women are masters of multitasking," said H2.

"That's what they say on Earth, and look where it got them," sniffed the wheelchair owner.

Everyone in the queue nodded.

At first, H2's foot rubs were a godsend to the old men who had spent a lifetime on their feet. The thought of cool liniment and gentle hands caressing their war-torn feet had them in their best leisure suits, queuing up the corridor, whistling, joking, laughing, some even singing the odd jocular song—until H2 developed the mood swings of a woman in labor.

Temper tantrums and silences were the downside to control, everyone knew that, but they had expected more of H2, a young woman with so much promise.

However, the burden of leading was wearing her down. She, holding fast to her "we all sit on the john the same" ideology, had no idea how to reflect on failure, or cast blame. She clung to her beliefs like shit on a shoe, but after several "improvement plan" failures and a small revolt from the outlands, she was beginning to doubt herself, and the effort of hiding it was exhausting.

The revolt was crushed like an egg carton. She called it "cushioned and absorbed," and despite telling herself it was a job well done, it wasn't how she wanted to do things.

She didn't want to crush anything, let alone absorb; she wanted to expand, make this world a better place, a utopia of equality.

She expected more happiness, more solidarity, more cheering, maybe a letter of gratitude or two, but the people complained and moaned even when she called them comrades.

Cynicism and disillusion were rising in H2 like dry rot, and unless things changed, she too would soon start calling the so-called comrades "the masses" under her breath.

Those close to her, with no idea of what it was like to grasp a dream and then watch it turn sour, did their best to encourage. Some tried to understand, while others (mainly the footmen) blamed "the hormones," an excuse they picked up from Earth.

H2 squeezed a corn with a tut.

"Is one having a hot flash?" said the doorman.

"It's nothing to be ashamed of," said a squeaky voice from the back.

"We are not Earth women; we don't have such things," said H2.

"Really?" The doorman cocked his eyebrow.

"What would you men know? You've as much hormones as a wheelbarrow. You can't even raise a sweat let along anything organic."

"No need to be so mean," said a voice from the back.

"That's it, I'm done," said the foot owner, removing his foot from H2's grasp.

H2 tugged it back. "Not quite, there's a bit of dry skin that needs scraping," she said.

"Scraping!" shrieked the wheelchair owner, looking behind at his comrades in horror. "No one mentioned anything about scraping."

"It's very helpful for concentration," muttered H2, pulling an implement from her pocket.

"Is that a potato peeler?" croaked the doorman.

"No," said H2.

"Looks like a potato peeler," said the wheelchair owner.

"It's not." She twirled the potato peeler's head. "See? It has a rotation element. For ingrown toenails."

"Reverse!" shouted the wheelchair owner. "Now."

"No room," automated the wheelchair. "Even for cat swinging."

"Who cares about cats? I want out! My ingrown toenail ain't gonna be potato-peeled by anyone, even by our so-called esteemed leader."

H2 looked up. "You have an ingrown toenail?"

"Ow!" yelped the foot owner.

"Sorry, wasn't looking," muttered H2.

"Wheelchair, get me the pickle out of here!" shouted the wheelchair owner, following up with a wealth of Earth swear words.

The wheelchair began to spin, confused. "*F* word excluded, *F* word excluded . . . does not compute, does not compute."

"Just leg it!" snapped the wheelchair owner.

"No leg, only wheel, no legs, only wheels."

"Great flaming Alien," shouted the wheelchair owner. He made to walk.

A hand landed on his shoulder.

"Perhaps you should chill—relax."

The footman stopped. DBO, it seemed, had appeared from nowhere.

She lifted the potato peeler from H2's hand. "Perhaps it's time to reverse the massaging"—she motioned H2 to a seat—"and for you to have a good old-fashioned foot rub yourself."

DBO looked about the room. "Any takers?"

"Happy to, ma'am," said the doorman.

"Don't call me *ma'am*," muttered H2 with a tug at her socks.

The massage did soothe; despite the papery fingers, the coughing, the heaving, and the mild nose dribbling, the doorman was an expert. He knew every nub, every nook and cranny of the foot, not to mention the ankle. He could find the G-spot in seconds, the F-spot in minutes, and the infamous but elusive Y-spot in a record fifteen minutes.

Sometimes he hit all three together, stunning the foot owner into the sort of pleasure coma that involved more sighing and moaning than an Earth adult movie; in fact, many suggested that was where he'd picked up his so-called special abilities.

"Show-off," muttered one.

The doorman, who considered himself to be just that little bit more than a footman, began to flounce, massaging with arm actions on par with an orchestra conductor.

"Just get on with it," squeaked the voice from the back.

He pulled his famous hypnotizing pelvic move, following up with his new arse-to-heel jab and almost did his back in.

"Oooooh," murmured H2.

Her head fell back, her face a picture of bliss as she sighed and slipped into a coma of ecstasy.

"Well done," said DBO.

"Arrrrr," murmured H2.

"You'll get extra for that."

"Extra what?" said the doorman.

"Whatever . . . you know . . . you get, you'll get that, plus a bit more."

"I get food, lodging, and free rein of the BBC."

"And the internet," squeaked the voice from the back.

"Not that it's worth much these days. Everyone's all lockdown crazy," muttered the wheelchair owner.

The doorman slid a blanket over H2. Then he stood with an erectness that stopped DBO.

The wheelchair owner rolled his eyes at the others. "I did find an amazing link."

The footmen groaned.

"Zoom."

"Zoom?"

"Yes."

He pulled out his watch.

DBO stared at a sea of Earth faces.

"You're on mute," shouted one.

She looked up. "Alice found this as well."

"Who do you think showed her?" said the doorman.

None were aware of Deidre lurking about the corridors of power, earwigging behind the room with a view by her favorite watercooler spot. She was sniffing out a "Why such a big statue?" story.

She had many angles . . .

An "Is this how public funds are wasted—leading to the state of the roads?" article, *for the market stall owners.*

"Has our leader gone loony?" *for the masses.*

"Is this what we recycle for?" *for the idealist.*

And . . .

"Does our leader know what she's doing?" *for her own pleasure.*

She was even thinking of following up with a piece about Legless, hinting at some sort of collusion, perhaps bribery . . .

Then she heard it: the disappearance of someone—followed by the telltale sign of a crisis: the lining up of footmen.

Something is afoot, she thought with no idea about puns.

Chapter Twelve

THREE HOODIES

Some memories are so ingrained they are burned into the reflexes."–Beryl's driving instructor manual

Beryl was sitting in the front passenger seat of a Volkswagen Up. It was small, powerless, but great for teaching.

Behind the steering wheel sat Mandy, a young-looking blonde with a shaky left hand and an even shakier foot. It wasn't her first lesson, but by the way her hand shook, anyone would think it was.

Mandy, foot on the clutch, gripped the hand brake, turned on the ignition . . . and stalled the car.

"Jesus wept," she hissed with a mild Australian twang.

Beryl, her face a mask of patience, said nothing.

In fact, so patient did she look that many on Planet Hy Man would have struggled to recognize her—apart, that is, from her hairdo.

A plastic co-op bag fluttered by, wedging itself between a windshield wiper and the windshield.

Beryl, with a sigh, jumped out to clear it.

She paused, staring at the dead-end street, the boarded-up shop, the overflowing bins . . . parking here had not been the brightest idea she'd ever had.

She scrunched the bag into a ball and tossed it at a nearby bin; it missed.

She moved to pick up, then stopped . . .

Was there someone behind her?

More than one?

She turned to see three "hoodies" loitering about the car with no intention of moving on.

One lad shoved the other into the car, and the learner sign wobbled; they laughed and pushed again.

Beryl sighed.

On Planet Hy Man, she'd have had them bouncing off the walls with one kick in exactly the right place, but here on Earth, her legs were as good as jelly beans.

"Keep it moving, boys," said Beryl.

"Aye—and whose gonna make us, gran?"

"She's not your gran," snapped Mandy.

"Just leave 'em," Beryl mouthed.

"Leave 'em?" said Mandy. "They've dented the car!"

"Dent? You call this a dent? I'll show you a dent," said the tall hoodie with a menacing gesture.

The hoodies walked around the car jeering at the "Drive like a Pro" painted on the side.

Beryl pulled her best intimidating face and waited. *These three bozos have the brains of a banana. Five minutes and they'll be away.*

The hoodies sauntered over. The tall one flashed a look at Beryl. "Pfff—grandma."

She'd heard it all before.

"Granny-poos," laughed his sidekick.

Even that . . .

"She's no grandma," said the tattooed one, "she's as barren as a Brillo pad."

The hoodies fell about laughing like it was the best joke ever.

"You know what a Brillo pad is?" said Mandy.

The tall hoodie called her a tart; the others followed.

"Pussy."

"Yeah—pussy, pussy, meow, meow . . ."

Mandy's eyes flashed. Beryl stared. For the first time, she noticed what looked like the line of a superb wig.

Mandy turned the ignition on and revved the engine.

The three hoodies stopped in their tracks.

"Let's see who's a pussy now," she growled, her accent broadening to a strong Australian growl.

Legless made his way to the Glasgow ferry. He was heading for Jimmie's Arabic Tea Shop. He had a whole day ahead of him, a fantastic speech, and, as usual, no Beryl.

She was busy, helping folk with a patience that niggled him. If only those on Planet Hy Man could see her now. The esteemed leader, not only sharing a car but teaching. They'd be choking on their hemp teas.

Beryl loved cars; she could change a tire quicker than unplugging a hair dryer. Which, at first, Legless had found strangely erotic.

He was as useless with cars as she was with changing a bed. Which, strangely enough, Beryl found erotic . . . it was a sight to behold.

The first time she saw it, she pushed him down on the bed and messed it up so badly he had to find new sheets.

Now, when he changed the sheets, she wasn't even there. By the time he pulled out a fresh set, she was out the door clutching a mug of something hot, phone to her ear, consoling some distraught student driver—or worse, taking a pizza order to god knows where.

He stood on the deck of the ferry, the wind whipping about his nether regions as the Dunoon coast disappeared to a speck. He wondered about his day.

Beryl had no idea he was meeting Archie and DJ, a couple of Identities. She had no idea because she wasn't listening when he told her; she was on the phone talking down a student who was hyperventilating before a driving exam.

He looked out onto the water dark and grey, gulping his powdered coffee—the sort of coffee Beryl screwed up her nose at.

He scrunched the empty cup to a ball and tossed it at the bin, admiring his perfect aim. He had made her happy last night. *That's something to brag about,* he thought, *take to the meetings.*

Chapter Thirteen

THE ALIEN WHO LOVED ME

"The women weren't exactly miserable, but they weren't full of beans either."–Legless's novella, A Shag Too Many

When Legless first arrived on Earth, he hid in a cave by a small Scottish village and remained there, secretly servicing unhappy women.

It wasn't hard; he came out in the early mornings when men were at work and women were hanging out their washing.

Sneaking up behind a woman to "service," as he put it, was easy back then. It was 1950, and women on the whole had little experience of a good service—at least the ones he met. In fact, many took to washing on a grand scale, changing beds daily, despite the rain—most were not sure why.

He stayed in the cave until discovered by a religious camper who mistook him for a spiritual apparition. Apparently, the cave he lived in was where Saint Columba lit fires and built an altar to pray and ponder.

Legless had no idea about altars; he just saw it as a good place to put his mug while he lit a fire.

Legless traveled Scotland, England, and Europe, even did a stint in Butlin's as a ballroom dancer.

He was a quick learner with a body that surprised him. Back then he could walk into a room and, with one look, one swish of his pelvis, have women eating out of his hands—as long as he didn't talk too much.

Earth men hated him.

The first generation of Identities grew fast. Robust, tall, and strong, they spread across the world, some inviting him to their new country, welcoming his stories of Planet Hy Man and advice on how to make a woman happy.

Nicholas, an Identity from Australia, begged him to visit.

"I cut hair," he said. "Great way to meet miserable women—they always think a perm will solve their problems."

Legless looked up from his writing implement. He was sitting in the so-called lounge of the ferry and could hear a distant radio from somewhere outside.

The Eagles . . . He smiled. "Take It Easy" was playing. He hummed as memories of Australia flooded back.

It was the seventies—*his* time.

He was lean and tanned with hair in all the right places, and with a Rod Stewart's arse and a James Bond's confidence, he could really work a room.

He hung out in bistros "clocking Sheilas" with the Italians and Greeks, men who knew a thing or two—mainly how to pull off a John Travolta haircut.

Saturday Night Fever was big back then, along with flared jeans and medallions so big you could knock a cat out with them. And Legless in jeans so tight he could barely fart had a John Travolta strut down to perfection. He even learned to play footy, kick a goal, mark a ball, and pose in photos to make his arms look muscular.

Driving was easy back then. Sixty was speeding, roads were clear, and "coppers," like women, were laid back and easy to win over and liked a beer or two.

Legless watched the dark waters of the Clyde splash onto the ferry windows.

Blistering summers, barbecues, flies, driving through the bush in a Holden Kingswood, his hand on a Sheila's thigh, both of them hot and sweaty . . .

He could almost taste the heat.

He sighed.

Australia was the place to be back then: plenty of out-of-the-way places for a secret fumble. Until, that is, he met Karen.

Chapter Fourteen

SPEECHLESS TROUT

"Beryl had no idea that Mandy had the ability to put a stunt man to shame." Legless's memoir

Beryl, stunned as a bludgeoned trout, was speechless.

She had no idea Mandy was anything other than a blonde learning to drive because her pain-in-the-arse partner had told her she couldn't. A blonde determined to prove her partner wrong despite his leaving her for a redhead just this side of the legal age.

In fact, she had no idea that a woman on Earth could drive like Mandy let alone move like a stuntman.

As she watched Mandy pin the tall hoodie against the bins with the car, Beryl wondered what else she didn't know about this woman who up till now had said little apart from ask who Beryl's hairdresser was.

Mandy reversed, revved the engine, and charged again at the hoodies.

The hoodies scattered.

Mandy pulled up beside Beryl. "Get in."

"What?" said Beryl, and for the first time, she noticed a hint of a five-o'clock shadow.

"I said get in."

Jimmie's Arabic Tea Shop had changed over the years. Thanks to health and safety, smoking was now restricted to the outside, the hookah to a dark corner at the bottom of the garden so cold it required dressing for the Antarctic. A dark corner at the end of a dodgy footpath lit by nothing but the smoker's mobile phones—not an easy thing to navigate when clutching a hookah.

Archie called it "Skidding access to Skid Row," which no one found funny as he usually cracked such a joke mid skid—anyone's but his.

Archie, despite looking a bit like an apple on legs, had the balance of a seasoned yogi; he could do anything on tiptoes, including avoid a skid.

Skid Row was the most exposed corner of the ground. Whatever wind blew into Glasgow, the corner not only captured it but trapped it into a whirlwind, making incognito talking a breeze and smoking a hookah as challenging as threading a needle blind. It was as much fun as skidding down the Skid Row path dressed for the Antarctic.

DJ and Archie, huddled by a gas heater trying to make the best of some out-of-date strawberry tobacco, watched Legless stumble down the path with a tray.

Legless placed the tray on the table, and DJ jumped to balance the table while catching an about-to-topple mug. "Easy . . . ." said DJ.

Legless plonked himself down and glumly pulled a sugar sachet from the tray.

"What's eating you?" said Archie mid suck of the hookah.

"Beryl didn't even eat the toast I made her this morning."

"Probably saving the world," said DJ.

Legless threw him a *hardly* look.

"What did you expect? You hooked up with Planet Hy Man's finest, a true leader."

"I told you she doesn't do that anymore." He shook his sugar sachet limply.

"Once a leader, always a leader," muttered Archie.

"She's not a pickling leader, she's a driving instructor."

DJ and Archie glanced at each other.

"There's something afloat, I can feel it," said Legless.

Archie spluttered.

There had been talk of third-generation Identities driving about flagrantly abusing the road signs. Legless had no idea, and Archie wanted it kept that way.

He needed to sort these lads out, and the last thing he needed was *her* interfering; one whiff of sugar and she'd blow the Identities' cover sky-high like a virus on Facebook.

Beryl, for the most part, avoided sugar.

One cube of the stuff and she was off, shoving anything sweet she could find into her mouth like an alcoholic with the first drink. Mars bars had her delirious, Snickers dancing like a lap dancer, while the mere hint of Pepsi turned her into a motormouth and had her giving away secrets on Facebook.

She was always on that thing, showing off her successful drivers, but under the influence of a rum and Coke, she took several "I am alien" selfies that had Legless deleting like mad.

"There's always something afloat with her," said DJ. "Why don't you ask her?"

Archie kicked DJ under the table; the teacups juddered.

"I saw that," muttered Legless. "You think I'm an imbecile—just like *her*?"

"I think you'll find all men are imbeciles with *her*," huffed Archie.

"What's an imbecile?" said DJ.

Archie nodded at Legless trying to open his packet of sugar.

"Oh, I see," said DJ. He grabbed the packet and, with the ease of ripping off a Band-Aid, opened it.

Legless grabbed it in disgust. He shivered. "Why the frig are we sitting here anyway? There's a perfectly good log burner inside and no one beside it."

"We are here because of all this health-and-safety shit." Archie gestured with the tip of his hookah. "Now give a man peace while he's smoking, will yer?"

"You hate those things," said Legless.

Archie coughed. "What would you know?"

"Unless, of course, you've something to . . . well . . . discuss out of earshot?"

Archie spluttered. "Just smoking." He handed the pipe to DJ.

DJ sucked. "Aye, just smoking,"

Legless sipped his tea. "Well, friggin' hurry up. Even my tea is cold."

DJ passed the pipe to Legless with a cough. "Don't let it go out."

Legless blew a pillar of smoke into the air. "Won't be long before shared sucking will be a thing of the past."

"Must you put it like that?" said DJ.

"Once that virus kicks in, this"—he waved the nozzle in the air—"will be as illegal as slapping a policeman."

Chapter Fifteen

HILDA

"Human men and Planet Hy Man men are as different as soya and Stilton, one being an acquired taste and the other being best served with a bottle of red."–Beryl

Hilda plunged into a tunnel, where her life flashed before her.

It was not a pretty sight.

She squirmed like a worm on a hook and, mid squirming, plopped smack into a large corduroy couch. Its cushions engulfed her.

The room circled; noises faded in and out as Hilda, resisting the urge to throw up, tried to right herself. She had no idea what had happened to her, just as she had no idea about portals or the ribbed feel of corduroy—or, for that matter, couches that sucked her in.

She knew of telespraying, and what she had just been through was nothing like it. It was more like . . . something out of an Earth sci-fi film.

Hilda swallowed hard. She waited for her eyes to adjust, for her body to stop pulsing as the thick, stifling smell of disinfectant filled her nostrils.

Telespraying is a controlled transfer from one world to the next, leaving the land-ee feeling like a ruffled cat—a few minutes and a shake of a head was all it took to get one's bearings.

Portal riding, however, left the rider feeling like she had just been on a roller coaster and dumped into an out-of-control lift, then plummeted a hundred floors down and back up again—leaving her stomach behind like last night's dinner.

Throwing up was generally a given.

Hilda, with her knees about her chest, belched.

She looked about and tried to press herself upright; a cushion toppled onto her head as her backside slid further between the back and the seat.

She gave up with a flop.

The TV blared; a Scottish voice as easy to understand as a barking dog filled the room.

"You're listening to the news on BBC Scotland . . ."

Shit, thought Hilda. *I am on Earth!*

Chapter Sixteen

MOONING

"Throwing a moony has little to do with tossing."–Hoodie (name unknown)

Beryl jumped in, and before she even shut the door, Mandy charged off with the sort of screech that stopped cats in their tracks. And as a particularly scraggly ginger tom jolted behind a bin, Mandy wrenched the car around the corner.

She sped up the hill.

"Take it into third," said Beryl.

"Third? Not on my friggin' watch," said Mandy.

"It won't make it up the hill in fifth—you need to take it down a gear."

Mandy threw a glare at Beryl. "Just watch me!"

"It'll stall . . ."

The car, however, didn't. It screeched up the hill with the sort of speed that had Beryl swearing every pickle she could think of.

"Look out!" she shouted as they swerved past a cyclist . . .

A car overtook them with a prolonged honk of a horn, and the shorter of the hoodies stuck his head out of the car and gave Mandy the finger.

"Well, I never," said Mandy.

"Just ignore them," said Beryl.

Mandy slammed her horn.

"I said ignore them," shouted Beryl.

Mandy stuck her head out the window. "Get stuffed." Her hair fluttered in the wind, sliding back from her forehead.

The hoodies screeched a U-turn.

"Why didn't you just ignore them?" said Beryl.

"Nobody fingers me," snapped Mandy, adjusting what Beryl could now see was indeed a wig.

"I think you'll find it's *give the finger*," snapped Beryl.

The hoodies shot past again, this time one baring a pimply white tattooed bum.

The sort of tattoo unfamiliar to Earth people.

Legless pulled out his speech with affected panache.

Archie rolled his eyes at DJ.

Legless stopped. "I saw that."

The two men shuffled uncomfortably.

"There's no need for a speech now," said DJ.

"What? But it's my turn," said Legless. "I've sat through everyone else's, applauded, encouraged, even fed back . . ."

"More like bitched," said DJ.

"I did not *bitch*."

"You had some Identities in tears," said DJ.

"As if." Legless looked at Archie for support.

"You were pretty mean at times." Archie sighed; he was still smarting from Legless's jibes about his recently grown ponytail.

Archie, unlike Legless, had a full head of hair, which recently he'd grown to wear in a ponytail, while Legless, his hair falling out like he was on chemo, had shaved his.

"If you're gonna stand up and talk, then at least know what you're talking about," snapped Legless.

"We've all got to start somewhere," said DJ.

"I was the first, damn it; I know what I'm talking about."

"Aye right."

"I've done my research, been about," he said, looking from one to the other. "Don't I deserve some respect?"

The two men looked at him like he was talking through his arse. In fact, if they didn't feel sorry for him, they would have said as much.

A year ago, Legless was top billing. Identities came from everywhere to hear him speak, as far as Canada, Australia, and even Mongolia.

He not only had conquered the great Beryl but continued to do so, and the Identities marveled at him—until, that is, the camper van arrived.

Identities read minds like humans read mobiles, and Legless's was full of great times with Beryl, until their relationship took a nosedive. He tried to hide it, control his thoughts, but even an Identity of Legless's caliber could not have kept that up for long.

The Identities saw it all: the lonely visits to the planetarium, the solo trips to the co-op; the unopened tea cupboard, and the most humiliating of all: Beryl driving off in the camper van, forgetting about him.

Soon Legless had as much appeal as a day-old espresso.

Some softhearted Identities felt sorry for him and wanted to help. Some even arranged "enhancement meetings," brought in speakers who taught innovative ways to "pleasure" the modern woman.

Legless had no idea that they were trying to help, that they felt sorry for him. He just waited his turn, prepared his speeches, and arrived at his meeting with his latest rolled up in his hand.

The Identities put him off with more excuses than a partner who'd gone off sex, hoping that one day Legless would see the light, realize that he was as out-of-date as a rental video.

Until that is, Legless started to find fault with them . . .

"There's more to pleasing a woman than, well—the Legless method," said Archie quietly.

Legless tossed the hookah nozzle at the table, his temper flaring. "There's nothing wrong with the 'Legless method.'"

"It's hardly a method," said Archie.

Legless turned to Archie, a caustic "ponytail" comment on the tip of his tongue. Then he caught Archie's eye and stopped.

"Well, I don't hear Beryl complaining," he muttered.

"Why do you think she took up teaching?" muttered DJ.

"Only this morning I successfully mounted Herself—" said Legless.

"Pfff," said DJ.

"—like a lion."

"Aye right."

"Doesn't matter now," said Archie. "There's no more pickling meetings."

Legless stopped, his speech flapping in the wind. "But what about the women?"

"What about 'em?" said Archie.

"Will they not roll up and, you know, make a fuss?"

"Hardly," said Archie.

Legless looked from one man to the other.

"Lockdown starts tonight," said Archie. "Have you not heard?"

"Shit," said Legless. "Forgot about that."

Chapter Seventeen

THE CARE HOME

"Nothing reeks like failure."—Hilda

Hilda, like many on Planet Hy Man, had seen Earth on her H-Pad, and she had no desire to be there.

She huffed and grunted with her knees about her chest. She tried to free her backside, then gave up with a flop and looked around the empty room as run down as the Courtyard of Greatness and as out-of-date as Legless's chat-up lines.

There was a Victorian photograph of a pier on the wall, a whiteboard with the day and a smiley face beside it, a plastic flower arrangement on a nest of tables, and, next to the TV blaring the news, a dark cabinet filled with Victorian china dolls, board games, and a selection of tattered Stephen King paperbacks.

There was an air of beige about it.

A middle-aged woman with a Margaret Thatcher hairdo sprayed to the max appeared. She slid a plate of biscuits on the table and with a "where is she?" caught sight of Hilda squashed up like a hobbit.

She laughed, grabbed Hilda's hand, and, with a robust pull, lifted her to her feet.

Hilda staggered, adjusting her "market stall onesie," which on Earth looked more like an eighties orange jumpsuit.

"That couch has swallowed more folk than an alligator," chuckled Morag, the Margaret Thatcher look-alike.

This couch swallows? thought Hilda as Morag led her to a firm chair by the window.

Hilda fell to the seat with a grunt as an ancient, wizened woman appeared clutching a Zimmer frame uselessly, swinging it inches from the ground.

She stopped, eying Hilda. "You're in my chair."

"It's not your chair," said Morag.

"It is too. *She* said it is."

"*That* is not a *she*," said the Morag. "That is a doll."

The hoodie sped off, turned into an empty co-op car park, and screeched to a halt.

Mandy drove on.

Beryl looked back to see the three hoodies fall out of the car in hysterics.

Mandy took a left, a right, and another left, pulling into the Park Hotel car park with a sharp brake.

Beryl's pale blue beehive jolted against the car ceiling. "What the hell was that?"

Mandy switched off the engine.

"Just who the frig are you?" snapped Beryl.

Mandy unclipped her seatbelt.

"I thought you said you couldn't drive."

"In a manner of speaking," said Mandy.

Beryl, her patience as thin as plastic wrap, was on the verge of shouting "What the hell does that mean?" when her gaze strayed to the care home across the road, and she caught sight of a familiar hairdo at a window.

Her eyes fixed on the spiky hair.

It can't be . . .

The figure at the window righted her beehive as two women in black waitress outfits walked past. They knocked on Beryl's window.

Beryl rolled down her window with a grimace.

"Have you heard?" said the grumpy-looking one.

The spiky hair moved . . . Beryl saw a flash of orange . . .

"Everything is shutting down."

"What?" said Mandy.

"Lockdown. Starts tonight at midnight."

The doll dressed like Queen Victoria took up a whole shelf.

Queenie, unlike the other dolls sitting upright and untouched, was squashed into a fetal position, like she had been rammed in with a rush.

Her china face was pressed against the glass door, her bun of hair flattened and framed by an arm freakishly twisted like it was broken.

The face looked like it had been made up in the back of a horse box while the horse was happily nudging. The splintered cracks on the face were covered in blotches of talcum powder, cheeks and lips rouged like a clown giving her a sort of surprised Ronald McDonald leer.

Hilda stared at the false eyelash dangling from one eye like a spider and assumed both were Earth robots.

The Zimmer-clutching woman, aptly called Serenity, turned toward the doll with reverence and curtsied.

"Mum, it's a doll," said Morag. She sighed and turned to Hilda. "Who are you visiting? I don't think I've seen you before."

"Queenie says she's from outer space," said Serenity.

Morag rolled her eyes.

"To protect the equilibrium."

"Goodness sake, Mum."

"Didn't you, Queenie?" Serenity dragged Queenie from her shelf and sat her up on a chair. Queenie flopped at the middle like she'd been punched in the stomach.

Serenity pushed her back into the seat. Queenie flopped to the ground, her right foot trapped in the back of the chair. Her skirt flopped over her head.

The three women stared at the tea-stained lace bloomers the care home staff had tried many times to remove and wash with no success.

The only person allowed to touch Queenie was Serenity and, at push, her daughter.

"She's never been the same since her fall," muttered Morag.

"I did not fall."

"You were on your knees."

"I was just resting; been dancing." She skipped a jig, nearly tripping over Queenie.

"Mind!" yelled Morag, swiftly lifting Queenie and wrenching her leg free.

"She was found outside that student's place—Jimmie's Arabic Tea Shop," said Morag.

She stuffed Queenie back onto the shelf, swiftly ramming the door shut before Queenie tumbled out. "You've heard of it?"

Hilda shook her head. "How she got there, no one knows."

"I caught a taxi," Serenity shouted over the news. She opened the glass door, and Queenie tumbled to the floor like a sack of potatoes.

"Leave it."

Serenity ignored Morag.

"We're just about to have some tea."

Queenie flopped like a rag doll; a false eyelash fluttered to the floor.

Morag grabbed Queenie. "Let me take it home. Give it a wash, sort the makeup."

An arm cluttered to the floor.

"Fix it up."

Serenity bent for the arm. "*It* is a *she*," she grunted, "and *she* likes herself just as she is."

Serenity, overbalanced, clutched the TV to right herself; both wobbled.

Morag grabbed her mother and motioned her to Hilda's seat.

Hilda stood, catching sight of a car driving into the Park Hotel car park opposite. Then she caught a flash of a pale blue beehive in the driver seat . . .

Morag waved.

Serenity made for Queenie, snatching at her bun.

"Mum, it's dirty, unhygienic. Let me have it."

They tussled; Hilda marveled at Morag's set-in-stone hair.

Queenie's head flew across the room and skidded across the nest of tables with a spin, knocking the dried flowers for six.

It stopped, the eyes freakishly catching Hilda's like in a Stephen King film.

Serenity marched to the table, picked up the head, and, with a glare at her daughter, rammed it back onto Queenie's torso.

The head tumbled to the ground; its eyes rolled to the side, catching Hilda yet again.

"I'll get the superglue," sighed Morag like she had done such a thing a million times before.

She turned to Hilda. "Keep an eye on her? Won't be long."

"Don't forget the tea," shouted Serenity. She turned up the TV to a deafening screech.

"What?" shouted Hilda.

Serenity smiled.

Hilda, with one eye on the car park below, gingerly smiled back.

"She is not really a queen," said Serenity.

A flash of a blue—a beehive hairdo got out of the car.

Beryl looked up.

Hilda ducked.

Serenity dragged the one-armed, headless Queenie across the room. She peered out a window.

"Queenie is an Identity."

The Park Hotel car park was the place where Beryl often met pupils.

In fact, so successful was the arrangement that other teachers soon followed, meeting for coffee at the end of the day and swapping driving stories.

The receptionist even took bookings for them on the sly.

Beryl looked up at the window again; the spiky hair had vanished. Serenity peered down with an intense stare.

Beryl gave a tentative wave.

Chapter Eighteen

CORDUROY COUCH

"Legless's rolling-on-and-off method of pleasure was as out-of-date as a rental video."—Identity unknown

Hilda looked at Beryl standing in the car park, a spitting distance from the window. She could almost smell her.

"Pfff—*her*," huffed Serenity.

"You know her?"

"She taught Morag to drive."

Hilda stopped. *Beryl teaches?*

A giant of a woman slid out the other side of the car.

Hilda frowned. *Did Beryl just laugh?*

"No one knows who she is," said Serenity with a two-fingered wave.

They watched Beryl head into the hotel with Mandy.

"She's from outer space," said Serenity.

"How do you know?"

"The Identities."

Hilda turned to Serenity. "Identities?"

"Yes."

"Of course, no one believes me. They call me senile."

Hilda's face softened. She nodded. *Serenity was as senile as the news-reader on the TV.*

"Your Queenie performance is pretty impressive."

Serenity laughed. Acting like a nutcase was as natural to her as pulling off a sock.

"I have heard of Stephen King too, you know," said Hilda.

"He's my favorite," said Serenity.

Beryl headed into the hotel, telling herself she was seeing things, that the stress of Mandy's driving was playing tricks on her.

She drove like a rally driver . . .

She collapsed into a chair. Mandy joined her, her large square hands resting on the armrest.

Beryl stared at them, her thoughts drifting back to the trans people at the Edinburgh International Book Festival again. Once she realized Mandy wore a wig, it was so obvious; she wondered why she hadn't seen it before.

"Mandy," she said, "can I ask you something?"

A tiny elderly woman strutted in, followed by her male instructor.

"Bleeding China," she said. "Here's me on the cusp of a license, the chance to get my hands on Henry's Aston Martin, and fucking COVID hits."

She caught sight of Beryl.

"I'll be gar-gar by the time it's all over," she heaved. "Over there"— she gestured to the care home—"sipping piss-weak tea."

"Let's head outside," said Mandy.

Hilda, her soya snack of three hours prior now settled thanks to a volley of belches, headed into the Park Hotel.

The last thing she needed was to lose Beryl.

Before Morag returned, Serenity had her slipping out the emergency exit in a down-and-out overcoat and clutching a Costa coffee.

The jacket came from the "unclaimed" cupboard, a dark, dusty place that had Hilda wondering what she had gotten herself into.

Hilda slipped it on with a "must I?"

Serenity stood back with a "perfect."

Hilda slid her fingers into the pockets and pulled out a dried-up, snotty hanky. She recoiled with a gag.

Serenity, with an "it's contagious" sniff, tossed it at the bin. "It's your cover," she said.

"It's disgusting," said Hilda.

"No one will notice you."

Hilda looked confused.

"You look like a homeless person, and they're invisible. Trust me."

She stopped.

"Something's missing." Then she grabbed the Costa coffee mug from the bin and, with a quick un-scrunching, thrust it into Hilda's hand. "Don't throw it away."

Hilda looked confused.

"You'll know what to do, and when."

Serenity had been dancing with the Identities for a year before her fall. A year of bliss and chocolate. A year of jiving with Identities, some young enough to be her grandson, others old enough to share the same memories. The good old days of glamorous ashtrays, perms, and Brylcream.

In fact, some of the old Identities still wore the stuff, filling the dance floor with a scent that had Serenity and her peers reliving the good old days of rock-and-roll dances and seatbelt-free cars.

After her fall, the dancing and the meetings stopped. She, with a gammy leg, was put into a care home for a "well-earned rest," a "holiday."

Her family, assuming she'd lost it, that she was wandering aimlessly, thought she'd remain in the home for good.

Serenity was determined to go home once her leg was better.

She was as lucid as a surgeon at an operating table; she had the memory of a crossword champion, the moves of a chess player, and the firmly held belief that she had met Legless for a reason.

Reading discarded copies of Legless's *The Apparatus of a Woman* and *The Spark Plug Odyssey* had inspired her to stop sitting and live . . . stop caring about the past and jump.

They were just so *boring*. They made sleep seem like a prison sentence . . .

She planned to escape, dance till she dropped, until she saw Beryl's pale blue beehive appear from her daughter's car like an apparition from Legless's *The Spark Plug Odyssey*.

It was just as he described . . .

She realized she was in the care home for a purpose. Just what that was, she had no idea, until she saw her daughter pull Hilda from the couch.

Over the years, the corduroy couch had managed to suck in wheelchair pushers, cleaners, daughters, and partners, and when the consultant landed knees to nose, the staff talked of dumping it . . . even burning it.

Serenity put up a fight. She liked the couch as much as Izzie did; it was their patting place. But after Izzie's famed panic attack, she'd started to see things at night . . . glowing under the cushions.

No one believed her, but she was determined to find out what was going on, even sprawling herself across it while screeching "Over my dead fanny!" when the removal men appeared, which surprised everyone.

Her shouting "fanny" was as likely as her flipping a somersault.

"I knew I was here for a reason," Serenity said to Hilda. "Guess it was you."

"I'll be back," said Hilda.

"I know," said Serenity. "You'll need the couch."

Chapter Nineteen

THE PARK HOTEL

"It can take a lifetime to find who you are—and but a moment to jump."—Don

Hilda headed across the street to the hotel. The receptionist, an elderly woman, took in Hilda's spiky hair and made-to-last, water-proof-as-fuck work boots and, assuming she was a lesbian with DIY abilities, immediately warmed to her.

She had spent most of her life with a man as silent as a goalpost. Not that her husband was bad or anything; more that he simply wasn't there. He hadn't touched her in years; now a widow with no one to cook for, she often wondered about women. Would living with, caring for, loving a woman be any different?

"If it's a room you're after, you've no chance, luv."

Hilda warmed to the "luv."

The receptionist glanced at Hilda's apprehensive face. "Or is it a lesson?" She pulled a book from under the desk. "You'll need to schedule the next open appointment," she said, flicking open her calendar. "Who knows when that'll be, though"—she looked up—"the way things are going."

She gazed at Hilda's confused face and assumed it was fear. "If you're nervous, don't be; Beryl's the perfect teacher."

The two waitresses appeared clutching a tray of clean cutlery and napkins, talking of lockdown and setting Hilda into a spin of confusion. They sounded fearful, anxious, angry, and yet they laughed, making jokes about the PM's "toilet brush haircut"—a heady mix for someone like Hilda to interpret.

Hilda, with no idea what a PM was, assumed he was the messy blond-haired man she'd seen on the BBC news. A prime minister who seemed to know what he was doing despite always looking like he had just jumped out of bed.

"The PM said it's for the best," said the jovial waitress.

"That jumped-up twat," said the grumpy waitress. "He has as much an idea of what to do as how to use a hairbrush."

"None of us do."

"All those buggers coming from other countries—what the hell were they thinking of letting them in? Too late to stop it all now . . ."

The women stopped, looked at Hilda's spiky hair, and assumed she was a militant lesbian.

"Another candidate for Herself," said the receptionist with a genuine smile.

Hilda basked under her warmth.

"God knows when that'll be," muttered the grumpy waitress.

"Beryl's booked up for months," said the jovial waitress.

"I was talking of lockdown," snapped the grumpy one.

"Beryl?" said Hilda. "Where can I find her?"

Chapter Twenty

THE SPY WHO LOVED ME

"A moony is as conspicuous as a fart in a church."–Mandy

Beryl and Mandy headed toward Victoria Promenade, Mandy sticking to Beryl like denture grip, feeling the need to explain, and Beryl perplexed . . .

Hilda, her senses on overdrive, her eyes glued to Beryl's back, followed.

Beryl was her only hope. She had no plan B.

Dunoon was not a busy place; homeless people were rare, and it didn't take long for Hilda to feel, well, obvious—like a wart on a nose. Her onesie was as out of place as a codpiece on a receptionist. She wrapped her coat more tightly about her despite the sunshine.

She began to sweat like a boxer.

Despite watching Earth's TV, she was completely unprepared for the sight of so many men: their aroma, their facial hair, their different sizes and weird shapes. Men with round stomachs hanging over belts, men in jackets too tight to do up, men with ponytails, bald men, some with glasses, some laughing, and all strutting about like they owned the place.

Beryl stopped.

Hilda panicked, feigned sipping coffee, and gagged. Whatever was on the bottom was as fresh as Queenie's makeup.

Mandy turned around.

Hilda, thinking on her feet, pulled a calculator from her onesie and pretended it was a mobile.

"That's not a mobile," said a little voice.

Hilda, a verbal telling-off on the tip of her tongue, turned to catch sight of a small boy who barely reached her waist. His tiny face and sweet milky breath stopped her short.

She put her fingers to her lips. "I'm a spy," she whispered.

His face lit up. "A spy?"

Hilda nodded as that queer feeling of warmth hit her again, until the mother appeared and dropped a coin into Hilda's empty coffee cup.

"What's that for?" said Hilda.

"Coffee," the woman said, eyeing her grubby overcoat. "Or a wash." She dragged the boy away.

"He's a spy, mum."

"*He* is a *she*," said the mother.

"Why does she look like a he then?" said the boy.

"She's homeless," sniffed the mother.

"Is that the same as a spy?" said the boy as another passer-by dropped a coin in Hilda's coffee cup.

Chapter Twenty-One

THE CALCULATOR

"Her onesie was as out of place as a codpiece on a receptionist."
—Serenity

Under Earth's atmosphere of car and takeaway fumes, Hilda's calculator had upcycled into the sort of deluxe, super-duper, high-powered H-Pad that made an Earth CCT camera as out-of-date as blackboard and chalk.

Quicker than the crack of a whip, the calculator connected with Alice, sending her receptors into overload.

Alice lit up like a Christmas tree.

She could see, hear, and smell everything Hilda could, and Alice had no sense of smell; it was missing from her sensory data.

Alice reeled over new earthly sensations as Hilda, unaware, continued to use her calculator as a pseudo mobile. She saw everything; it was like 3-D film with smell-o-vision . . .

Hilda passed the Boathouse, a small café heaving with last-minute orders of chips, pies, burgers, and rolls filled with sausages, bacon, cheese, eggs, and tomato ketchup.

"You all right?" said Verruca, watching Alice circle like a dog on the scent of something shaggable.

"I think I can smell meat. At least I think it's meat." She sighed. "No wonder you lot miss it. If I had a mouth, it'd be watering by now."

She stopped.

"Hang on, she's moving."

"Who's moving?" said Verruca.

"Hilda," said Alice.

"Hilda?" said Verruca.

"Hilda!" shouted Cyborg.

The sportswomen, mid arguing with the statue builders, stopped. *Hilda?*

Hilda passed a dog tucking into a bone.

Alice stopped. "Oh, that is disgusting."

"You can see?" said Verruca. "Where is she?"

Alice watched as an elderly lady tripped in front of Hilda. Hilda stopped to help.

"Great pickling grief," said Alice.

"What's happening?" said Verruca.

"She just stopped to help."

"No."

"Get out of here . . ."

"As if."

"She's grabbed her."

"Pfff, that'll help," said Cyborg.

Alice flashed her sights onto Legless's rump.

The women stared.

"Where do you think she's landed?" said Dozy.

"Where do you think she got that coat?" said the voice from the back.

The elderly woman slapped Hilda away, calling her a "lesbian hobo."

"Earth," muttered Verruca.

The door to the room with a view opened.

Deidre crouched behind the watercooler, her pencil poised.

A footman doing his best to run shuffled out, leaving the door ajar.

She heard gasps, then *Hilda, Earth* and *Zoom* in the same sentence, and she stopped.

This called for something bigger . . . and something way older than a pencil and paper.

The three Identities now inside Jimmie's Arabic Tea Shop were sitting by the wood burner as the waiter/cook/cleaner/student gave the remains of the fire a good rattle and slammed it.

Legless, sulking, said nothing, completely unaware that his legs were in the way of the waiter/cook/cleaner/student.

Finally he had a corker of a speech that would have those know-it-all Identities on their knees, but thanks to friggin' lockdown, his plans were as fucked as his prostate. He sighed. What was coming of this place—health and safety screwing up a decent smoke, meetings canceled, the world closing down because of some virus that sounded like a Russian spy in a James Bond film?

The waiter/cook/cleaner/student sidestepped Legless's legs, lifted the empty cups, and, with a pointed flick of his towel, began to wipe the table.

"Could we have a coffee?" said Archie. "Perhaps with cream?"

"We're closing soon."

"Just a quick one."

"It's never quick with you lot."

"An espresso then?"

He glared at them. He had the toilets to clean, the floors to mop, the cashing up, then he had to cycle across the friggin' city to the college, pick up all his stuff, and . . . *Jesus*—move in with his mum.

He looked at his watch. "You want me to fire up the coffee machine five minutes before closing time?"

Archie and DJ looked at him blankly; they were reluctant to split up. Talk of lockdown had them anxious. When would they meet again?

"I just cleaned the friggin' thing and you want me to make espressos?"

"Well, yes."

The manageress/mum appeared, a tiny woman with the look of someone who managed with exasperation. Who not only cleaned up after the waiter/cook/cleaner/student but sorted his mistakes and dealt with his unhappy customers. She slid on an apron, and after tying it around her tiny waist, she eyed the men.

There was something weird about these men, and she could never be arsed to find out. Jimmy, the owner, thought they were fantastic, the bees' knees, always giving them freebies, allowing them to "stay on." Well, he wasn't here and she was, and the last thing she needed on the eve of lockdown was being held back by these bozos. She had to clean up, lock up, pick up her son, make sure there was enough toilet paper in the house, and god knows what else.

There seemed so much to do . . .

"We're closed," she snapped.

Archie looked at her, trying to make eye contact, appeal to her womanly nature, his ESP working overtime.

Hands on hips, she stood her ground. "I said we are closed."

"You said closing."

"*He* said closing," she said, gesturing to the waiter/cook/cleaner/student. "I said closed—too much to do."

Archie, flashing his best puppy dog eyes, tried a fatherly ESP . . .

"Sweetheart."

"I'm not your sweetheart."

"Just, my bunions are playing up," said Archie, "and a coffee would fair set them right."

Untouched, she snapped, "Don't try that malarky with me."

DJ stood. "Let's go. Let this lot clear up."

"Thank you," said the manageress/mum.

DJ stopped and touched her arm. "And perhaps when lockdown is over . . ."

"In your dreams," she snapped.

The waiter/cook/cleaner/student chuckled.

The three Identities stood to go, sliding their damp jackets back on as the pair headed into the kitchen.

"What's bunions got to do with coffee?" muttered the waiter/cook/cleaner/student.

"Fuck all," muttered manageress/mum.

Legless turned to Archie. "Should have left it to me. I could have gotten you a hot chocolate and at least an hour."

"In your friggin' dreams," barked the manageress/mum from the kitchen.

Beryl and Mandy headed away from the street, past Dunoon's very own Hard Rock Café and the Boathouse café, and on to the Victoria parade, which ran along the sea loch. It was their usual walk after a lesson and often led to a coffee and egg roll.

It was a clear afternoon with not many people about, yet still neither seemed to see Hilda following behind.

Hilda, still clutching her complimentary coffee (now with several coins), watched as they took a seat on a park bench and hid behind a tree.

A ton of questions reeled through her mind until Mandy caught her eye, dwarfing Beryl like a wrestler beside a ballerina.

A queer feeling hit Hilda deep inside.

A breeze ruffled Beryl's beehive. She eyed Mandy's slight Adam's apple. *Why did I not notice before?* "You're not really a woman, are you?"

"I am too. Just waiting for the hormones to kick in," said Mandy.

She lifted her wig.

"I am in transition."

Beryl touched her shaved hair. *It's so soft.*

"I had no idea," said Beryl.

"Most don't."

"That a scalp could be so round, so beautiful."

Mandy laughed with a blush. "That's what shaving does to you."

Beryl nodded, curious, until Mandy mentioned her operation.

Beryl asked her to stop. "What about your partner? Does he know?"

"A mere ruse," said Mandy.

Beryl's face stiffened. "Ruse? What are you, a spy?"

Mandy coughed. "I blend in like a priest in a mosque—or should I say a nun." She sighed. "I've been laughed out of more dressing rooms than your hairspray collection."

Beryl bristled.

She hesitated. "It's not easy being an Identity, let alone in transition."

"You're an Identity?"

"Growing up was hard enough."

"You really are an Identity?"

"Not feeling human, hearing other women's thoughts, not knowing why."

"I can't believe you're an Identity."

"But when you feel like a girl despite what's between your legs doing its own thing . . ."

Beryl's face softened.

"I thought once I started to transition, it would be different; I'd be seen as a woman." She turned to Beryl. "Those idiot hoodies sniffed me out."

"Those were Identities too?"

"In a manner of speaking."

Beryl sighed.

"Third generation . . . total morons."

"There must be others like you," said Beryl. "There always are. Even robots come in groups—there is never just one."

"You would think," said Mandy.

Deidre pulled out her out-of-date sucker recorder. It went back to the days of spaceships. In fact, she'd found it on one, near the abandoned Art Centre—a center that once housed geriatric footmen with little to do but cut their toenails and see to their bunions (an all-day task due to their inability to stand on one foot).

The spaceships were forgotten like the four-legged creatures.

Deidre liked to go there and think, tinker with the out-of-date kitchen, imagine what it was like sailing through space with no idea where to land.

It appealed to the writer in her, unlike the masses, who didn't even look at her Look Back and Wonder series—most used the paper it was written on to line their underwear drawers and shoeboxes.

She found several thin manuals in the john, during days when the diet on the spaceship had men sitting on it more frequently than blinking.

The potato peeler in the kitchen fascinated her; it took a long time for her to work out what it was. Potato skins on Plant Hy Man were considered a delicacy, the best part of a potato; in fact, peeling any veg on Planet Hy Man was unheard of. To them, it was like throwing away the cherry of a cupcake.

For while, she contemplated such an object, until she came across a decoder and the sucker recorder.

The decoder was the sort of instrument that decoded noises from space.

And the sucker recorder was so called because of its ability to not only stick to a wall (with suckers) but *suck* the noise behind it, along with its own sucking sound (the main reason it remained a prototype).

Deidre, intrigued, took sucker recorder home.

She figured, if she stuck one on the wall of the room with a view, she could record in-depth whispering. All she needed was the shuffling of a footman to camouflage the sucking sound—a mere bribe away.

Chapter Twenty-Two

THE GODDESS

"You've been mooned!"–The bumper sticker of a seasoned mooner's car

"I thought if I found my father, then perhaps . . . I could somehow fit in, find a place."

Beryl's face softened. There was a time when she'd thought like that.

"I wouldn't worry; fathers aren't all they're cracked up to be." She looked at Mandy, who seemed so sad . . . "Maybe Archie can help. He's in touch with Identities all over the world."

Mandy's face burned. She had said too much. "Why don't I get the coffee this time," she nodded to a nearby burger van. "The usual?"

Hilda, unaware of a dog sniffing at her rear, watched Mandy stand and head toward her.

She pressed her back against the tree.

Mandy strode by.

Hilda caught her breath.

Mandy's scent lingered.

Hilda watched Mandy, the goddess, stride self-assuredly across the park.

She was stunning, a pure powerhouse.

Hilda couldn't take her eyes off her. She wondered what to do and then thought of all those stupid James Bond films Cyborg liked to watch on the sly.

Mandy stood at the van, a familiar feeling swirling in her imaginary womb. At first she thought it was her hormones, hunger, or perhaps the wind whipping about her thighs . . .

She flashed a smile at the round-faced van owner.

He smiled back with a "the usual?"

She nodded.

She could hear Hilda's thoughts; in fact, they had hit her like a sledgehammer.

What would James Bond do now?

She had no idea who owned those thoughts, let alone what James Bond had to do with things, but she knew it was all mixed up with Beryl . . . and a dog?

The van owner slid two mugs onto the bench. "Two coffees, two sugars, and lots of hot milk."

Mandy nodded a "cheers."

"And two egg rolls." He winked. "Not too hard." He nodded to the ketchup tray. "Help yourself."

He winked again, this time with a full-on, brand-new-set-of-dentures grin.

She winked back, feigning a coy smile.

Beryl's Nokia vibrated in her pocket—an H2 vibration.

She looked about. She could see Mandy in the distance clutching two coffees and a bag of something.

She quickly flicked open the phone.

"Hilda's disappeared via a portal . . ." messaged H2.

Beryl looked up. *Portal?*

"Suspected on Earth," added H2.

Shit! thought Beryl.

"No, wait a minute . . . Glasgow? Hang on. What was that, Alice?"

Beryl waited . . .

"Sorry, Dunoon," messaged H2.

Beryl, using a variety of pickles, swore under her breath until Mandy's large frame blocked the sun.

"Something wrong?" said Mandy.

Beryl faked a smile and shook her head.

Mandy plonked herself down beside Beryl and handed her a coffee. She didn't need ESP to see something was up.

"How old is that thing?" She gestured to Beryl's Nokia.

"This?" said Beryl. "Who knows?" She slid it into her pocket. "Must get a new one."

Mandy, picking up something about a *portal* and some *cow called Hilda*, passed over an egg roll. "Everything all right?" she said.

"Oh, absolutely," muttered Beryl.

She bit into her roll; yolk oozed from the side. She wiped her mouth.

"Any idea what a portal is?" she said with a casual air.

Mandy, with a mouthful of egg, began to talk of *Doctor Who* and telephone booths.

The dog barked.

Hilda jumped, stumbled, and turned to find the squashed face of a boxer inches from her nose, its hot, rhythmic breath fanning her face.

It was the size of a horse.

It took a moment for her to realize it wasn't a robot—that it was actually breathing and, God forbid, drooling.

It barked again.

She looked at the globules on her sleeve and almost gagged.

It pushed its nose onto her arm and sniffed, its earthy warm breath close to her neck; the nuzzling turned to licking.

Hilda froze. Was it about to eat her?

"Of course, the best example of a portal is *Star Trek*," said Mandy. "*The Original Series*." She sighed. "The dynamics between Kirk, Spock, and McCoy, and the costumes; always fancied myself as Uhura . . ." She stopped, catching sight of Beryl gazing ahead not even pretending to listen.

Mandy followed her gaze and spotted a large dog nuzzling what looked like . . . a stunned spiky-haired . . . man? Or was it a woman?

"Hilda," muttered Beryl along with another selection of pickles.

"Hilda?" said Mandy.

"Shhhh," hissed Beryl. She looked about. *Now where did that cow go now?*

The dog overpowering Hilda pushed her to the ground behind the tree—out of view.

Hilda had no idea what to do. A wet tongue was as foreign to her as a McDonald's, and the dog weighed a ton.

She struggled, tried to push, and then stopped. The fur felt smooth, the body warm. She looked at its face . . .

It wasn't going to eat her at all.

She stroked his back, then stopped; something felt hard against her leg. *Is that its member?*

Beryl, frozen to the park bench, stared at the tree, wondering where the hell Hilda had disappeared to. She waited and listened for several minutes, but all she could hear was the young voice of a girl shouting . . .

"Dumbledore, Dumbledore . . . Oh, there you are . . . Stop that! I said stop that. Bad boy! Very bad boy!"

Finally, after a "where are you?" text from Legless, she left Mandy for home.

Legless was in the camper van chopping onions when he heard the PM on the radio. He—deciding to make the best of things, as Archie suggested—was home early, feeling hopeful and preparing a "reliving of romantic times" meal in the camper van.

After several jokes with a Tesco "checkout chick" called Sheila and two heaving bags of groceries, he had made a plan. A cozy dinner for two, Beryl's favorite: French onion soup, spaghetti, homemade garlic bread, and a side salad with plenty of olives.

He sliced open a pepper with a crunch.

Perhaps lockdown would change things, bring him and Herself closer together.

He turned up the volume, then returned to his chopping board, mincing garlic with precision and sliding all into the pan.

The PM talked of China and the virus.

Legless stirred in the ground beef, dusted it with herbs, and listened.

China?

His memories went back to a brief fling with a Chinese woman. *Or was she Japanese?* He smiled. There were so many.

He slid the lid on the pan, trying to remember . . .

Great pickled pepper, she was from Thailand. What an idiot. He sighed. *She sure knew how to massage . . .*

The camper van began to steam up, and he opened a door wondering where Beryl was. She was late, even for her . . .

He quickly jotted down a note.

The Great Thai massage . . .
It was all about the oil with her, and the warmth of it. Listening to her warm
the oil in her hands was always the beginning of something, well, spectacular.
She called it Hawaiian.
I called it heaven.

Hilda, trapped under the horse of a dog, drool forgotten, was busy trying to dodge its member when she heard a child's voice shouting, "Dumbledore!"

Hilda looked up, catching the tiny face of a girl grabbing the dog's collar with grim determination.

"Bad Boy!" the girl hissed. "Very bad boy." She pulled him off.

Hilda dusted herself with a sigh.

The little girl looked at the strange woman wearing the sort of outfit even her mother wouldn't be seen dead in. A mere seven-year-old with a way-too-vivid imagination for her own good, she wondered if Hilda had escaped from a circus . . . or perhaps she was a spy? Either way, the funny woman didn't look like the sort who knew what she was doing.

"He's harmless really. Just a bit stupid." She patted Dumbledore. "See?"

Hilda sat up and tentatively stroked. "A total pussycat."

Beryl appeared, flying through the camper van door like a whirlwind.

Legless slid his notebook away and looked up.

She stopped, oblivious to the "steaming up" from Legless's cooking. "What are you doing?"

"Cooking," he said.

"In here?"

"Thought we'd relive some old memories."

"Not writing then?"

"I am making your favorite," he said.

"Did you not just slip a notebook away?"

"No."

She collapsed at the table. "Oh, bugger—who cares?"

"What?" said Legless.

"I said who cares?"

"Oh," said Legless.

"I've had a big fat pickle of a day," said Beryl.

Legless sighed. *It was always a pickle of a day with her.*

Beryl, her mind still on the disappearance of Hilda, pulled out her phone yet again.

"Can you not just put aside that thing for one minute?" said Legless.

Beryl looked at the blank screen. *No messages from "up there"—pickling nothing.*

"I thought we could have a cozy night in the camper van, just the two of us—bring back some memories."

Beryl, flicking through her messages, engrossed, didn't even nod.

"I've opened a nice red—you fancy one?" said Legless.

Silence.

"I've cooked spaghetti."

Beryl looked up. "What?"

"I said I've made your favorite," shouted Legless.

Beryl's phone rang. She looked at Legless with a "just a minute" and headed out the door to answer.

Legless sighed.

He may as well have shoved a pizza in the oven and eaten in the cottage in front of the TV.

Chapter Twenty-Three

MIND READING

"There was a feeling of manly aloofness about Mandy that I couldn't put my finger on."—Hilda's blog, An Alien in Paradise

Once Hilda started to pat, she couldn't stop. It felt so good, so different to anything she had touched before, and so deliciously warm . . .

She rubbed around his ears. "Ooh, he likes that."

"You could do that all day," sighed the girl.

Dumbledore nuzzled Hilda's neck.

Hilda laughed. "Who's a big scary boy then?"

"He does that to everyone, doesn't mean anything," said the girl.

"Y'big softy," Hilda muttered into his neck.

The girl eyed Hilda, who was beginning to look more like someone who sat in the streets begging for money . . . the sort her mum steered her away from.

"I need to go now." She tugged at Dumbledore.

"Just one more pat," said Hilda.

"Mum's calling," lied the girl.

Mandy, now alone, was still sitting on the park bench, pondering her future. She worked and lived in a hotel, but thanks to lockdown, that would soon change. She was already getting panicky texts from her coworkers.

She hadn't long been in the UK, didn't know many people, and for the first time felt unsure about what she was doing. What was the point of it all?

She tossed her cup at the bin, watched as it missed, and then heard the thoughts of the little girl as agitated as a dog being dragged to the vet.

She looked at the tree, catching sight of a little girl, a large boxer dog, and Hilda's spiky hair. She walked over and took in the little girl's exasperation, Hilda zoned out on patting . . .

Dumbledore barked.

Hilda rubbed his head.

"I need to go now," said the little girl.

"Who's a good boy then," muttered Hilda.

"Hilda?" said Mandy.

Hilda stopped.

Their eyes met.

Hilda, catching sight of the sort of face she could wake up to every morning, froze.

"Beryl has told me all about you," lied Mandy. She flashed her best smile, made a connection, and held out her hand.

Hilda took it, the grip almost crushing her fingers.

As the girl raced off with a relieved "bye," Mandy plonked herself beside Hilda and leaned against the tree with a sigh.

Hilda didn't move. She could feel the warmth of Mandy's body beside her and didn't want it to end. It was delicious, like her scent.

Mandy stared out onto the sea loch at the edge of the park; a few children were swinging, laughing.

Hilda wanted to say something, anything, and yet she was tongue-tied, exhilarated, *and* apprehensive. She was sitting so close to the most magnificent being.

Hilda's mind raced; a thousand thoughts were pushed aside as a feeling of warmth welled inside her—a patting-a-dog warmth.

She sighed, unaware that her mind was as readable as a Kindle on audio.

Mandy was on hormone therapy, which gave her not only frequent hot flashes but also overwhelming rushes of thoughts followed by periods of blankness.

Hilda's past flashed like a newsreel in Mandy's mind. She saw so much she was feeling a little sick. She flashed a half-hearted smile.

Hilda beamed back.

Mandy stood.

Hilda began to follow.

"Don't follow me," she whispered.

Hilda did anyway, right down the main street of Dunoon, just like Mandy knew she would.

Chapter Twenty-Four

HARPER

"A Nokia by another name still needs a charger."–Glaswegian market stall owner

Mandy stared out of the large bay windows and onto the loch. It was a beautiful sunset, and she, unlike the rest of the staff, was watching it.

The rest of the staff, all dressed for a night of work, were staring at Antonia, the manageress, who looked as uncomfortable as a politician caught in the wrong place.

She had recently given up smoking and was seriously considering opening the emergency pack hidden in her desk.

"Tonight's canceled," she said in a rich Italian accent.

None looked surprised, although all were disappointed. Tonight's event was a hen night, a closed affair with cocktails, male performers, and a "pleasure products" stall. It had been planned for months, a highlight in an otherwise dull winter.

The hotel was situated on the corner of Dunoon's Main Street, and Antonia had worked there since she first moved to Scotland.

Back then, it was a family-run business full of locals and regular holidaymakers. She stayed on when the useless son took over and ran it into the ground, and she became a manager when a company bought the hotel, counting every penny, including overtime—or, rather, the lack of it.

She sighed.

What's going to happen to me now?

She loved her job; it was her escape from dinners with her mother, a woman as frivolous as daytime TV. In fact, that's what she did all day: sit and watch the friggin' thing with a picture of her no-longer-here husband by her side.

Antonia looked at her staff. Most were from another country, some making plans to head back, others at a loss as what to do.

"They're packing up the hen do—perhaps you can help," she said.

"Help 'em pack up? I need to pack myself," said a young woman.

"You're not getting kicked out," said Antonia.

Silence.

"I mean—there will be some reshuffling."

A few grumbled.

"The seasonal staff . . ." She looked at Mandy and stopped. "There is talk of furlough."

"So you *are* kicking us out," said a local girl.

"Well not tomorrow, not in the foreseeable . . ." She stopped. "Look, things will work out."

Even she doesn't believe that, thought Mandy.

Mandy headed back to her room and slammed the door. "We don't have long," she snapped.

She looked about the small damp bedroom. *Where the hell is Hilda?*

She focused her mind . . .

Mandy believed in fate, the god of galaxies, kismet—all that stuff—and despite not liking the "soppy Hilda," Mandy knew she was here for a reason. She could be useful. How? Mandy had no idea, just as she had no idea how ruthless the real Hilda could be.

She smiled; she knew where she was. She headed for the bar.

"You call this a rabbit?" said Hilda, clutching a pink vibrator (still in its plastic bag).

Mandy stopped and turned to the lounge, catching sight of Hilda's muscular back.

"I mean, a rabbit? Is that not cute and fluffy?"

"Exactly," said Harper, the young salesman.

Hilda turned the vibrator in her hand. "Very primitive."

Harper's thin face pinched with distaste; he snatched the vibrator. "That is our best seller."

"Pfff, hate to see your worst," muttered Hilda.

"Come on," said Mandy, "leave the poor fella to pack."

"Just trying to help," said Hilda. She picked up a business card and turned it about like a specimen. "I could double your sales in a day."

Harper, with an "as if" look, shoved the last of his merchandise into a box. "I think you'll find that we are the best sellers in the business." He rammed the box shut, sparking a rabbit to rotate inside.

"Rotations—so yesterday," said Hilda.

"Come on," snapped Mandy.

"Rotation is everything," snapped Harper.

"Hardly; my women have way more sophistication."

"Sophistication? We're talking pleasure here, not business suits." Harper shoved the box into his trolley with a tut. "What am I talking to you for? What would you know? The last time you had a 'moment' was probably the last pandemic."

"Last what?" said Hilda.

"Come on," said Mandy. "Antonia's coming."

"Oh, ha-ha, very funny," said Hilda.

Mandy looked at her. "I was speaking literally. If she sees you, she'll have a fit . . ."

Mandy stopped; Antonia was standing in the doorway with the sort of look that leads to yelling.

"What's going on?" snapped Antonia.

"I'm just trying to help," said Hilda.

"Will you stop with the helping?" hissed Mandy.

"I mean, this man here is selling rotating rubbish."

"Will you shut it?" snapped Mandy.

"What woman wants that?"

"I don't see any women complaining," snapped Harper.

With a long sigh, Antonia headed into the lounge. She had way too much to do, bugger-all time to do it in, and a mother who was always on the phone whining about "stocking up for doomsday."

"This is not the time or the place . . ." Antonia stopped. He hadn't even started to pack up. "You need to get a move on, we're closing."

"A sausage would have more effect," muttered Hilda.

"Sausage!" yelled Harper. "How dare you. I never touch the stuff, and as for my girls—"

"I'm sure she didn't mean real sausages," said Mandy.

"Actually, I did," said Hilda.

"I told you we are closing," said Antonia. "I am not going to say it again."

"I could make you a fortune," said Hilda.

"As if," snapped Harper.

"You need to leave," said Antonia.

"Honestly, give me a month and you'll have women eating out of your hand."

"I said you need to *leave*," hissed Antonia.

Hilda was confused. She was only trying to help . . . even her delicious Mandy looked pissed off.

"What would a man like you know?" said Harper.

Hilda stopped. "Man?"

"Yes—what sort of a man gets about like you?" said Harper.

Hilda looked at Mandy. *How could he call her a man?*

"Just get out," snapped Antonia. "All of you, now."

"She started it," said Harper.

"And take your friggin' sausages . . . I mean vibrators . . . with you."

Harper packed up his things quick smart. An Identity himself, he had heard of Mandy, seen her turn up for a meeting or two—but her companion?

What sort of an Identity hangs around someone like that?

Hilda was a woman's name, but she looked as much like a woman as "the Rabbit" looked like . . . well, a rabbit.

In fact, he didn't think she was, even after he gate-crashed Hilda's mind. Her thoughts were as feminine as a pickup truck, messy, mannish, aggressive, hoovering up information like an industrial vacuum cleaner with an empty bag.

Until, that is, Hilda looked at Mandy and went all gooey . . .

He righted himself.

Mandy, an Identity? The man—now woman—is an Identity? What did that make Hilda?

Without even thinking, Harper ESP-ed Archie. After all, he was the boss; he'd know what to do. And those two were trouble, he could sense it

Chapter Twenty-Five

ARCHIE

"Selling a vibrator is selling a dream."–Hilda's blog

Archie was sitting in Tesco drinking a soya latte. DJ, who'd just parked the car, was making a meal of lockdown.

He, seeing several people pushing overflowing trolleys like the Armageddon was about to start, had headed straight for the toilet rolls with manic purpose.

Archie had other concerns. In fact, he was so engrossed in his thoughts he didn't notice the cleaner's cart rattle past.

The cleaner paused like he remembered something . . .

"The car is in the garage."

Archie looked up.

"And . . . the meter is still running?"

"There's no need for all that," said Archie.

"Oh, and my batteries are flat," said the cleaner.

"I said there's no need for passwords . . . and those are out-of-date," said Archie.

"Oh," said the cleaner, disappointed. "I have waited for years to do that too."

The cleaner leaned on his cleaning cart, eyeing Archie's ponytail with a critical look.

Archie ran his fingers through his hair with a blush.

"Aren't you a tad early?" said the cleaner.

"I think you'll find he's late."

"Late? He *is* coming from Dunoon."

"It's hardly the Antarctic, and *he* said it was urgent."

"Honey, everything is urgent with him." The cleaner looked at his nails. "Had me hoarding toilet paper like we've a diarrhea outbreak, and it *is* only us in the house."

He watched a trolley pass overflowing with toilet paper rolls, bread, and tins of beans.

"Panic buying—ridiculous."

"One packet of toilet roll per customer," barked a stern voice over the intercom.

"I mean honestly, as if we're gonna run out of things. This is Britain, luv, hardly a Margaret Atwood book . . ."

The manager walked past, young and fit, the sort that belonged on the cover of a magazine. However, Archie, unlike Legless, didn't notice.

He sipped his latte and spluttered. "Soya's not what it used to be."

"Can't stand the stuff," muttered the cleaner. "Makes me want to throw up."

Archie eyed the cleaner. "It makes you sick?"

"In a manner of speaking. Himself thinks it's the dog's bollocks." He smiled at Archie. "I told him dog bollocks has nothing to do with it, does he laugh—does he fuck? He didn't even crack a smile."

Archie laughed so loud the chatter in the café stopped. The manager turned on her heels, quickly catching the cleaner in her sights.

"Those toilets won't clean themselves," she barked. "Remember, we're closing early."

An elderly man on the next table looked up, his fork poised over his haddock. "You're closing early?"

The manager stopped. "You've time to finish that," she said. "Although I wouldn't waste my time with a pudding. It's lockdown, remember . . ."

The cleaner watched her back disappear into the kitchen. "How could anyone forget?" He turned to the elderly man. "Don't know what's eating her. Heard the boyfriend maxed out her card—again."

He smiled at Archie with a tilt of his head. "Why don't you try a beard with that thing?" He gestured to the ponytail. "Very *Game of Thrones.*"

Archie looked at him; he had no idea what he was talking about.

"So *in* at the moment."

"Just tell your pal I am here," said Archie. "We don't seem to be making a connection."

"Don't worry," he said with a reassuring pat. "He's coming. Although I wouldn't bother; he's in a bit of a huff. Apparently, some lesbian slagged off his vibrators."

"That's why I'm meeting him."

"No. Seriously? Tell me more—*he* never tells *me* anything."

Harper finally arrived with a packet of "rough-as-fuck" toilet rolls, a plastic bag full of Sainsbury's finest coffee, a scrunched loaf of bread, and a packet of four cans of Heinz baked beans. He dumped the toilet rolls on the table with a "sandpaper stuff was all that was left."

"Chaffed to buggery then," chuckled the cleaner, sliding a cappuccino his way.

Harper glared. "Sugar?"

"With that waistline, hardly," the cleaner said, then, catching the glare of the manager now behind the till, minced off.

Harper looked at Archie (the boss, as he liked to call him). "I told Himself she was a lesbian to keep things, well, discreet." He looked about, gesturing for Archie to come closer.

"That man is as much a lesbian as Himself over there is a cleaner."

They looked at the cleaner behind the counter flicking a J-cloth about like it was a scarf.

"He waves a bit of air freshener about the bathroom and calls it clean."

"Just tell me about the, er, non-lesbian," said Archie.

"He goes by the name of Hilda," said Harper.

Archie sucked in his breath. He had memories of Beryl, high on sugar, talking nonstop about "that cow who ruined everything."

"His mind was an open book," said Harper.

"*He* is a *she*."

"She?"

"Yes."

"But I saw it all, there in his mind."

"Don't think so."

"Including"—he pulled Archie closer—"the portal." He sat back. "Like in *Star Trek*."

Archie looked confused.

"TV show," jumped in the elderly man. He slid the last of his haddock into his mouth. "Hardly portal material."

"More *Doctor Who* if you ask me," said the cleaner, appearing from nowhere.

"I don't think I did," said Harper.

"Hmm, that lesbian has really got your goat." The cleaner patted Harper's arm.

"You better get moving," Harper said, nodding toward the dark face of the manager behind the till.

"Pfff, *her*—a clear case of not getting any for so long you've forgotten how to do it." He flicked a cloth about the table. "You men finished?"

"I am," snapped the elderly man.

Archie, his intuition working overtime, stared at the aisles. He could see DJ in the distance queuing behind an overweight woman with an equally overweight trolley.

What is that Hilda doing here? What does she look like? Is she as bad as Beryl made her out to be? And the portal—is it still open? Will there be more from that place? Oh, God, and lockdown . . . is that going to make it all more difficult?

"Tell me more," said Archie.

"More? He . . . she completely trashed my stock, boss."

Archie winced. "Don't call me boss—we're not the Mafia."

"Said they were as out-of-date as, well." He eyed Archie's ponytail. "Why don't you try a beard with that thing?"

The cleaner lifted a cup, then put it down. "Exactly, that's what I said."

"Those toilets won't clean themselves," yelled the manageress from the till.

The cleaner trotted off with a tut as DJ appeared, a tad exasperated. "It's like a Boxing Day sale out there. Got the last packet of these"—he gestured to his trolley—"and a pizza for tea."

Archie said nothing. His latte was swirling around his stomach along with every anxious feeling possible.

"What you gonna do now, boss?" said Harper.

Archie threw him a dirty look, then turned to DJ. "We need to see Legless and that Beryl," he said, "while we still can."

DJ looked at him. "What about the pizza?"

"Better make the most of it," huffed the elderly man, pushing his chair in with a huff. "This place is friggin' closing down like a vibrator with flat batteries."

Chapter Twenty-Six

MANDY AND LEGLESS

"Selling vibrators is no different than selling burgers: it's all in the packaging."–Harper

When Legless first saw Mandy, he dropped his ladle into the soup.

Beryl had been on her phone while he was "heating things up," his notebook as forgotten as the friggin' time.

Normally she'd be on him in a flash, telling him to keep his memoirs to a thought—the last thing they needed was his writing "giving the game away."

Not this evening. She didn't even notice his spaghetti, smell his warm bread. She, with her face in her phone, charged outside to talk, only reappearing hours later—his soup cold with a skin on top, his bread as hard as a calloused heel, and his spaghetti as limp as his appendage.

———

While Legless stood in the camper van kitchen—ladle poised—Beryl stood next to his shed waiting for Hilda and Mandy to arrive.

For a year she had been on Earth, thinking about her home with only Legless to share the memory, and his was as out-of-date as a telephone directory.

She thought she was in control of her feelings, that her heart was hard, that her head was full of politics, that she was thinking like a leader—until she saw the silhouette of Hilda, whose familiar march stopped Beryl in her tracks.

Beryl's heart skipped a beat; her stomach lurched. For a moment, she was home.

She wiped a small tear from her eye, pulled a militant stance, and watched as Hilda loomed closer.

She looked different.

Is she smiling? Did she just laugh?

Mandy waved at Beryl.

Beryl gave her best curt nod. She looked at Hilda.

Hilda looked at Beryl.

Beryl's hatred and anger melted like ice cream. Resisting the urge to hug, she held out her hand.

"Hilda," she said in her best gruff voice.

Hilda nodded.

Legless was cooking up a storm when Beryl waltzed into the camper van.

Legless, adjusting the heat, turned with a "where have you been" on the tip of his tongue, then stopped as Mandy appeared by Beryl's side.

His jaw dropped, along with his ladle, which sank to the bottom like a shoe in quicksand.

"Hi," said Mandy.

"You've enough for three?" said Beryl.

He turned to his soup, taking his time to fish out the ladle. "No."

"There's always enough," said Beryl. "You cook for an army."

"Well, not today." He dropped the ladle in the sink with a crash. "There was a rush at the co-op—the world is in a panic."

"That's why I said Mandy can stay here," said Beryl.

"Her? Here?"

"Yes."

"Where?"

"They can stay here in the camper van . . ."

"They? What do you mean *they*? I thought you said *three*."

"I wasn't including you," said Beryl.

"You never do," huffed Legless. He returned to his soup. He had as much chance of "getting his end away" now as the PM of getting a haircut. "I thought we could, you know, explore the tea collection," he said.

She looked at him. "I've tried them all."

"I've new ones," he said.

"I'm more a coffee person," said Mandy.

"May as well toss it to the birds then," muttered Legless.

"No need to be like that," said Beryl.

"Like what?"

"All moody."

"Moody? I'm just in the middle of making a cozy meal for us, looking forward to some . . . you know . . ."

The door crashed opened and Hilda appeared, clutching several bags of "pilfering," as she called it.

"Hello, Legless," she said.

He stopped. "What the pickling hell is she doing here?"

"I did say three," said Beryl.

"May as well ask the whole friggin' sheltered housing complex, let them stay too."

"Happy to see you too, Legless," said Hilda.

Legless huffed. "Why her—why now? Is this part of some plan you haven't told me about?"

"There's a portal," said Mandy. "And she was in it."

Hilda dumped her bags on the table with a clink. "I think you'll find it's *riding a portal*."

Legless turned to Beryl. "Portal?

"Think *Star Trek*," said Mandy with a glare at the bags.

"I wouldn't recommend it," snapped Hilda. "Still feel a bit sick."

"But what about deliveries?" said Legless. "How are you gonna manage that with these two shacked up here?"

"Oh, forgot about that," said Beryl.

"If it's too much trouble, we can go," said Mandy with little conviction.

"Go where?" said Hilda. "A park bench?"

"Yes, well, if you hadn't upset that young man, we could have stayed on—bought some time before you were discovered."

"I was just saying I could triple his sales," said Hilda.

Mandy glared at Hilda. Thanks to her, they had nowhere to stay.

"What would you know about sales?" said Beryl.

Hilda looked at her. "I am an entrepreneur."

"An entre-fucking-preneur—you?" said Legless.

"I am a great success on Planet Hy Man," said Hilda. "All the women come to me and none complain."

Beryl's heart sank. *Hilda was a success . . .*

"What do you sell—deep-fried soya, yesterday's underpants?" snapped Legless.

Hilda glared at him. "Vibrators."

How did I miss that one? thought Mandy.

Beryl huffed. *Friggin' Hilda . . .*

Hilda pulled out a bottle of Islay, followed by several bottles of Etienne Dumont Brut Champagne, a bottle of Croft sherry, a bottle of Cava, and several cans of Irn-Bru.

"I told you not to take anything," snapped Mandy.

"What's the point of coming from another planet if you can't bend the rules? Besides, it's hardly taking," said Hilda. She pulled several crisp packets from her pockets. "More relieving, just desserts and all that," she said with a toss of a salt-and-vinegar.

The crisp packet slid across the table onto the floor. Mandy picked it up with a glare, while Legless surveyed a bottle of Jura with an impressed look.

"They did kick you out," said Hilda, retrieving several nut packets from under her top followed by a fistful of Nescafé sachets. "What did they expect."

"They kicked me out because of you," snapped Mandy. "And if they see this, they won't let me back in."

"Typical," said Beryl, turning a coffee sachet in her hand with disgust.

"What?" said Hilda, opening the bottle of Jura. She sniffed and pulled a face.

"You—you never do what anyone says. You do the opposite."

Legless grabbed the whisky and poured. "Better get rid of the evidence then," he said as Hilda struggled with a packet of nuts.

A few hours later, the camper van was rocking to Wham! on full pelt. Beryl, with the sort of gyrating that would make any lap dancer proud, was singing off-key, and Legless, his soup demolished, his spaghetti a delicious memory, was in a state of expectancy.

Hilda's lectures on the joys of a vibrator that "did more than rotate" were so vivid that Legless, under the influence of Jura malt and Irn-Bru, reckoned he was in with a chance.

Mandy was outside feeding Gina, Lollo, and Brigid leftovers, giving her mind a rest from reading. She, having never made it past the door of a meeting, had only heard of Legless, and as "the girls" pecked at her fingers, she pondered her discovery. He seemed to have no idea who she was.

She didn't hear the car pull up, the door slam, or Bark Twain barking, until "the girls" scattered.

"Visitors," she yelled. And when no one answered, Mandy poked her head through the kitchen window, stopping Beryl mid "Club Tropicana."

Archie filled the doorway.

No one noticed.

"Legless," he shouted. Then, catching sight of Hilda, he stopped. *She really does look like a man.*

"There is a portal," shouted DJ from behind, "from here to Planet Hy Man and back again."

The party looked up.

Legless, bleary-eyed, blinked. "*Star Trek*," he slurred, and with a raise of a glass, he shouted, "Cheers!"

Chapter Twenty-Seven

JURA MALT

"Beer makes you feel the way you ought without beer"—Henry Lawson, famous Australian writer

The next morning, Legless was sorting out logs for the fire with a thumping head, with Archie and DJ giving unwanted advice.

Having slept in the shed, they were up early, ravenous for coffee and food. They could hear Hilda in the camper van pacing about, full of beans, just as she was last night. While the others slurred more with each drink, becoming tactile and singsongy, Hilda had remained annoyingly sober, completely unaffected.

Hilda stared out of the window; an old man chopping wood was as foreign to her as a condom. The only thing she had seen a man do was shuffle.

She had seen many things on the BBC replays, but somehow, in the flesh, it was all so different—the noise, the smells, the people of all ages and all sizes, their accents, the swearing . . .

There was so much to learn.

She turned to Mandy facedown in her pillow. "Can you teach me to read minds?" she said.

"For the last time, it's not teachable."

Hilda lifted a Nescafé sachet. "Everything is teachable," she muttered with a useless shake.

Mandy looked up from her pillow. "Besides, it's not all it's cracked up to be; some things are best left unread." She flopped back into her pillow. "In fact, I'm glad to be losing it."

Hilda stopped mid shake. "You're losing it?"

"Hormones," said Mandy. She grunted, lying on her back. "Estrogen will kill the Identity in me—eventually."

"All the more reason to teach it."

Mandy looked at Hilda. "Why are you not hung over?"

Hilda resumed her sachet wrestling. "Because I was too sick to drink," she lied.

Mandy sat up, eying her with suspicion.

Hilda's frustration boiled. "These bloody things. Who on Earth invented such stupid . . ." She wrenched. "I mean what's wrong with a jar?"

"Just leave it," said Mandy.

Hilda stopped and looked at her friend. "I was gonna make you one."

"No need."

"But it's the least I can do."

Mandy, her head fuzzy, snatched the packet, ripped it open, and emptied it into a mug. "Just a drop of milk," she said.

"Oh—there's none," muttered Hilda.

Last night had been a night like no other for Hilda. She had never seen men dance before. Mandy had, and to her mind, it was way better under the influence of a whisky or two.

Tucking into the malt like there was no tomorrow, Mandy soon became more than squiffy, her accent broader and her face more animated. "Whisky makes you feel the way you should feel without whisky," she drawled in a nasal fashion.

Legless stopped mid Highland fling. He'd heard that quote before —in Australia.

"Should it not be beer rather than whisky?" He staggered.

"Yes," she said, "but we're drinking whisky."

He looked at her, her accent now as familiar as her face. Like someone from the past.

"I love a sunburnt country," she quoted. "A land of sweeping plains . . ."

Legless joined in.

"Here we go," said Archie, "another bleeding Aussie poem."

Legless stood on the table, Mandy followed as they quoted Dorothea Mackellar's famous "My Country," a poem every Aussie grew up with.

Hilda was mesmerized.

A drunk Mandy was easy to read, and Hilda's spy antenna was picking up signals like a sonar radar. There was something that needed to be rattled, a nub that was eating Mandy up—something elusive, yet so obvious Hilda could almost touch it.

Soon she was as curious as a policeman at an autopsy.

Legless threw his arm around her until the table crashed to the ground, not that it stopped him. Kicking the table's remains to the side, Legless jigged until he staggered.

"The bonnie, bonnie banks of the Yarra . . ."

Mandy laughed, Archie and DJ called him a show-off, and Beryl told him to sit down. But Legless, with a drunken urge to impress, pulled another twirl.

Hilda took it all in, sipping nothing. She was desperate to read minds. *What a bonus that would be.* She could really take control, despite Beryl pointing out it probably wouldn't work "back home."

Legless stopped mid twirl. "Back home? Here is your home, with me."

"Hardly," said Beryl.

"But you drive people about, teach, deliver—you're more human than I am."

"A mere stepping stone."

"You should go back too," Hilda said to Legless. "They're building a statue of you."

Legless stopped. "Me?" He turned to Beryl. "Did you know?"

Beryl blushed.

Didn't see that coming, thought Mandy. *Perhaps Hilda's mind is not as open as I thought.*

DJ and Archie started to laugh.

Mandy watched and for the first time saw the Legless who did not quite fit anywhere. Her face softened; she didn't either.

"Why friggin' not?" snapped Legless. He skulled his whisky. "I did invent the spark plug."

"Yes, well, the last time I saw *your* statue, it was covered in bird shit, your appendage stuck in a pumpkin the size of an elephant."

"You have pumpkin up there?" said Mandy.

"Of course."

"Not really *up there*, more to the side, just by the Milky Way," said Beryl.

"Hmm, not really," said Hilda.

Beryl threw her a "what would you know" glare.

"I saw a lot in that portal, and your coordinates, Beryl, are as off as Legless's dancing," said Hilda.

Legless scowled.

"It got me here," huffed Beryl.

Legless soothed Beryl with a touch. "Perhaps being sick squiffed your vision."

Mandy caught his eye.

Legless held it. *I know that face . . .*

Legless, shoeing "the girls" away, sliced a log in two, threw the pieces into a pile, lifted another, and took aim.

Charlton Heston, with a crow, began to strut.

"All right, we know you're there," muttered Legless. He sliced another log.

"I wouldn't do it like that," said Archie.

"Aye, well, you've central heating."

Chop!

Crow!

The axe wedged.

"Told you."

Legless wrenched the axe; it refused to move.

Charlton Heston, after a parade around Legless's legs, perched on the stump.

"Come on, ol' fella," muttered Legless, pushing him off.

"Here, let me," said DJ.

Legless thumped his foot on the stump. "I've got it."

"You'll do your back in."

"Don't you think you should leave?" huffed Legless. He wrenched; the axe gave way; he staggered back, sending "the girls" into a flap. "Lockdown and all that . . ."

"But nothing's sorted."

"They're with me, perfectly safe." Legless went for another chop and then stopped . . . in the clear light of a hangover he remembered where he'd seen Mandy's face before . . . she looked just like his lover in Australia, Karen.

Karen was the only woman he'd met without mind reading who never knew of the meetings let alone joined one, and whose brain was as impenetrable as Fort Knox. She was that confident.

He met her when he was cleaning cars for a living, and did such a great job of hers that she came back for a wax and polish, and asked him out for a coffee.

Legless thought back to that day. How their eyes met, how she ordered for him and told him to "tuck in your shirt," which at the time he found endearing.

Legless had fallen for a giant version of Beryl with short hair. A woman who pouted the same, stood the same, and even shagged the same—something Legless had no idea of until Archie pointed it out (the pouting and standing, that is).

They were sitting in Jimmie's Arabic Tea Shop at the time. Legless was reminiscing about Australia in the seventies, boring Archie stupid until he pulled out a Polaroid of Karen leaning against his Holden Kingswood like she owned it.

Archie took one look at her athletic body in tight flared jeans and whistled through his teeth. "All she needs is a Beryl beehive and she'd be a twin."

"What?" said Legless mid tea sipping.

"She's the image of Beryl."

Legless snatched the photo and stared at it. "Don't think so."

"And by the sounds of it, just as bossy," said Archie.

"That's just one Polaroid," said Legless, sliding the photo back into his wallet.

"A Polaroid speaks a thousand words," said Archie with a poignant pouring of tea.

Legless never talked of her again, and he didn't realize Archie was right—until, that is, Mandy came along.

Beryl looked out from the bedroom window. Legless had something on his mind, she could tell. She often wondered about Legless's past; he was so evasive about things. He was a restless sleeper most nights, but the previous night, his muffled groans and jostling limbs had her wondering.

"Up the Yarra," he shouted more than once in his sleep.

What are the memories that have him running marathons, laughing out loud, moaning like a porn star, or yelling like a football fan?

What the pickle did he get up to on Earth? And what the hell is the Yarra?

Chapter Twenty-Eight

SPILT MILK

"A sugar sachet is as easy to open as a jam jar."–Hilda

Hilda, still impressed with Mandy's ability to open a sachet, dove out of the camper van to find some milk, expertly skidding past "the girls'" shit. She made a beeline for the cottage.

The kitchen was empty. Hilda looked around the tiny space, examining, for the first time, the eating habits of those on Earth.

Hilda's curiosity gnawed inside her like a tunneling worm, like a miner on the promise of gold.

She was learning to read Mandy and felt she was getting closer to something.

The truth was, Mandy talked in her sleep, and Hilda, an insomniac, heard everything, not that it made sense.

I mean, what the hell is a Yarra?

She opened the fridge, lifted a packet of bacon and sniffed, poked at a tub of margarine, picked at a bit of cheese, and almost swooned with the taste. In fact, if she hadn't heard Beryl's footsteps upstairs, she would have gulped down the lot.

She grabbed the milk, made to head out, then stopped and stared at a shelf full of glossy hardback cookbooks: *Twenty Ways to Cook a Tomato, There's More to a Mushroom Than Garlic, Getting to Know Your Blender,* and several others.

In the middle, hardly visible, was a notebook. She pulled it out and stared at the cover. It looked like a child's coloring book.

She ran her fingers across the handwritten title written in crayon:

An Alien in Melbourne: A Memoir

She stopped. *That's where Mandy came from.*

She opened it.

Being an Alien does have its downsides, one being that women like Karen want nothing to do with you when they find out.

They don't understand and take things the wrong way . . .

Hilda flicked through the tea-stained pages peppered with the odd cartoon drawing. Men in tight shorts kicking footballs, women under seventies hair dryers idly flicking through magazines with "Nicholas's girls" in florescent crayon underneath, a Holden Kingswood's car with "the ol' girl" in fancy script beside it, cricket bats, cricket balls, barbecue, and a men's barbecue apron with bra and suspenders painted on.

Hilda had little idea what the drawings were, but they intrigued her. Some even made her laugh.

She stopped at a page littered with drawings of a woman looking very much like a caricature Beryl—minus the beehive.

Hilda chuckled until she began to read . . .

I almost made it, almost turned human, until she found out.

We had spent a year together, and it was all food and sport . . .

"Footy" is a weird game played in the winter by men in shorts so tight they'd rip with a mere fart . . . not that anyone minded.

Those men were heroes.

"Aussie rules," they called it, but as far as I could see, there were bugger-all rules, just a lot of grabbing. Men leaping in the air to catch a ball, which is called a "mark"—something I thought pens did.

Karen did try to explain. Every Saturday, we'd head down to the oval, shiver in the queues by the food vans for a meat pie and sauce or donuts with hot jam. Aussies loved them. I just burned my lips they were so hot.

Summer it was cricket, where every man talked about whipping the pommie's arse, and tennis on TV, which we'd watch with Karen's mum and eat fish and chips.

I even met her family, spent a Christmas around the table eating a big fat juicy leg of lamb, which to be honest I didn't enjoy. Karen's mother is a lousy cook, and Karen's not much better . . . but their dominating humor made up for it.

In the end, it was so bad I learned to cook, which made barbecues easier. I could blend in.

I never felt at home with men; they were as alien to me as Aussie rules. I found the whole standing-around-with-a beer thing as comfortable as a set of piles.

Learning to cook helped. An apron with painted-on bra and knickers can do wonders for an outcast.

While everyone kicked a footy about or lobbed a cricket ball, I could stand by the burning meat, tong in hand, doing my best to blend in like a true Aussie.

Beryl coughed, stomping from her bedroom to the bathroom.

Hilda slid the notebook into her pocket and headed out.

Mandy was looking out the window, admiring Legless's ability to chop wood with a hangover, when Hilda came back.

Hilda, catching sight of *her* Mandy, threw her best full-on wave, then attempted a "footy kick" like she saw in the notebook.

She skidded across some hen shit; milk flew into the air, "the girls" scattered and squawked, Charlton Heston sprung into manic parading, Sophia dove for cover, and Bark Twain slept through it all.

Mandy laughed her head off—a big, loud, throw-your-head-back cackle—just as Legless did the same.

DJ clocked it. Archie, however, already knew: Mandy was the image of the woman in the Polaroid.

Hilda, mid lunge, stopped. *So that's what floats your boat,* she thought.

She threw another skid, scattering "the girls," waking Bark Twain and setting him into a frenzy of tail chasing.

Mandy's laughter echoed across the garden.

Hilda, like a child with an audience, hammed it up, clowning about like she had never done before.

Mandy cheered her on . . .

Legless looked at Mandy and realized she sounded just like he did.

It took several moments for it all to sink in; that Mandy was his, and that she had come to find him like many others.

Shit, he thought. *Am I that blind?*

"Yes," said Archie, reading his mind.

"I thought I only bred boys," said Legless.

"But she was a he," said Archie.

"She was a he?"

Archie nodded.

"That explains the builder's frame. Mind you, her mother was a giant—a basketball player." He laughed. "Making a goal for her was like posting a letter, a mere plop . . ."

He sighed at the thought.

He stopped, catching sight of Beryl crashing about the kitchen . . .

Shit, thought Legless. *Beryl will go nuts when I tell her.*

That night, while the others slept, Hilda read Legless's notebook.

She saw a different Legless, a man who felt not only out of place but lost in the sort of relationship that was crushing him.

The sort of woman who bullied him, sending him back to the only place he felt comfortable: the Identities and their meetings.

It was heady stuff, the sort of stuff she could use to control and manipulate . . .

She continued to read, struggling to picture Legless's descriptions of a country as foreign to her as, well, Scotland.

She wanted to know more. What was a *Kingswood,* a *Yarra,* a *googly?*

It took her five minutes to log into Mandy's phone—it turned out *Yarra* was the password—and over the next few nights, while the others slept, she explored.

Within hours, she was hypnotized by the internet, browsing like a singleton on Tinder . . .

She googled everything, even the Yarra, which turned out to be not only a password but Melbourne's famous river. She spent hours on

Facebook and YouTube, Instagram at a push; TikTok videos had her confused and a little seasick.

She absorbed everything, scanning, reading, and gasping at Mandy's Facebook page, her Australian "mates" and her mother alluding to some sort of "bastard *runaway* . . ."

"Tell him he owes me half a century of alimony," she messaged more than once.

It was then that she saw it . . .

"Tell that bastard father of yours he owes me."

"But Legless has no money, Mother," Mandy messaged back.

"That's what he says."

"And he's actually quite sweet."

"Sweet? That so-called *man* is anything but sweet. What did he say when you told him?"

"I haven't yet. Not sure how. It's complicated; there's another woman."

"There's always another woman."

Hilda stared at Mandy sleeping without a sound. *So that's why Legless seems on edge and she acts all girlie around him.*

Chapter Twenty-Nine

THE CHANGING OF A LEADER

"Bearing all has little to do with underpants."—Mandy

Legless had spent the past year wondering if he should tell Beryl about the great Aussie romance, and if so, how?

Over the next few days, he did try, but getting her attention was as easy as hypnotizing a hen, and by the time he did, he chickened out.

Beryl was all over the place—sharing a bathroom with your archenemy can do that to a person—but when that archenemy turned into a comedian who happily made coffee for everyone, including her, Beryl's head spun in more directions than a clothesline in a hurricane. And the presence of Archie and DJ, camped out in the shed, constantly whispering to Legless until she appeared, didn't help. It was like they knew something and itched to tell.

After a few days and way too many silences, she snapped.

Legless was making a curry at the time, toying between egg or chickpeas, when Beryl stomped into the kitchen. "When are those bozos gonna leave?" she said.

Legless, mid garlic peeling, looked up.

"Here I am dealing with the new 'anything-for-a-laugh' Hilda, and that lot are whispering like schoolgirls."

"Hardly schoolgirls," said Legless.

"As soon as I walk past, they stop."

"That's just an Identity's way," said Legless.

"Not to mention the pickling portal," muttered Beryl, peering into Legless's pan . . .

"Oh, that—that's all under control," said Legless.

"Last thing we need is more Hilda-ites pitching up—floggin' vibrators."

"I said it's all under control. They're plotting a break-in," said Legless.

"A break-in, during lockdown?" said Beryl.

"Shh, don't want those two to hear." He gestured to the camper van.

She looked at Legless. "Mandy? As if she'd care. She's too busy laughing it up with Hilda."

Beryl huffed, snatched a ladle, and began to stir.

He took the plunge . . . "There's something I need to tell you."

"I just can't figure her out. Why pretend not to drive?"

"It's about Australia," said Legless.

"I mean what's that all about?" Beryl stared at the camper van.

Hilda appeared, pulling a stretch, then, spying Sophia, bent to scratch her ears.

"And as for her," muttered Beryl.

"It was a long time ago . . ." said Legless.

He stopped. Beryl had as much interest in what he had to say as what was under his underpants. He may as well have tried to pull her to bed . . .

"A few mugs of coffee and Charlie Chaplin over there thinks we're best buddies."

Sophia rolled onto her back and Hilda rubbed with a chuckle.

"It'll take more than a frothy milk to win me over," muttered Beryl.

Hilda was now stroking not only Sophia but Bark Twain.

Bark Twain eased his creaky bones under Hilda's hand for a pat; she rubbed with her best "I'm in heaven" look.

"I mean what has gotten into her?"

Legless looked at his woman. Was she blind? Did she have no idea that Hilda was in love?

He tried to explain.

"In love? Hilda?" Beryl laughed. "That's as funny as us getting married."

Legless tossed the garlic into his pan and, deciding on eggs for a curry, headed out.

Hilda's mind was a whirlwind of swear words and messages she'd spied from Mandy's mother—who, to be fair, sounded a trifle angry and nothing like her sweet Mandy.

While Mandy was chopping wood, Legless was chopping garlic, and Hilda, halfway through Mandy's texts, was confused. She had no idea what *alimony* was and was in the midst of googling said word when Mandy's phone died.

She plugged it in, waited for what seemed an eternity, and then, realizing Mandy would soon be back, decided to find out. Alimony was the key, she knew it . . . just as she knew who to ask.

She strode out of the camper van and, catching Beryl watching, feigned a stretch, following it with a casual pat of Sophia . . .

Legless made his way to the hen house and began to rummage.

Bark Twain sniffed behind him.

Sophia, stretched out in the sun expecting another stroke, looked up with a "seriously?" glare as Hilda made for Archie and DJ. Then, ruffled and unsatisfied, she followed.

Archie and DJ, sitting on bales of hay, didn't hear Hilda enter. Engrossed in a Zoom meeting with other Identities, they were trying to come to grips with screen sharing.

Finally, the plans for the care home appeared on the screen.

They peered at it like it was Fort Knox.

"There is but one entrance, and it's as visible as a traffic light," said Archie.

"What about the gents'?" said one.

"There is no gents', it's gender specific," said another.

"Don't you mean unspecific?"

"Whatever; it has no external entrance."

Legless, moving about the hen house next door, heard every word, including Hilda's "I'm here" cough.

"Aye, but it'll have a window—health and safety and all that," said one.

"A window the size of a cat flap," said another.

"Well, you got any better ideas?" snapped DJ.

Hilda coughed again.

"Yeah, forget the whole friggin' thing."

"And have more Hilda and her vibrators? Not on my watch. No one will come to our meetings anymore."

Archie sighed. "I hardly think the ability to do more than rotate could compete with our commando dancing."

Sophia appeared with a "you haven't finished" screech of a meow.

Archie and DH turned to see Hilda, knowing by the look on her face that she had heard it all.

"Well, gentlemen," she said. "Can either of you tell me what *alimony* means?"

Silence . . .

Legless stopped his hand mid clutching a warm egg from under Gina. *Alimony?*

Archie sucked in his breath.

DJ swore under his.

Alimony was a dirty word to an Identity. It was the sort of word that sparked indigestion, palpitations, and brewer's droop. It was the elephant in the room, the N-word for Identities; the mere mention of it could render an Identity impotent for months, and as for "child support?" Archie had seen Identities suffer strokes when that was mentioned.

"Shit," hissed Legless.

Gina threw him a glare.

He headed outside.

"Why on Earth would you want to know about alimony?" said Mandy, entering with an armful of chopped wood. She caught Hilda's eye.

Hilda looked away. A strange feeling hit her; she had no idea it was guilt.

"Have you been reading my messages?" said Mandy.

Hilda looked at her feet. Her throat felt dry.

"Have you been at my phone?"

She gulped, and if she could have blushed, she would have. However, the only thing she could muster was a lie, and when that didn't work, she headed out for milk.

Mandy followed and dragged her into the camper van; words were spoken, most yelled, as tensions of the past week erupted in the sort of screeching that stopped Beryl mid peering into the fridge and wondering where all the milk had gone.

"Well, I hope you're pleased with yourself," yelled Mandy.

Silence . . .

Beryl headed outside.

Bark Twain barked.

"I trusted you," shouted Mandy.

"Well, I trusted you too," said Hilda. "Why didn't you tell me you're Legless's offspring?"

"Who isn't?" DJ laughed, looking nervously at Beryl.

"Exactly," muttered Archie.

Beryl, grim-faced, said nothing. Mandy was so young-looking that Beryl had just assumed her father was some idiot, like DJ.

Chapter Thirty

FATHERLY LOVE

"The love of a father is often underrated."—Bunnie

For the next two days, while the others worked on portal removal plans, Beryl stewed.

She thought of the hours she had sat in the car with Mandy. Granted most of it she spent teaching, but there were times when they sat and chatted—women sharing men's stuff. She realized now there was very little sharing, just her going on about Legless and Mandy pumping her for more info.

Beryl had been done over like a kipper, played like a deck of cards.

For days she spoke to no one, flying into rages at Legless over nothing. All he had to do was flick the kettle on and she glared.

She was completely unprepared for the pain she felt. She regretted letting her guard down, falling for Legless yet again, and listening to Mandy.

"Am I not enough?" she wanted to scream at Legless, but instead she stomped out the door with a "get that shed tied up pronto" yell.

Like it was her shed . . .

Legless withdrew to Mandy, spending his days in the camper van.

Legless found his bond with Mandy quite different from one he'd had with any other Identity.

Turns out Mandy had read all his books, even *The Spark Plug Odyssey* and *Sugar Is the Noose around the Universe*, and claimed they were excellent bedtime reading.

She knew more about him than he did himself . . . and she didn't treat him like an idiot. She understood the whole being different thing.

Hilda, in the throes of Earth emotions—love being the main one, along with a spot of guilt—watched it all. She was still smarting from Mandy's verbal abuse, and for the first time in her life, she wanted to make amends.

She even felt for Beryl, a woman past her prime with a man who seemed to have no idea how to help, and the weird thing was, she had no desire to exploit.

She even toyed with the idea of helping, although she still hadn't figured out how to do that without getting an earful of abuse.

Chapter Thirty-One

THE TENT AND THE HELMET

"The making of a statue requires the skill of an artist and the tact of a politician looking for votes."–The ambitious statue worker

Within an hour of Hilda's disappearance, Verruca's garden was cordoned off with a "Nothing to See Here" banner that flapped in the wind.

H2, a woman of immediate action, ordered a bright orange "danger" tent to be erected over the singed hole where the shed had once been, then held a summit.

Alice, using "wide-o-vision," projected H2's face onto the tent's flapping wall, distorting it into an off-putting sneer.

Calling the sportswomen and the statue builders to pull together, she talked of "the portal holding no prisoners," sparking a rumble of confusion. "Anyone could be next," she said.

It didn't take long for Verruca's home to look like a crime scene from an Earth movie.

Her garden, trampled within an inch of its life by masked sportswomen and robots, was now a mud slide, her greenhouse a hub for digger robots as foreign to her as a Chinese takeaway.

There were so many bodies Verruca lost count, and not a soya-tom in sight, just the odd remnants of the shed and a selection of vibrators embedded in the mud.

Cyborg took charge of the robots. For the first time *ever*, he strutted an "I told you so" strut, like he knew something—which he did, like he had warned—and his joy of being right was on the verge of blowing a fuse in his head.

In fact, if it wasn't for Hilda not being there for him to "rub it in," he probably would have.

Her disappearance was fantastic, yet a small fly in an otherwise delicious ointment of smugness.

Verruca told him not to "crow, go on about it; nobody likes a show-off."

Cyborg couldn't give a toss. It was not like anyone had liked him before.

"Friendship is for women," he said. "You lot made sure of that."

He turned his head with a judgmental squeak to Verruca.

"Those robots have been microchipped within an inch of their lives, merely command based . . ."

A miniature tank robot edging along the Legless statue attempted to climb its rump. Deaf to the shot-putters' "Go the other way," it continued until with a swift flick she had it overturned like a helpless sheep on its back.

Verruca watched as a four-legged robot followed, marching over the tank robot like it wasn't there.

" . . . as focused as an Earth missile," muttered Cyborg.

"Forgot about the microchip."

"Some woman's idea . . . of . . . curbing a revolution," said Cyborg.

Verruca said nothing.

Decades ago, when Beryl and Verruca were still working as a team, they watched the building of a turtle robot army. Although the turtles were miniature, they were still a force best avoided. Following their destruction, it was agreed the friendship chip for robots was to be rationed to a few elites, such as Alice, and the infamous 33 Robots, leaving old-style robots like Verruca's lonely with few to connect with.

"Those robots feeling anything is as possible as your soya-toms surviving . . . all this."

Verruca looked out onto the quagmire of mud. She caught sight of an upright vibrator valiantly rotating . . .

The lead sportswoman trooped across, lifted, switched off, slid into a bag, and, with perfect aim, tossed into a distant wheelbarrow.

Verruca, with a deep sigh, headed into the tent.

Inside were tables covered in diagrams, a beverage corner, benches littered with specimen jars, Petri dishes, and microscopes with lab assistants peering in, occasionally admiring the robust fertilized earth of Verruca's Garden.

"She knows her manure," said a studious-looking lab assistant.

"Aye, she does that—not many could pull off a vegetable patch over a quarry. Not with all that effluent under it," said her best buddy.

"Surprised she set up here."

"Me too. I mean who would want to live on top of a pile of robots? Not to mention the other stuff . . . lubricants and things?"

The best buddy shivered.

Verruca stopped. "Wasn't it cleared?"

"Cleared? You must be joking."

"No one clears a quarry."

"But I grow potatoes in that stuff," said Verruca.

The two assistants blinked.

"To eat," snapped Verruca.

They looked at each other.

"I'm sure there's nothing to worry about," muttered the studious lab assistant.

Her best buddy nodded. "Definitely."

Verruca looked at the two young faces hardly out of nappies. "I've been growing my veggies over a dump of festering robots . . . their effluent and oils leaking into my compost, my soya-toms—my potatoes —my pumpkins!" she screeched.

"I wouldn't call it a dump," muttered the studious lab assistant.

"I would," shouted a militant-looking woman mid diagram surveying.

"We could be wrong," said the best buddy.

"Don't think so," yelled the militant woman.

The lead sportswoman stumbled in with several limbs of ancient robots under her arms. One with red painted nails clutched a glowing potato seedling covered in mud.

The two assistants returned to their microscopes.

"As I said, we could be wrong," muttered the studious lab assistant.

"Yes, definitely," said the best buddy.

"Wrong? That's a Mae West arm if I ever saw one," snapped Verruca.

"And what's that when it's at home?" said the militant woman.

"A very-old-but-not-to-be-ignored robot from the days when men ruled," said Verruca.

"Where do you want these?" said the lead sportswoman.

"Men, rule? Don't make me laugh," said the militant one.

"They called themselves cleaners, but that was just a front . . . ." said Verruca.

"The first H-Pad was made out of a Mae West torso," said the studious lab assistant.

"Where shall I put these?" said the lead sportswoman.

The best buddy looked at her pal. "Really?"

"So what," snapped the militant one.

"And my robot spent hours in the shed," said Verruca. "Above that," she added, gesturing toward the offending limb.

The lead sportswoman spied an empty space on the beverage bench. "I'll just put them here then," she said.

"No!" shouted several women.

"You can tell," muttered a voice from the back.

"Definite glow," said the buddy.

The lead sportswoman stopped, dropping her cargo on the floor like it was poison. "Glow?"

"Not to mention Hilda," said Verruca.

A few snorted. *Pfff—her*.

"She made her toys in the shed."

The tent fell silent.

"By *toys*, do you mean *vibrators*?" said the sportswoman.

Verruca nodded. "Even tested them—in this very spot."

The women dropped their tools and stared as the shot-putter marched in from the garden clutching the shell of a glowing miniature turtle, one of its legs still attached—and rotating.

"Look at what that four-legged so-and-so dug up . . ." She stopped and glared at the women. "What?"

The appendage slowed with a whine.

No one said anything.

"It's an arm." She looked at it. "Or a leg. Nothing more."

Silence.

She gestured to the beverage bench. "Shall I put them here?"

"No!" shouted several women.

"Hilda made her vibrators here . . ." said the lead sportswoman.

The appendage dropped to the floor.

"*And* tested."

For the first time ever, the lab technicians were stumped by technology; seriously scared.

They put on extra gloves and extra white jackets, doubled up on the Teflon aprons. Despite a wheelbarrow full of bagged vibrators, no one had actually put the two together, until that is, Verruca pointed it out.

Now they couldn't stop thinking about it.

Was whatever had blown up the shed and had various bits of buried robots glowing contagious—poisonous? And if so, had it affected their vibrators and . . . well . . . other things?

Those in the tent worked furiously to isolate the source—or, in layman's terms, "find out." Soon the tent was a den of unbagged "toys": heaving, rotating, and vibrating loudly enough to drown out the odd rumblings from beneath the Legless statue, which was now as forgotten as a Mae West robot.

No one noticed the slow sinking, the engulfing of the earth about the sides; they were too busy trying to reassure themselves that Hilda's vibrators were as sterile as the womb of a Planet Hy Man woman.

Two days later, a helmet-shaped cleaning robot, under the orders of whoever had given them, was brushing about the edges of the Legless statue's rump.

He was a meticulous four-legged robot, first using a broom followed by a brush and shovel attached to its back, which Verruca thought unnecessary but didn't have the heart to say.

It was a slow, irritating process to supervise, which is why no one did, including Verruca's robot. In fact, the mere mention of "the Helmet" had many pulling a bored, glazed face.

Mid sweeping around Legless's rump, the Helmet stopped to pull the brush and shovel from its holder when a small flutter of soil dropped on its back.

It stopped.

A clump followed with a thump.

The robot circled to shake it off.

The statue shuddered.

The robot skidded.

The statue shook, shivered, trembled, squeaked, convulsed, rose, and then sunk deeper into the mud.

The robot tumbled off and rolled toward the tent, hitting the side with a thud just inches from Cyborg's robotic feet.

It blinked.

Cyborg blinked back.

The Helmet jumped to its feet to begin the rebalancing process by circling.

Cyborg, having never seen such a process before, stopped to watch.

The statue vibrated, juddered, this time with more force, sending the Helmet's broom across the garden with a plop. It landed by Cyborg's feet.

The robot looked up to catch sight of a giant pumpkin rising between the sinking thighs of Legless's statue.

"Call . . . call . . . call . . . arch . . . archeo . . . the digging people," he yelled.

The shovel followed; propelled into the air with the speed of a football, it cracked across the Helmet's back . . .

Splat!

"Danger, danger . . . shovel . . . an implement of meager ability . . ."

The brush followed.

Cyborg looked up and muttered, "Oh, shit," as it smacked into him instead.

The statue workers watched from Verruca's kitchen window. H2's "pulling together" meant they had been demoted to caffeine production and biscuit searching—not an easy task in Verruca's kitchen. Her biscuit tin was as empty as a Hilda promise: just four moldy cheese biscuits as ancient as the days when cheese came from real milk.

In disgust, they tossed said biscuits out the window, sending a nearby crow flying off in disgust. They were as down as a pair of socks with no elastic.

Watching your statue plummet to ground can do that to a statue worker.

Chapter Thirty-Two

DIGGERS

"There is more to a toothbrush than bristles."–Woody

The "digging people" were three women with wild hair and woolly jumpers. They looked and acted like no one else and were, to quote Woody, in a class of their own.

Where they'd gotten the idea for woolly jumpers, no one had any idea, as they were too aloof to ask, although Woody had his suspicions: they looked just like the Archaeologists he'd seen on Earth TV.

Their training was so intense that only three qualified; once qualified, they upped the training to impossible levels that even Alice couldn't fathom.

They even claimed to have decoded another language from the bowels of the tunnel, calling it *script* . . .

They were so intelligent they pulled apart and rebuilt H-Pads "for a laugh," and they not only played quizzes but reinvented them—in script—just because they could.

The digging people spent their time investigating the old tunnels under the city, which had been blocked after the death of Bette the cleaner, or "Our Bette," as they liked to call her.

At first, a toothbrush was used to "caress the evidence"; once the caressing was completed, a sniffer was installed.

The tunnels had been considered death traps, until the sniffer was invented. An ingenious up-cycling of the vacuum cleaner that elevated the status of the three diggers to Archaeologist (with a capital A) and *digging* to *excavating* (capital E optional).

A sniffer not only sniffed but hoovered, filtered, and spat, which led to reading and more spitting, along with an in-depth, laminated receipt of said reading.

The unblocking of "our Bette's" tunnel was a piece of piss with such equipment. Not that the Archaeologists told anyone how easy it was. They explored and recorded like they were discovering not only the great secrets of their world but secrets as complicated as an Earth's Rubik's Cube.

A cube they had not only reinvented but taken to another dimension altogether—the fifth invisible when complete dimension.

It was just after elevenses when the Archaeologists zoomed in on flying platforms, their hair flowing behind like superhero capes.

It was a sunny day with a warm wind, and the robots were stretching their legs outside the hub due to it being "as hot as an armpit" inside. They were loitering about, trying to understand the idea of laughing, when Cyborg, mid cartwheel and funny face, stopped, his jaw mechanically dropping like a digger lever.

The robots, thinking it was all part of Cyborg's "let's have a laugh" session, did their best. "Ha-ha-ha, ha-ha-ha," said a couple of four-legged sweeper robots who liked to think they were a cut above the Helmet.

The Helmet snorted with mechanical precision.

Verruca, emptying her morning tea onto the mud that had once been a garden bed, had seen it all before.

She had told Cyborg his "let's have a laugh" face was as funny as a set of piles, but would he listen? She slung her teapot dregs to the wind, then stopped, her jaw dropping too—with a little more finesse.

The Archaeologists liked to work incognito; everyone knew that and assumed they would arrive in "the dead of night," erect a "do not enter" tent, work under a lamp until dusk, then disappear again, perhaps leaving a fifth-dimension Rubik's Cube behind to rub in how smart they were . . .

Them appearing in public was as probable as Hilda wearing a knitted bikini, but there they were, circling the garden on flying platforms.

"Who let them use those?" snapped Cyborg, still a little full of himself.

The Archaeologists didn't look up, even when Cyborg called them "the digging people." They merely continued to circle, shouting to each other in script.

"F!"

"C!"

"Speak the language of our great Manifesto," shouted Cyborg.

They circled again, noses in the air.

"Ignore them," shouted one in script.

"I said—" yelled Cyborg.

"We heard."

"And choose to ignore."

It was Woody's suggestion that they film the Archaeologists causing the sort of uproar that only the promise of a flying platform could fix.

H2's leadership team did advise against it, but Woody believed in the caressing of evidence, and he felt Planet Hy Man had a right to see the toothbrushes in action.

"You've seen those women?" said Pete.

Woody didn't answer. He had been down in the tunnel once and found the women there to be a relief. They didn't even look up let alone coo over him like those in the market.

"We need to record and learn," he said, and before anyone could argue, he headed down the tunnel with the sort of confidence that had the team shaking their heads.

The three Archaeologists were packing up at the time, talking of incognito digs and toothbrushes, when Woody appeared.

They argued as they packed—or, rather, the chief Archaeologist known as Howard argued. Carter, the second-in-command, who many claimed knew so much her head hurt, nodded as passionately as possible while packing.

While Zelia, the last of the women to qualify, was brushing herself clean with a quiet intensity that irritated Howard.

"Don't know why you bother," Howard said. "You attract dirt like a torch attracts moths."

"Excellent analogy," muttered Carter.

With a sigh, Zelia stopped and bent for a box.

Woody made to help. But the box was so heavy he dropped it smack on his toe.

He hopped.

Zelia lifted it like it was a paper cup.

Woody stopped, staring at the elfin, almost five-foot girl propping a box that weighed a ton under her arm like it was a handbag . . .

"Jesus," he muttered.

Carter handed him her lunch box, then slid Zelia's on top.

Woody, with a groan, began to argue his point. "It's what they do on Earth," he said. "Film digs."

"Yes, well, we are not on Earth, and our work requires solitude," said Howard, slapping her lunch box on top.

Woody struggled to balance, wondering what the hell they had for lunch. "We have a right"—he grunted—"to see what you do with all those toothbrushes."

Howard retrieved the latest receipt from the sniffer with a crisp pull, peered at it, and turned to Woody. "The smaller the implement, the more scientific and the harder to comprehend."

Carter nodded.

Woody eyed the receipt. "Can I see that?"

"Absolutely not," snapped Howard.

They stomped to the surface, dumped their luggage at the Operator's room, then made for the room with a view, Howard arguing all the way. Even Woody's best smile didn't shut her up.

The Archaeologists barged in.

H2, staring out of the window, hands at her back, turned.

"We are not for public eyes," shouted Howard. "Archaeology is not entertainment; it is a science."

"Absolutely," said Carter with a look at Howard.

"Do you see Alice filming the egg popping labs?" said Howard.

Zelia stared out the window. She could see the emporium, and with her super-sharp bifocals, she peered through the window, catching a glimpse of a circling flying platform.

She sighed. How she dreamed of that: the wind in her hair, her big pickling jumper off and tied around her waist for the wind to flap . . .

"We go incognito or not at all," snapped Howard.

"Totally," said Carter.

H2 caught sight of Zelia sighing and followed the line of her vision, and her heart leaped at the thought of pleasing someone.

The flying platform did a backflip; the rider threw back her head with a laugh, and Zelia clapped her hands.

"Just ignore them," said Howard. "Those riders always over-egg."

"Over-egging is your department," said Woody, his patience a little frayed.

Howard and Carter glared at him.

"I heard those flying platforms need testing"—H2 threw a warm look at Zelia—"outdoors."

"Really?" said Zelia.

"Perhaps two birds and one stone?" H2 smiled at Zelia. "What do you think?"

"Oh, yes please." Zelia clapped.

"Making an idea sound smart doesn't take away the fact that it is but stupid," said Howard.

"Definitely," said Carter.

"We are scientists, not adventurers," said Howard.

Carter stopped. "I wouldn't say that."

"There are great Archaeologist adventurers on Planet Earth," said Woody. "Lara Croft, Indiana Jones . . ."

Carter sighed. "What I wouldn't give for a hat and a bit of leather."

Howard threw her a look. "Mere Earth fantasy." She sniffed. "Those films have as much to do with science as footmen have with feet . . ."

"Footman *do* do feet," said Woody.

Howard's face stiffened.

H2 jumped in. "We need a scientific review."

Zelia's face lit up.

"A good testing outside, perhaps near an excavation—by the portal site," said H2.

Carter smiled.

"But how will our packer robots keep up?" said Howard.

"You could use a packer flying platform for the necessaries," said DBO. "And if you need more, the packer robots could follow later."

Howard looked unconvinced.

"We've always worked with the packer robots; they understand packing. It's not a trivial thing, you know, it takes years to develop . . ."

"All right, Howard," said Carter, "we all know about your packing."

"They need guidance, someone to follow," said Howard, losing ground.

"Woody can guide," said H2.

Woody choked on his caffeine. "Me?"

"And Pete," said H2.

"Why me?" said Woody.

"Your leadership qualities," she said. "Women love you."

Howard rolled her eyes.

"And Pete's an expert with robots."

"Well, I wouldn't say that, ma'am."

"Don't call me . . ." H2 stopped. "I would, Pete."

Chapter Thirty-Three

THE PACKER ROBOT

"A holiday is nothing without decent packing."–Don

Packer robots were, to quote Howard, an Archaeologist's best friend. They were sturdy, good-old-fashioned transporters of all things in boxes and knew a thing or two about packing.

They had been around for ages, and although slow—like turtle-slow—they did pretty much what they were told, carried a ton, and always delivered their cargo intact.

The packer robots could carry boxes on their heads, strapped to their backs, in their pockets, and piled up in their hands; they could push packed-up trolleys like they were in a true duty-free airport passage, even through inches of mud. They were the transport elephants of Africa, the camels of the desert, the backpack of a back-packer, and the trolley of the supermarket all rolled into one.

To them, packing was an art that had Howard sighing There was nothing "haphazard" or "slapdash," as she liked to put it. They labeled things, wrapped delicate things with care; how they filled their boxes was just as important as where they balanced their boxes on their person, and Howard loved them.

"It the cornerstone of our work," said Howard.

"Wouldn't call it that," muttered Zelia.

"But we must move with the times . . . adjust," said Carter, "and help when asked."

H2 met Howard's eyes. "A robot can only do so much, and testing a flying platform would really up your status."

"And I'm fed up working in that dark place," burst in Zelia, "bent over like a turtle. Besides, I always wanted to fly."

Chapter Thirty-Four

THE FLYING PLATFORM

"Driving a flying platform takes more than standing."–Zelia

"Flying platforms, flying platforms," yelled Cyborg.

The robots charged out of the hub … .

Verruca, mid lubricating the Helmet's joints, looked up. "Flying what?"

"A small board," yelled Cyborg, "mid trial stage."

"Oh, that," said Verruca, wiping her hands.

The robots watched a fourth flying platform appear and begin to circle in a tipsy fashion. With two sniffers and a bag of toothbrushes strapped to the back, balancing looked to be a serious issue.

The packing had been done in a rush, shoved onto a fourth flying packer platform by a sniffy footman who was not too impressed with Howard. He knew a thing or two about feet; he had soothed many, trained with the best, and the last thing he intended to do was take packing orders from a jumped-up digger who, well, insulted the very fabric of a footman.

With the silence of a couldn't-give-a-shit teenager, the footman loaded up while Howard watched, cheesed off to her back teeth.

He heaved two sniffers onto the platform with an exaggerated elderly shake, pulled the belt from his trousers, wrapped it around their round body, and tied the sort of knot that a sneeze would unravel.

Howard gritted her teeth.

Packing in a precise "what goes in first is the last you need" manner was not only their first lesson but a must when working in a dark tunnel.

She stared at the sniffer trunks dangling freely like a lose appendage until the footman tugged his trousers up with a "finished" look.

"You can't leave it like that."

"This is emergency packing," he sniffed.

"That lot will be lost by the time we've left the city."

He looked at her with a "so?"

"And what about my toothbrushes?"

"Essentials only," he snapped.

She glared at him. *How could they be taken seriously with just a handful of implements?*

"As promised, the rest will follow," he added.

"You're taking the pickling proverbial," she hissed.

He ran his papery fingers through his hair with a tut, almost over-balancing.

"I can't work without my toothbrushes," she yelled.

The footman nailed a bag to the end of the platform with a "there."

She glowered at him.

He glowered back and then, with another tug of his trousers, shuffled off.

"Never upset a footman," whispered Zelia with a decisive shove of a toothbrush. "They have an elephant memory."

Howard moaned all the way to the site—until the circling began. It felt quite nice . . .

After a few loops around the bonfire, the flying platforms sped up.

"Perhaps you should slow down," shouted Verruca.

Howard ignored with a regal wave. She'd never experienced speed before and she rather liked it. Women appeared from the tent, some clutching mugs of beverages, others munching biscuits, most as pissed off as a lockdown teenager.

"Why should those up-themselves diggers get to test?"

"Like they're the favorites."

"Just because they can make a toothbrush work."

"Yeah, why them?"

"They did invent the sniffer," said Cyborg.

"And what's all that in the tent—camp pie?" said the militant woman.

"Well, yes, but—"

"We've invented more implements in an afternoon than that lot use in a year, and—" She stopped as Howard zipped past, her cheeks wobbling with the speed.

"No good will come of it," muttered the ambitious statue worker. "Takes years to control one."

"Can we stop?" said Zelia. "My feet are sliding all over the place."

"One more round!" yelled Howard.

Zelia, mid skid, threw her a dirty look.

Carter, feeling a little sick, grumbled.

The flying platform sped up, circling like water down a plug hole.

The packer platform wobbled.

Howard tossed her head back with a manic laugh—the faster the better. She pickling loved speed.

The women stared like stunned fish as the footman's knot loosened like a hair bun without pins.

A sniffer clattered to the ground.

The flying platforms circled faster, like dogs chasing their tails.

"And fly we shall," yelled Howard with a crazed look.

"There is no need to shout," snapped Carter, who was now trying to keep her breakfast down.

"I want to get off," shouted Zelia.

The second sniffer frisbeed into the air, taking the bag of toothbrushes with it.

Toothbrushes propelled into the air.

The sniffer crashed into a tree.

"Stop!" yelled Carter with a heave, her breakfast now bubbling like a cauldron.

Howard staggered to a hero pose.

"Time to park," said Howard.

The platforms continued.

"I said park," shouted Howard. "Now!"

Howard's platform overtook the packing platform. She zoomed past Zelia.

"I said stop, damn you!"

"I thought they were voice operated," muttered the militant one.

"They are," said the ambitious statue worker. "Just have to hear the right one."

Howard's flying platform pulled a U-turn, speeding off in the opposite direction, leaving Howard mid air . . . she tumbled to the ground.

"Ha-ha-ha, ha-ha-ha-ha," said a four-legged robot.

Cyborg turned to the robot. "Now is not the time for laughing."

H2 and DBO saw it all in the room with a view, projected onto the wall via H2's H-Pad.

"I just wanted to make them happy," muttered H2.

"I know," said DBO with a comradely pat.

"It was my idea."

"I'm sure it's sortable."

H2 turned to her confidant. "You think?"

"Everything is sortable. We just need to keep things under our hat . . . away from—"

"I'm going in," said H2.

"In? To do what?" said DBO.

"Sort things. I made this mess," said H2.

"Not so loud."

H2 looked at her.

"If Deidre hears of this, we are done for. Imagine the chaos when this gets out. The fear."

She stopped.

A shuffle came from behind the door.

"Who's that?"

"Merely passing," said a voice from behind the door.

"No one *just* passes that door; were you eavesdropping?"

"Didn't hear a thing."

"You sure?" said H2.

Suck . . .

"What was that?" said DBO.

"Nothing," said a voice from behind the door.

"Sounds like a decoder," said H2.

"As if," jested said a voice from behind the door.

Watching the fall of snotty women is never as enjoyable as imagined, and as Howard's flying platform made a beeline for the other platforms, the women gasped.

A head-on collision is not something you'd wish on your worst enemy.

"Jump!" shouted some.

Zelia, perfecting a perfect drop-and-roll, landed at the feet of Cyborg, her hair the sort of mess a flock of seagulls could nest in.

Carter's drop was more a dive bomb. She hurled herself onto the ground, landing with a roll-and-tumble motion impossible to stop, and was propelled across the mud—smack into the side of the Legless statue, where she bounced over his thighs and disappeared between his legs with a "Bugger and bollockkkkkkks!"

A few pulled faces, until . . .

Piff, puff, poof . . .

She was gone.

"Oh, shit," muttered a voice from the back.

The ambitious statue worker looked at Dozy. "And that is why we don't use flying platforms."

DBO opened the door with drama.

Deidre looked up, mid pulling the sucker recorder from the wall, as two footmen jolted into a futile "we're just passing by" gesture.

"So it *was* a recorder," said DBO. "Wait a minute—is that a sucker recorder?"

Bang! Crash!

The women turned to catch, on-screen, the packer flying platform and Howard's collide.

Boom! Bam!

Flames filled the screen.

"Looks like you have a crisis on your hands, ma'am," said Deidre.

"Don't call me—" H2 stopped. What was the point?

Chapter Thirty-Five

BOUND AND GAGGED

"In the end, with all their toothbrushes and sniffers, it wasn't the Archaeologists who found the portal. It was the portal that found them."—H2, Reflections of a Leader

It took several minutes for the smoke to clear, and when it did, the sight had those in the room with a view silent for some time.

Toothbrushes littered the landscape, some embedded in the mud, others suspended from trees and hedges like fairy lights. The sniffers lay in a collapsed pile, their trunks as motionless as snakes with full bellies, while the remaining two platforms continued to circle as the women shouted uselessly like football fans.

Alice tried to intervene, filming while dodging like a cartoon bullet, until those from the room with the view, feeling a little seasick, ordered a "stationary filming."

Finally, Verruca took one down with her lasso.

The platform put up a fight, bucking like a bull at a rodeo, until the women, joining forces, held on to the rope to bring the "so-and-so" down.

The platform tumbled to the ground, stopping the remaining flying platform in its tracks. Its lights went out with a fizz.

It paused, suspended in the air as the fire cracked beneath; then, in a subdued fashion, it parked by the tent.

Deidre's recorder clicked off.

"Well, I wonder what those in the marketplace will have to say about this," she said.

DBO turned to her with a steely glare. "Who's going to tell them?"

Deidre returned her glare. "When someone disappears, the public have a right to answers."

"We don't have any yet," said DBO.

"Well, I'll just let the public know that . . . then."

"And set them into a panic? They'll start pulling down statues again, and then where will we be?" said DBO.

"The public is entitled—" said Deidre.

"To what you print?" said DBO. "No one has the *right* to see that."

"I've won awards," said Deidre.

"In Hilda's time."

"We don't have time for this," said H2.

"At least they'll know," muttered Deidre.

"And what good would that do?" said a footman.

The three women turned to the two elderly footmen. One had a shake and the other a stoop.

They had forgotten the footmen were still there.

"They could help, change things. They have a right to the truth . . . their opinions," said Deidre.

"More hindrance than help," said DBO. "They don't know anything."

"Whose fault is that?" shouted Deidre.

"It's not a fault, it's a fact," said the footman with a shake, silencing the women yet again.

H2 skulled her caffeine, pondering DBO's words. "You're a leader in a crisis, you can't afford nostalgia. You need to monitor, censor, delegate—take a stand."

She had to act with a clear head, not think about the happiness of others.

"We need to know what we are dealing with," said H2 with her best blank face. "How can we do that if the masses flood the site?"

"*Pfff*, that's just an excuse," huffed Deidre.

"There is a time and place for public opinion, and, well, Deidre, you have no idea when that is," said H2.

She grabbed Deidre's arm, and DBO followed.

"Let me teach you," said H2.

"You mean shut me up, silence me."

"More fudging your reporting than silencing," said H2.

H2 didn't like to call it *imprisonment*, *silencing*, *gagging*, or any of the other things that Deidre screamed at her.

She called it "taking control—for the good of all."

Vegas appeared, clutching enough rope to haul a boat, while Mex, called in for the "rough stuff," pushed Deidre to a chair with a "still got it" gloat.

They strapped Deidre's torso to a chair, snug like a rally driver's seatbelt.

Deidre struggled.

Vegas moved to Deidre's hands and tied her wrists together at the back of the chair.

Deidre tugged and swore.

Mex held her down with another "yep, still got it" look.

Vegas threw them a "Judas" glare.

"You're screwing with my liberty," she yelled. "Thrusting my rights to the wind."

Vegas moved to Deidre's ankles.

"Liberty and saving are two different things," said H2.

"Just because they are *spelled* different doesn't mean they *are* different," said Deidre.

"But they are," said Vegas, tugging a crisp knot.

"One day you'll thank me for this," said H2.

"Thank you? I am gonna crucify you."

"Shall I gag her?" said Vegas.

"No," said H2. "Take her to *the* cupboard."

"*That* cupboard?"

"Yes, *that* cupboard."

"But it's full of trolleys waiting for wheel oiling," said DBO.

"You might have told us before we strapped her to the chair," muttered Mex.

H2 turned to the footman. "And find a pencil and paper."

The women looked at her.

"Yes, the good old-fashioned implement some still use on Earth."

With a bit of grunting, Deidre was placed in the old trolley wheel oiling cupboard, right beside a rather whiffy mop and an upturned trolley.

With a "there," she was squared in.

"You can shout all you like, no one will hear," said H2, discovering a side to herself she'd rather kept hidden.

"I *can* gag her," said Vegas.

H2 shook her head. Then she motioned to the footman. "Put the pencil and paper just out of reach."

With trembling hands, the shaky footman pulled a notepad from his pocket, followed by an inch-long pencil.

The women stared; it was as unimpressive as Deidre's old-fashioned recorder.

"Bit short, isn't it?" snapped Deidre. "For what I'm gonna write?"

"You sure you don't want me to gag her?" said Vegas.

The stooped footman, feeling a bit mean, slid a pen and paper inches from her fingers.

"Honey, by the time you reach that, we'll have saved the planet," said DBO.

Deidre watched them leave. "I can still see you," she yelled.

The door slammed shut.

"Still write things down."

She attempted a mouth grab at the pencil.

It dropped to the floor.

She swore. *By the time I manage to wriggle a finger free, H2 will probably be too old to massage a foot.*

At first, H2 planned to supervise on-site, "get her hands dirty," as she liked to put it, but ousting Deidre had changed her.

She finally understood that leadership was not always about being liked. In fact, being liked had nothing to do with it all; it was about decisions and delegation, which required spying and experts, and she knew just who . . .

Not that anyone was going to like it.

Vegas called it a stupid plan.

Even DBO had her doubts, and Pete was so against it he nearly walked out of the room claiming that they were "all turncoats."

But H2 had grown in confidence, and she realized that no one knew any better than her. She had seen the hippies in action. What they couldn't clean up was nobody's business.

And as for Pete? Well, he's just bitter about the past. He'll soon get over it.

Chapter Thirty-Six

TOFFEE AND CROWS

"The erecting of a tent in a hurricane is still easier than the erecting of a drunk."–Pete

Alice projected her face onto the flapping wall with wide-o-vision.

The women crammed into the tent, plonking themselves on benches and tables, while the robots lounged about the back like builders on a tea break. With the hearing of sheepdogs, the vision of eagles, and the memory of, well, microchips, they didn't even need to be in the tent. But H2 insisted.

Unimpressed, they all stared at her youthful face.

"We need to be strong for each other," she said.

No one said anything.

"Think of each other, and the planet."

A few pulled faces.

"It will only get worse if we don't."

"Here we go," muttered a voice from the back.

"And we will all suffer."

"Told you."

"Shhhh," hissed Verruca.

"Besides, I have reinforcements."

"What, a couple of footmen?" snapped Howard.

"An expert in the field of nature."

"Expert? That'll be as easy to find as a heart in a robot," muttered

Cyborg, offending just about everyone in the tent, including the robots . . .

That night, they waited by a campfire as instructed by H2. Apparently, reinforcements were coming on foot and would appreciate a warm welcome.

H2 had learned a lot from her time with the hippies, and contemplating by a fire was one of them.

"Bonfire building is team building," she said, "and while you're at it, ponder the stars, get a sense of nature."

It was a perfect night for a bonfire: still, clear, with just a whiff of a breeze and the moon in all its glory.

Most had never studied the stars let alone sat around an outside fire; a toasted soya at the marketplace was about as outdoorsy as most got. They soaked in the expanse of the dark, staring at the star-filled sky, waiting for a savior, hero, warrior, or whatever to appear. Apart, that is, from the "digging people," as Alice continued to call them.

They noticed nothing, and they hardly helped with the bonfire; they were not only one down but downhearted. In fact, so down were they that they couldn't even face their Rubik's Cube.

Carter was seriously missed. The sniffers, now as useless as a kettle without a plug, were going to be that much harder to reconstruct without her. And as for the toothbrushes, Zelia had spent the afternoon retrieving them with a heavy heart. Even a decent scrub wouldn't make them usable.

A four-legged robot appeared with a tray of teas on its back. The ambitious statue worker lifted a mug and sipped. "Never seen a man swallow a woman before."

Dozy grabbed a mug. "Me neither."

"Swallowing is but the action of a woman," said Cyborg. "Not that of a statue."

"What would you call it then?" said the ambitious statue worker.

"Portal transmission," said Cyborg.

Zelia stared into the night at a toothbrush grimly swinging from the top of a tree. *If only they hadn't packed in such a haphazard fashion.*

She was wondering about a ladder, where she could get one, when a large mechanical crow circled the tree. It landed, gripped the toothbrush, and flew off, circling about a distant figure on the horizon.

"Whatever it was, it had that Legless statue glowing," said the militant one. "Lit up like the emporium in the good old days."

Some nodded; others turned to the statue workers.

"Nothing to do with us," said the ambitious statue worker. She gestured to the four-legged robot. "Even he's lit up."

Zelia watched as the distant figure pulled something from her pocket and dropped it behind her. The crow made a dive, toothbrush forgotten.

"Is that a hippie?" said Verruca.

Hippie? gasped a few.

Two more figures appeared, followed by a couple of crows; they too dropped something behind. The crows made a dive.

"That'll be the toffee," said Verruca.

The lead sportswomen looked up. *Toffee?*

"Yes, it's a hippie thing."

The women stared at the crows, silent and still, as the figures drew closer.

"It's the only way to get a bird off your back," said Verruca. "That stuff will stick their beaks together for hours."

"Oh," muttered the shot-putter. "If only I'd known."

"Yes," said the lead sportswomen with a glare at Verruca.

The hippie colony had been called. They ransacked their greenhouse, consulted the library, and opened up the old spaceships until they found what they were looking for—in volumes.

Chapter Thirty-Seven

MIND FUDGING

"Tent pegs are far more important than they look."–Don

The hippies were but three. The head Alterationist, the cook, and Prudence (for a robot's point of view) had come, not to gloat, as the militant woman feared, or to start a battle, as others rumored; they had appeared because a portal was something that affected all on the planet.

They weren't the sort to hold grudges, as Deidre had written, to exploit, as she implied. They were more like the earlier hippie legends; zoned out on what was left of nature, chilled out on the good life and happy hot chocolate, developing new drills (vibrators) to smuggle across to Hilda—until, that is, they arrived at the campfire.

Nothing inspires gloating like needy confusion, and those by the campfire had it in spades.

The hippies took one look at the forlorn looks of the Archaeologists, the confused pissed-off look of the sportswomen, and the glazed, "nothing to do with me" looks of the statue workers and couldn't help themselves. Forgetting all of H2's advice, suggestions, and "try to remember when you knew little" words, they entered the campsite like a teacher catching students skipping classes with smokes in their hands.

In the dark, they sniffed about the site, the statue, and the remaining platform, claiming that it took "serious nature-fudging for such things as this to happen."

"And the worst thing to do in the midst of nature-fudging is to shout," said the cook. "And don't get me started on . . . rude words."

"Gets the lubricants bubbling," said Prudence (making things up to impress).

"Like oil on water," said the cook.

"Do you not mean fire?" said the militant one.

The cook threw her a look.

"Nature-fudging is a mechanical thing, affects the sparking of circuits," said the head Alterationist. "Very spreadable."

"On Earth, they call it *pollution*," muttered a voice from the back.

"Yes, well, we are not on Earth."

Silence.

"I thought we were here to find a portal . . . thing," piped up the studious lab assistant.

Her buddy nodded.

"Better to find what opened the portal," said Prudence.

"And I am wondering if perhaps it's the same as whatever sparked the platform to rise up," said the cook.

The remaining platform whined; Prudence soothed it with a stroke.

"Well, that's a given," snapped the ambitious statue worker. "Even Dozy over there worked that out."

"I did wonder about telespraying . . ." said Dozy.

The cook shot her a look.

"What would you know of telespraying?"

"I know a thing or two," huffed Dozy.

"Not everything is alterable," said the Alterationist.

"Telespraying could be," muttered Dozy.

"Telespraying is set in stone," said the Alterationist.

"This is not the work of telespraying," said the cook. "Too messy."

"Swallowing," said the shot-putter. "That can be messy."

"Only when you don't know what you are doing," said the cook.

"Toffee then?" said the lead sportswoman with a look at Verruca.

"*Pfff*, as if," said a voice from the back.

The cook lifted a pumpkin in her hand. It pulsated with a green glow. "And who is responsible for this?"

"I am," muttered Verruca.

"You surprise me, Verruca."

"And him over there," she said, gesturing to Cyborg.

"A robot follows orders, ma'am."

Verruca sniffed.

"I gather the soya-toms didn't survive," said the cook.

"How did you know about them?" said Verruca.

The cook headed into the tent. "Skid marks—dead giveaway."

The Alterationist followed with her best "I knew that too" march.

"What skid marks?" snapped Verruca.

"You need to be a cook to see those sort of skid marks," said the Alterationist.

"Well, what the pickle is the good of that then?" said Verruca.

The women followed the hippies into the tent, leaving the Archae-ologists glumly staring into the bonfire and Prudence loitering about the entrance.

She had been told Pete would appear.

She, like Pete, was a 33 Robot. There were only four on the planet, and she lived with the other two, Pope and Pot.

She had drawn the short straw, and now she would face Pete and a past that she and her comrades weren't proud of. And as she watched the last of the technicians enter the tent, she wondered . . . what was she going to say?

"What is a soya-tom?" said the studious lab assistant.

"Buggered if I know," said her best buddy.

"It's a high breed," said Prudence.

"And what's that when it's at home?"

"You'll soon find out," shouted the cook. She turned to Prudence. "And it's *hybrid*."

As the women entered the tent, they gasped. They had no idea just how bad it was. In the dark, the robot appendages glowed like fluores-cent glow sticks, pulsating like they were alive.

Some shuffled like they had committed a crime, others went for a "how were we to know?" stance.

The cook slung her satchel from a microscope, pulled out a *Portals for Dummies* book, and slapped it on the table. "Why didn't you start with just one robot?"

The Alterationist nodded.

The militant one stared at the book, then moved to open it.

The cook slapped it shut. "Instead of this . . . scrapyard affair."

The Alterationist nodded again.

"I mean this is a shambles. Look at this place."

"Bit hard to see in the dark," joked the voice from the back.

"Dark? This place is lit up like an Earth's Christmas tree," said the cook.

"When you get a microscope in your hand, you just can't help yourself," said the militant woman, making another grab for the book.

The cook caught her eye.

She held it and retrieved her hand.

"We hardly ever get a chance to see the past." She threw a glare at the Archaeologists outside. "So when we do . . ."

The others nodded.

The Alterationist picked up the forearm of a Mae West robot, its red-painted fingernail thrust into the air like the Statue of Liberty's beacon.

It pulsed.

"We were told it was an emergency," said the studious lab assistant.

"All hands on deck," said her buddy.

"Time was of the essence, *she* said," said the voice from the back.

"I doubt H2 said that," said the Alterationist, pointing the forearm into a dark corner. Light flooded the corner, startling a mechanical rat into a scurry.

"It's like a fog lamp," the Alterationist said to herself.

"Not now," said the cook.

"I mean look at it." She pointed to another dark corner. "We could light up our camp with this, make streetlamps."

"Exactly," murmured a voice.

"We don't have any streets," said the cook.

"But we do," said the shot-putter.

"Just sitting there to be used like . . ." murmured the Alterationist. "Free of charge—for all."

The cook ripped the appendage from the Alterationist.

"Only one thing could set off this sort of glow."

"Oh, I'm sure there is more than one thing," said the ambitious statue worker. "There is never just one thing."

"And nothing is free," said the cook. She pointed the arm at Verruca. The red nail lit up her face like a scene from a horror movie.

"You know what you've done, don't you?"

Verruca blinked into the light. "Well, if I did, I would not have done it."

"You opened things that should have been left closed."

"What things?" snapped Verruca, forgetting how evasive pickling hippies were.

"Effluent."

The women looked at her.

Verruca blinked, shielding her eyes.

"A soya-tom effluent."

"I did tell her," said Cyborg.

"You did not."

"One hint of a glow should have stopped you."

"Glow? I work in the daylight; nothing glows under that sun."

"Yes, but you knew it was a quarry. You should have been more careful, growing vegetables over all these robots. And as for soya-toms—"

Verruca blew a fuse. "Nobody told me about the quarry," she yelled.

"I did try to warn—"

Verruca turned to Cyborg and, with a glare of pure venom, tossed a turtle carcass at him, sparking off a rotating leg.

Thump.

"Ow!"

The cook, with a sigh, turned to her book to find the militant one with her nose in it.

The militant one looked up at the cook. "Bit out-of-date, isn't it?"

Chapter Thirty-Eight

KAREN

"Fire up the barbie!"–Australian Tourist Board

It all started with FaceTime . . .

Two days of sulking and Beryl was getting nowhere fast. Trying to adjust to the whole "Legless has a daughter" thing had her as touchy as a tooth abscess.

She decided to go for a walk.

Not something she was generally fond of. In fact, mentioning it had Archie and DJ raising their eyebrows with a "really?"

Beryl was strictly a car-to-the-shop sort of person, but she was fed up with everyone whispering like they knew something she didn't, itched to tell, but couldn't.

It was like she was back on Planet Hy Man walking the halls of power, encountering backstabbing at every corner—or was she just paranoid, as Legless claimed?

Archie looked at DJ. They had just left the camper van, and the last thing Beryl needed to see was what Legless was up to.

"Why not wait, have a chat with Bunnie?" said Archie.

"Pfff—her."

"She'll be here any minute. You could have a woman-to-woman sort of thing."

"As if," said Beryl.

"She is a good listener," said DJ with little conviction.

"That woman's idea of listening is to music with headphones. Even then she can't make it through one song without shouting."

"Singing," said Archie.

"Screeching," said Beryl. "The hens have better voices."

"She's not that bad."

"I'm off," said Beryl. She headed out the shed.

"Go the other way," shouted DJ.

And when she didn't, Archie nudged him.

"I'll come with you then," said DJ.

Beryl passed the camper van. She could hear Mandy and Legless inside.

She stopped.

DJ took her arm. "Come on, let's get that heart pumping."

"Mum," said Mandy.

"How about we head up to the Benmore Garden?"

"Why would I want to go there? It's shut."

"You did say a walk."

She heard Legless use his soft voice; she moved closer.

"You need to stop bragging," drawled a deep female voice. "No one cares."

She looked at DJ. "Who's that?"

He shrugged. "Fancy a coffee?" he said feebly.

"You mean you don't?" said Legless.

"I stopped caring years ago," said the Australian voice.

Beryl made to spy through the window.

DJ tried to stop her; she slapped him. He tugged at her sleeve; she pushed him away.

"Bollocks," he muttered as Beryl stared through the net curtains of the camper van.

Her heart lurched.

Legless, with the sort of boyish look Beryl vaguely remembered from their shagging-in-the-trolley-oiling-closet days, was all cozy next to Mandy, staring at the smallest flat-screen TV she had ever seen . . . while pickling *Hilda* was making coffee with her usual annoying hum.

They were FaceTiming with some loudmouth Australian.

"Let's go back to the shed," said DJ.

"Shhhh," hissed Beryl.

She caught sight of an older, Mandy-like face on the screen. The woman had the look of an athlete, fresh, healthy, with long, thick "shampoo add" hair—the finger-running-through kind.

Mandy called her mum.

Legless laughed. And if Beryl's heart hadn't been pounding so much, she would have realized it was a nervous laugh.

"Aye well, you would say that," said Legless.

She gulped. *Since when did he say "aye"?*

"Let's take you back," whispered DJ.

The first time Legless saw Karen, his heart stopped, his stomach turned, and his member shot up like a flag up a pole.

Karen had swept Legless off his feet, and as he stared at her sunburnt face, the memory warmed him.

Australia in the seventies had confused Legless. The "footy," the TV, the lingo—all of it had him as bamboozled as a sheep coming out of anesthetic—until he met six-foot-tall Karen, an athlete who not only thrashed women at sport but men as well.

Many saw her as a freak. Legless, however, thought she was brilliant.

She had a handshake that could crush a finger, a kick that could propel a ball across the seas, and an aim so perfect men were speechless.

For the first time since he'd left Planet Hy Man, Legless felt a connection with someone other than an Identity, someone who could help him fit in.

Nicholas the hairdresser warned him not to get involved. An Identity himself, he had seen it all before. Identities trying to assimilate, forget their roots . . . it never worked.

"There is more to an Identity than a human can understand," he said.

"But I am not an Identity," said Legless.

"Forgot about that," said Nicholas. "It must be even worse for you."

Legless nodded.

"You'll need to tell her; you can't keep sneaking to meetings forever."

"I'm giving up the meetings."

"What? But how can you? Everyone needs to be with their own kind."

"I am going to start fresh, become a human."

Nicholas shook his head. "No Identity can stay away for long."

"I told you, I'm not an Identity," snapped Legless.

"You'll regret it," he said, and he was right.

Legless couldn't keep away from the meetings.

He craved the honesty, the chance to talk about his home, who he was.

Within six months, Legless was sneaking off like he was having an affair, and just like an affair, it was a relief when he was found out.

Karen saw it as a betrayal, as him being unfaithful.

Legless tried to explain. "It's entertaining, nothing more."

"Call it what you like; in my book, you're fooling around with other women."

"But nothing happened."

"That's what you say. If it's nothing, why go and be with all those women? Aren't I enough?"

"No one is enough. We all want more."

"Just leave," she said.

"I'm an Alien," he blurted out.

She glared at him. "Always thought there was something different, just couldn't put my finger on it," she lied.

She hadn't a clue.

"Seriously, I am," said Legless.

"So am I." She sighed. "I want children, and the last thing I want is to have them with a nutcase who calls himself an Alien."

"You never mentioned children."

"You never mentioned Planet Hy Man."

Legless retreated to Nicholas, the hairdresser, with mixed feelings and confusion.

Nicholas was in the middle of a perm at the time. He caught sight of Legless's slump and stopped.

"What's up, kid?" he said, despite being half Legless's age.

"It's over—she wants me to leave."

Nicolas placed a hair dryer hood over the permee and handed her last month's *Cosmopolitan*.

She looked at it with an "I've read this already" look.

He handed her an old *Cleo*.

She opened it to the centerfold and, without a blush, stared at the male nude.

"She says she wants a man who does more than wash cars for a living."

"Well, I can understand that."

"She said there is only so long a good shag will last."

The permee looked over her centerfold with a raised eyebrow.

"Pfff, that's got to hurt." Nicholas shoved a comb into a sterilizing jar. "Has she met someone else?"

"No. At least, I don't think so."

"They always meet someone else."

"She says it's her, not me."

"She's met someone else," shouted the permee.

Legless tugged him away from the permee. "She knows."

"Shit."

"She says she wants kids with a normal man."

"Bollocks." Nicholas stopped. "I thought she was allergic to nappies, kids, and 'all that shit' . . ."

"Not a nutcase." Legless sighed.

Nicholas looked at him.

"She doesn't believe me. Thinks I'm nuts."

"Phew!"

"What do you mean, 'phew'?"

"No one wants our cover blown."

"But she thinks I'm doolally, a fruit loop, and she'll tell the world."

"They all think that. It's the way they cope."

Soon after he left Karen, he headed back to Britain via several countries and just as many backpacks, feeling lonely but light.

Legless's mixed feelings confused him. It was a relief when Karen ditched him—trying to be something he wasn't had just about killed him—and yet he missed her.

He had no idea they'd made a child. He thought his balls were as dried up as a prune. Turned out there were a few seeds left after all.

When Mandy wanted to know why he'd left her mother, he found it hard to explain. He didn't want to blame Karen, despite her having called him a moronic fantasist.

He knew the truth; he saw it in her eyes. He repulsed her, scared her, and she never let him near her again.

He did his best with a shrug. "She was a woman ahead of her time."

Mandy searched his eyes.

"She didn't want to be tied down," he said.

Mandy nodded. "You mean with an Alien."

"Well, yes."

Karen glared at Legless just like she used to years ago when he made other women laugh.

She hadn't aged that much, he thought. In fact, she looked pretty good. Then she mentioned . . . alimony.

Legless sighed. He'd forgotten her mean streak.

"The best thing I ever did was let you go," she shouted.

He stared at her hard eyes. "Let me go? I escaped."

Chapter Thirty-Nine

THE CRUSHING OF THINGS

"Looking 'good for your age' doesn't gloss over a dickhead."– Mandy

Beryl walked away crushed.

How could she compete with a woman like Karen, the mother of Legless's child, who she hated to admit looked way younger than her?

She headed into the shed.

Archie looked up from his laptop and called her a ball-breaker.

Beryl, assuming it was something positive in a "man spy" sort of way, huffed.

"You're a pussycat compared to her," said DJ, which didn't help.

"You're calling me a cat?"

"Compared to her," said Archie.

"Like Sophia?"

"As I said, compared to her."

She looked at the two Identities with no idea what they were talking about.

Bunnie's face flashed onto the screen. "It's a compliment," she said.

Beryl huffed again.

"Not her, you."

"Oh," said Beryl.

Hilda handed coffee to both Legless and Mandy, catching a glimpse of Karen's hard face. "Biscuit?" she said, moving for the tin.

Karen turned to her daughter. "What's with all that lipstick?"

"Mum."

"Told you to tone it down."

"I have spent a lifetime in a man's body; the last thing I want to do is tone things down. I want to celebrate," said Mandy.

"Spent a fortune on operations."

"My money."

"And the hormones," said Karen.

Hilda stopped mid biscuit tin opening. She caught Mandy's eye; her face softened.

"Cost an arm and two legs."

"I said not now, Mother."

Karen turned to Legless. "This is all your fault."

"How?"

"You abandoned your responsibilities," snapped Karen.

"You never told me. I'm no mind reader."

"Well, according to you, you are," said Karen.

"Jesus," he muttered.

Chapter Forty

RUBIK'S CUBE

"A robot can only get away with so much."–Woody

The Archaeologists, alone by the campfire, glumly tossed their Rubik's Cube from one to the other. They didn't notice Woody and Pete, let alone their much-loved packer robots, marching onto the site.

The packer robots circled the campfire, waiting for a "just over there" command; when none came, they started marching again.

Woody, spotting Howard by the bonfire, made a swift dive into the tent, while Pete took charge of the packer robots, ordering them to drop their cargo near the entrance.

He caught sight of Prudence.

She threw him a coy wave.

He glowered back.

DBO was transported back to the days when she was in the hippie library. She would have loved to catch up with the Cook and the Alterationist, find out what was new, until Vegas reminded her that it had only been a year since she had been there.

"You never did like that place, did you?" said DBO.

"It's not a case of liking—more not being suited," said Vegas.

They stared at the images beamed in from Alice: two disheartened Archaeologists tossing their Rubik's Cube back and forth like they couldn't give, well, a toss.

Howard with an underhand throw.

Zelia with a "fuck off" fling.

The packer robots marched between them like toy soldiers.

"Just over there," said Pete.

They dumped their boxes inches from Howard's feet.

"No! Over there," shouted Pete, "away from the fire."

Howard didn't bat an eyelid, even when a robot caught the side of her head with a robotic "sorry."

"Show us inside the tent," DBO ordered Alice.

Alice passed Prudence, gazing at Pete, then zoomed into the tent. She stopped when she reached the cook and grabbed her *Portals for Dummies* from the militant one. "It's a series," she said.

"It's out-of-date," said the militant one.

"And there are sequels."

The militant one grabbed it back. "Pfff—but who wrote it?"

"Legless."

The tent hushed . . .

H2, Vegas, and DBO looked at each other.

"He knew about portals?" said Vegas.

"A mere theory, ma'am, nothing more," said the footman with a stoop.

The footman with a shake looked at him. "Hardly a theory. Where do you think telespraying came from?"

"A power shower?" said Vegas.

The footman with a shake turned to her. "Well, yes, it did to a degree, but there are only so many showers one can take."

"Don't listen to him, he's talking through his nostrils. Legless was a pure blowhard," said the footman with a stoop. "Why she has that pile of trash is a mystery to me."

They turned to the projection on the wall . . .

"It warns about the mixing of genes," said the militant one.

"But that's our bread and butter," said the studious one.

They bent over the book.

The sportswoman followed. "'Thou shalt not bugger about with the soya gene,' it says here." She glared at Verruca.

"Pfff," said Verruca. "There is no mention of soya-tom."

"But there is of toffee," said the lead sportswoman.

Verruca's face stiffened.

"Beware the shirker."

"Doesn't mention toffee."

"Those who withhold."

"Still no toffee."

"Especially the toffee-holder."

Verruca bristled. "I don't hold any and I don't shirk."

"But you knew?" snapped the lead sportswoman.

"That's not shirking."

"Let's stick to the portal," said Woody.

"This woman stood back and watched the attack of the birds, and she could have easily stopped it."

"Like I'm going to whip up a spot of toffee for *you*."

Woody, having spent a lifetime with two larger-than-life rugby-playing brothers who punched rather than talked, had mastered deflection before he could walk. "There are side effects of sugar," he said, veering to the evils of Scottish tablet. "I mean look at Beryl."

"Pickling *Beryl*."

"She's the cause of all this."

"Exactly."

"Even says here," says Woody, "right next to the unplugging of a portal: 'Never leave the unplugging of things in the hands of Beryl.'"

The woman started to laugh.

"'The chances of her getting it right are as likely as . . .'"

He stopped.

"Go on . . ."

"'Her letting her hair down.'"

Woody, smug as a dog with a catch, shut the book.
The women sighed.

"That man's a master," muttered DBO.
"Played right into his hands," said Vegas.

Pete and Prudence held their gaze.

The 33 Robots were designed with a thought microchip that had the ability to adapt, evolve, or, as some would say, mutate like a virus, and these chips had changed them both: Prudence into a robot with a conscious, and Pete into a robot with gender issues and extremely long false eyelashes.

She had heard of his market stall, how Earth had transformed him, but she wasn't prepared for the complete fifties look. Pete was trussed up in a corset, which, despite the flexibility of Teflon, was crushing his innards. He strutted rather than marched.

She felt the need to be nice. "Do you ever look in a mirror?" she said.

"You're asking me that now?"

"Well, I . . ."

"We are in a crisis."

"Yes, I know, but . . ."

"I haven't seen you since you buggered off, left me in the lurch, and now you ask me about a mirror like I don't use one?"

"Just wanted to help." She gestured to his pointy bra. "It's not very convincing."

He adjusted it. "Don't hear any complaints."

"Yes, but . . ."

"Who cares?" lied Pete.

"I am happy to advise," said Prudence.

Pete flushed. "Advise—you?"

Prudence stammered as Woody appeared. He grabbed Pete's arm and, with a "you're needed," dragged him into the tent.

The three 33 Robots had evolved in the hippie colony to feel such things as comfort, pleasure, and choice. Understanding guilt, however, was thin on the ground.

It had taken them a long time to face what they had done, and when they finally did, they merely justified it.

Pope called it survival.

Pot called it necessary.

And Prudence believed them, until she saw Pete.

She stared at the tent, her so-called "justified" feelings melting. Did they really need to leave Pete the way they had?

Pope told her she was chosen for a reason, that she was the only one that could "pull off" a meeting with Pete. "It's that flowy way about you," he said. "You don't bristle like we do."

Was he right?

A queer feeling welled up inside her, a putting-it-right sort of feeling.

I could help, she thought. *Starting with those ridiculous eyelashes . . .*

She pushed the tent flap open and made to walk in.

"Bugger," said Howard.

She stopped.

"That nearly landed in the fire."

Prudence turned and caught sight of Howard blowing the Rubik's Cube, brushing away ash.

"Who cares?" muttered Zelia.

Howard looked up. "I never thought I'd hear you say that."

Zelia grabbed the cube and tossed it high into the air, straight for the line of packer robots standing to attention.

They lunged forward with no idea how to catch.

Prudence, with a perfect dive, seized it. Heat seared her palms; she juggled, blowing furiously, as the packer robots jostled each other to help.

The cube flew from hand to hand—until she saw a glow shining through in a crack of the cube. She dropped it.

The cube landed on its corner, balancing like a ballerina.

The packer robots backed away.

Prudence stared . . .

The Rubik's Cube pulsated with a florescent glow.

A glow that had nothing to do with landing in the bonfire.

The cook pulled out more books, including her *How to Live with a Portal* book, several recipe books, and a *Gardner's Guide*. With a pointed look at Verruca, she opened the *Gardner's Guide* to the "The Elusive Tomato" chapter and thrust it at Verruca.

Verruca flicked through the pages, completely fed up. All she was trying to do was elevate the tomato.

"It's the acid," said the cook. "Highly unstable."

"I thought I'd accounted for that." She stopped at a chapter on soil fertilization and blushed.

"Too much of a good thing," said the Alterationist. "You were too kind, fertilized the soil to the point of crumbly."

"I did say," said Cyborg.

"Porous to the point of sievelike," said the cook.

"I thought I was crossing new boundaries, creating something new and great." Verruca said glumly. The whole world, it seemed, was against her.

"A soil too crumbly is as bad as a soil too dense, especially over a quarry," said the Alterationist.

"Got our work cut out here," said the cook.

"For the last time, I had no idea about the quarry!" snapped Verruca.

KUNDALINI YOGA

"A ponytail on a man is nothing without a beard."—Archie

Beryl was doing a spot of Kundalini yoga—or "yogurt," as she pronounced it—when all hell broke loose around the camper van.

She had taken up yoga to find the sort of Zen feeling that Pete had cryptically talked about before he ended up back on Planet Hy Man. Her emotions were all over the place, swinging like a monkey on a tree, and isolating with people you wouldn't sit next to on a bus didn't help; neither did her friggin' shoulder stand.

Her stomach slumped to her chest; she adjusted with a grunt, trying to ignore the commotion outside.

"The girls," as Legless liked to call his hens, were screeching about the camper van like they were dancing on hot coals, while Charlton Heston was crowing like someone had cut his balls off.

She stretched her feet higher, pushing her beehive askew, and inhaled . . .

Once the whole saga of that "Aussie tart" and her mother came out, Beryl's jealousy raged like a toddler with a newborn brother.

She felt she had lost Legless, and in front of the worst person possible—Hilda, a woman who had taken her "everything."

Legless did his best, but Beryl was as reasonable as a stroppy teenager and believed nothing he said . . .

"Earth's atmosphere finally has your innards," he yelled, "stirring up erratic emotions that defy logic."

She looked at him.

"It's a female thing," he said.

"What are you talking about?"

"Hormones, or rather the lack of them."

Beryl wanted to punch him. Then he said it—the very thing that would curdle any woman's juices.

"It happens to all women of a certain age . . ."

Beryl nearly spat out her coffee.

"HRT is the answer," he said, "and I'd lay off the coffee."

She stopped mid breath of fire. *Coffee has nothing to do with it.*

Bark Twain was barking himself hoarse, and Gina had sparked a fight with Lollo.

"Can't you hear?" shouted Hilda at the top of her lungs.

Beryl's legs flopped over her head in a "thank goodness that's over" inversion.

What the hell is going on?

Archie was in the shed, joining a Zoom meeting with Don and Bunnie at the time.

They were not exactly enthusiastic about his plans, as Beryl irritated the hell out of Bunnie. In fact, they argued about it constantly; Don claiming it was their duty to help.

Bunnie was yet to be convinced that raiding a care home during lockdown was really "the answer" despite Don insisting it was their only course of action.

"Men always say that when they're done thinking," said Bunnie.

"Can you think of something better?" he said, and when she couldn't, he signed in to his Zoom meeting.

"How's Beryl?" said Bunnie.

Archie pulled a face.

"It's a lot for her to take in," said DJ.

"Yes, but we mustn't let her hamper things," said Archie.

"Such an illustrious plan," sighed Bunnie.

"We haven't explained it to her yet. But I suppose if needs must . . ." He turned to DJ. "You could always do your worst."

"What's that supposed to mean?"

"Nothing," he said. "Just, well . . ."

"He means for you to try your charms on Beryl, woo her," said Bunnie.

"Woo her for what? A seat here in the shed? It's not like there are any meetings just now."

"You're all we've got," said Don. He eyed Archie. "She's hardly going to go for him."

"Cheers," muttered Archie.

"Why don't you grow a beard with that thing?" Don gestured to Archie's ponytail.

"Beryl hates beards," said Archie.

"So do I," said Bunnie.

"Maybe I'll grow one," said Don.

Bunnie rolled her eyes. "What she like, this daughter?"

"Interesting," huffed Archie.

"Bit mannish," grumbled DJ.

"Maybe I could give her a few tips," said Bunnie.

Archie looked at the plump, powdered face and said nothing.

Legless charged in, took one look at his woman doubled over like a folded mattress, and stopped.

"Since when did you start doing that?" he said.

She sat up, a smart answer on the tip of her tongue, when Mandy hollered, "There is no use shouting."

"You'd better come," said Legless.

Beryl rolled onto her side with a glare.

"Seriously, we need you."

Beryl looked at him. "Oh, *now* you want the old fuddy-duddy."

"I never called you that."

"You thought it."

He grabbed her hand, tugging her outside. "How do you know what I think?"

"I just do."

They raced into the garden, skidding past Bark Twain circling "the girls" in a manic fashion, past Charlton Heston majestically strutting, spoiling for a fight, until Bark Twain made a dive for him.

Legless crashed into the camper van.

Mandy and Hilda jumped.

Beryl appeared, catching sight of the miniature TV screen . . .

She gasped.

On the screen, lit up by the flashing neon Closed sign from the hotel across the road, was "the couch."

It took several flashes for Beryl to make out that someone was on it.

"We connected to the security camera," said Mandy with a look at Legless.

He smiled and nodded.

"Isn't that illegal?" said Beryl.

"Look," said Hilda.

Beryl strained her eyes to see a woman in a fetal position, looking as confused as a drunk trying to negotiate a TV remote—she was definitely from Planet Hy Man.

Beryl watched as she blinked, attempted a stretch, tried to get up —the couch sucked her in tighter.

"That's the third time she's tried," muttered Mandy.

"Bugger of a couch," said Hilda.

"Looks like a digger," said Beryl.

Mandy looked at her.

"Archaeologist," said Hilda.

"You have Archaeologists?" said Mandy.

Beryl nodded. "Carter."

"Called *Carter*?" said Mandy. "And what's the other one called, Howard?"

Hilda looked at her. "Well, yes."

Carter wriggled like a cat in a toddler's arms, then, with a glazed look, gave up with a flop.

Portal traveling, it seemed, had her as zonked as a ton of spliffs on an empty stomach.

Archie barged in, followed by DJ.

"What the hell is going on with those hens?"

"Girls," corrected Legless.

"We were in the middle of a Zoom meeting, sorting your shit . . ." He stopped. "What's that doing on TV?

"We connected to the security camera," said Mandy.

"Isn't that illegal?" said Archie.

"Why didn't we think of that?" muttered DJ.

Archie threw him a look.

Gina appeared at the window with a squawk.

Sophia, curled up on the camper van window, lifted her head with a "what now?"

"If you're gonna raid something, at least do it properly," said Hilda, expertly opening the window to knock Gina off the sill.

"We are working on a plan," said Archie.

"Lockdown will be over by the time you have a plan," said Hilda.

"Wish we'd thought of it," muttered DJ.

Archie threw him a glare.

"Are you still there?" came Bunnie's voice from the shed.

Chapter Forty-Two

THE FIGHT

The "Sorting out who's in charge is as easy as sorting out the seating plan of a wedding."–Archie

Portal tapping, as Hilda called it, had an adverse effect on Legless's animals. Apart that is, for Sophia, a tough-as-old-boots cat that had the ability to make even the prickliest of settings look as comfortable as a fluffy pillow. She could find a beam of sunshine in any dark corner and scare off even the toughest of dogs with a look. She was impervious to most things and, when in need of attention, did not give up until she got it.

Legless's "girls," however, had picked up the vibes of something unearthly, and they remained disturbed for as long as Carter was onscreen, or rather the portal. They were as unsettled as an expectant father in a waiting room. Unable to sit still, they cackled and jibed each other, which no amount of rounding up by Bark Twain could sort.

Hilda stroked Sophia, mesmerized by her ability to sleep through it all.

"All systems go then," said Archie. "We could have the home raided and that thing dismembered in jig time."

"Aren't we jumping the gun here? We don't even know what the portal looks like," said Legless.

"And it's the only means of getting back," said Hilda.

"There are other means," said Beryl.

"Then why are you still here?" said Mandy.

Beryl huffed.

"Beryl's here 'cause she's needed," said DJ. "Could even be that couch."

"A couch—a portal? As if," said Mandy.

"We'll know when we get there," said Archie. "We Identities have a few senses up our sleeves."

Mandy rolled her eyes.

Gina appeared yet again at the window, followed by Bardo, which sparked a frenzy of pecking and squawking. Feathers flew like a burst pillow.

Archie turned to Legless. "Can you not sort these friggin' hens out?"

"My girls," said Legless, "are merely barometers."

Hilda, with a sigh, opened the window and shooed them away. "Not being funny, but you men aren't all you're cracked up to be."

Charlton Heston, reclaiming his strut on an out-of-reach beam, flapped his wings . . .

"Cock-a-doodle-doo!"

"Try doing that without balls," said DJ with a look at Hilda.

"Merely sacks of hormones," said Hilda.

The men squirmed; even Mandy looked uncomfortable.

"We've done away with all that on Planet Hy Man—very liberating."

"I'm quite fond of my hormones," said DJ. "They haven't let me down yet."

"There's hormones and then there's hormones." Beryl looked at Legless.

"I merely *mentioned* HRT," muttered Legless.

"You've gone on about it like a dripping tap."

"Maybe if you listened," said Mandy.

Beryl flushed, her emotions rolling around like a boat in a hurricane. The past few days had taken their toll on her; she felt old, past it, and as powerless as Gina's ability to lay a friggin' egg.

She looked from Legless to the youthful Mandy standing oh-so-close.

"That's right, you two stick together."

"Easy, Beryl," said DJ.

"Toss me aside like an unwanted banana skin."

"I wouldn't call you that," said Mandy.

"And what would you call me?"

Mandy, still smarting from her mother's so-called visit, was in no mood for Beryl's dramatics. "As cold as ice."

Hilda blew threw her teeth.

"Needs must," said Beryl with a glower.

The two women eyeballed each other . . .

"Cock-a-doodle-doo!" screeched Charlton Heston.

"I thought you'd be nicer," said Mandy.

"Leaders aren't meant to be nice," said DJ.

"You should have seen her when she was younger," said Hilda. "Do anything to get what she wanted."

Beryl turned on Hilda. "So did you."

"That's what Legless said," said Mandy.

"He would," said Beryl.

"Was kinda hoping he was wrong."

"Yes, well, he wasn't."

"Come on, guys, we've a world to save," said Archie. "A portal to find, rejects to return."

"I wouldn't call our top Archaeologist a reject," said Beryl.

"We need to work together," said Archie.

"Pfff—with *her*."

"It's a tough mission," said Archie. "We need everyone."

"With super-duper Mandy here, I may as well take up knitting."

"Cock-a-doodle-doo . . ."

"You said it," said Mandy.

"Are you saying you don't need me?" said Beryl.

Mandy shrugged. "Your drama is a bit tiring, not to mention unnecessary."

"I'm sure she didn't mean it," said DJ.

Hilda felt an urge to soothe her archenemy. "Perhaps she just means at your age, you could take a back seat . . ."

"A more advisory position," said DJ.

"Why don't you just shove me into a wheelchair with a packet of incontinence pads?" snapped Beryl.

"No one's saying you're incontinent," said Legless.

"Wheel me into that god-awful care home?"

"Let's just leave care homes out of it," said Archie.

"You *are* going to raid one," said Beryl.

"Perhaps you could go undercover then," said Mandy.

No one said anything.

"That's right, rub it in," shouted Beryl, "make fun of the old girl. Well, at least I don't need hormones for my bits and pieces."

"I think you'll find you do," said Mandy.

Beryl glowered at Mandy. Then, with a pointed push, she stormed out of the camper van with a slam that not only shook the van but the miniature TV screen, pulling it from its plug.

Archie grabbed it.

"You can shove it up your arses!" yelled Beryl, silencing "the girls." Even Sophia looked up.

"Are you still there?" shouted Bunnie.

Chapter Forty-Three

THE COLLAR

"To wear a collar is not the same as to collar someone."–Bunnie

Bunnie stared at the empty screen in disgust. She was just about to turn it off when she heard Izzie trot up the stairs.

Izzie jumped on Bunnie's knee. Bunnie ran her hands over Izzie's head, then stopped. "Don," she yelled.

Don didn't answer.

"Where the hell is her collar?"

He appeared at the door, a mug in each hand. "She has a collar?"

"Of course she has a collar. All dogs have one."

He shrugged.

She ruffled Izzie's neck. "That collar has been with Izzie since I got her. It's an heirloom."

"It's just a collar."

"Been everywhere with her," said Bunnie, "even to space and back."

Don slid the mugs next to the laptop. He'd forgotten about Izzie's trip with Mex.

"He was up and back in jig time, according to Eunice," said Bunnie.

"I remember now."

"Swallowed a component," said Bunnie.

"Yes, it's all coming back to me."

She looked down at Izzie's white puffball face. "If only she could talk."

Don said nothing. Izzie was a mystery to him. The only thing he knew about Izzie was how much his mother loved her visits. She'd even sent him back once to collect her when he arrived without her. "A visit is not a visit without Izzie," she said.

Sometimes Don wondered if she loved the dog more than him.

The others in the care home loved her too, even the carers. As soon as he appeared, the residents were out in force, squabbling over a pat. The last time he'd taken Izzie, she was there for ages and was so patted out she hid in that god-awful corduroy couch . . . which apparently swallowed people up "like an alligator."

"Loved that collar," muttered Bunnie. "Guess I'll need to get a new one."

Don looked down at Izzie. She blinked.

"If only she could talk," he muttered.

Chapter Forty-Four

THE SECOND COMING

"Never ride a portal with your eyes closed."–Carter

Archie stared at the TV screen, which was now blank.

He plugged it in, waited for it to fire up, and turned to the others. "Maybe one of you should go after her."

"Well, I'm not," snapped Mandy.

They looked at Hilda.

"Me? I'm the last person she wants to see."

"But you're from the same planet."

"Yes, but everything I say comes out all wrong. I'm not equipped for all this *nice* malarky."

"I'll do it," said DJ, and with a slam of a door, he headed out, rattling the TV from its perch yet again.

Mandy made to grab and missed.

Carter, lying on her back, her stomach still churning, attempted to look up with a belch.

She stopped with a grimace.

Her hair was trapped in the crevice of the couch.

She chanced a wriggle, a gentle tug, and stopped.

She heard a cough, shuffled footsteps.

She peered into the evening shadows and caught a wave of some sort of metal frame around the doorway, followed by . . . a leg . . . a silhouette.

Carter strained her eyes. *A woman?*

"Oh, another," muttered Serenity.

Another? thought Carter. She blinked, then belched. Then it all went dark.

A few hours later, Carter woke to a sea of blurry faces, her hair free, a cup of something bitter at her lips, and a faint whiff of disinfectant and pee.

Not that she knew what the smell was. She had no idea about incontinence, just as she had no idea where she was.

She had her long-distance vision, and she could make out a closed door, a TV, and women bent and doddery, but everything up close was like peering through a frosted windscreen.

The voices were old and crackly, one deep with a cough, the second in a weird accent (Glaswegian), and another in a high voice, who seemed to make as much sense as a robot on its last legs. At least her hair was free.

She felt a tug—someone brushing.

"Ouch," she spluttered, spraying tea.

"Told you, can't give tea to the comatose," chirped the high voice.

"It's to wake her up," said the Glaswegian.

"It will choke her," said the high voice.

"She's not comatose, she's awake. Aren't you, luv?"

Carter looked at the blurred faces, as disoriented as a teased and tossed-about kitten. "Ouch! My hair."

"Gimme that brush," snapped the deep voice.

"Just freeing a few knots. She's so pretty," said the high voice.

"She needs a drink. Coming from outer space is thirsty work," said the Glaswegian voice.

"You and your outer space," said the deep voice.

Carter felt the hot mug at her lips again. She gagged; the liquid was bitter, tart, unlike anything she'd tasted.

"Need sugar, luv?" said the Glaswegian voice.

"Sugar's bad for you," squeaked the high voice. "Gives you diabetes. Look at Molly, ankles of an elephants."

"That's my circulation, *and* it's hereditary," said the deep voice.

"Give it here," said the Glaswegian voice.

Carter heard the cluttering of mug stirring, then felt the hot, sweet liquid on her lips. She gulped.

Her stomach settled.

"Arrrh . . ."

Her eyes focused on the papery skin of the three faces.

The three faces stared back at her.

"More?" said the Glaswegian voice.

"How about a biscuit?" said the squeaky voice.

"She doesn't need a biscuit," said the deep voice.

"Some chocolate?"

"Just give her a minute," said the Glaswegian voice.

"I've some tablet."

"A minute ago you were talking about diabetes."

"Here," said the squeaky voice. A biscuit was pushed between Carter's dry lips.

She coughed, spluttered, then stopped as a sweet coconut taste exploded in her mouth.

"Hmmm."

"It's a Nigella recipe."

"Don't be ridiculous. You can't bake—certainly not a Nigella Lawson recipe. Half of them don't even work. I mean just because a good-looking woman parades herself on TV with a spatula and underwire . . ."

"There's more," said the squeaky voice.

"Don't give her anymore." The deep voice coughed.

The taste lingered on Carter's lips. "Oh, yes please."

A few hours later, Carter was sitting on the very same chair Hilda had been on a few days ago, staring at the same car park, wondering if the high voice who had finally gotten the knots out of her hair had any more biscuits.

She had a little face and a big smile and she brushed hair like she was pulling teeth. Getting her to stop was like trying to halt a flying platform, but Carter, a true scientist, knew when not to say too much.

She nodded in what she thought were the right places, quickly assessing that the little face was called Dolly, who, to quote the other two, was not only "doolaly" but as "nutty as a fruit cake."

The one with a funny accent was called Serenity, and the one with the deep voice who had a grudge against Nigella Lawson (whoever that was) was called Molly.

Molly, a large woman with a sort of breathlessness that required a lot of leaning on her metal frame, had a son called Don whom everyone seemed to like. Apart, that is, for Molly.

Not that Carter knew much about sons. She knew as much about sons as she did Zimmer frames.

Watching Serenity walk with it inches from the ground had Carter wondering if it was an antenna for signals or an implement to hang socks on, perhaps even a weapon, until she saw Molly use it properly . . .

After several more biscuits, Carter had come to, quickly making deductions and assumptions.

She realized "doolally" was code for "irrational," along with a host of other words—"barmy," "daft," "dippy," "bonkers," and "fruit loop"—all of which the two other women used every time Dolly left for another biscuit.

She fed her constantly, moving from biscuits to tablet.

Carter couldn't get enough. Condensed milk was as foreign to her as a blow job and just as exhilarating. In fact, if she knew what an orgasm was, that would be how she would describe the delicious sensations in her mouth.

Every nerve tingled with delight, each bite an explosion to the senses, and when she sucked . . . her mouth became a pleasure dome.

She couldn't speak, only moan.

Carter's portal trip had been way rougher than Hilda's. In fact, Hilda's journey was a stroll in the park compared to Carter's roller-coaster ride.

The portal, fired up by the rummaging of the women, was as feisty as a caged lion. It ripped through the dimensions of the solar system like a tsunami, taking no prisoners.

Carter had arrived with her lunch in her throat, her hair like a kookaburra's, and her head spinning like a whirligig. Coupled with a packet of coconut biscuits and a ton of tablet, Carter was as high as the Legless statue, jabbering on about not only it but also flying platforms and nutty diggers in a sort of hysteria that had the three women in a panic.

"You've given her too much," snapped Serenity.

Carter eyed the woman's bun of grey hair and started to giggle.

Dolly stared at her. She was as gaga as a pregnant woman on gas, and Dolly, an ex-midwife, knew the signs. "She needs some toast."

"Don't be ridiculous," said Molly.

Carter hiccuped. *Perhaps Howard is "doolaly"?*

Dolly beamed. "I've a toaster."

The other two rolled their eyes.

Toaster? "Is that a robot?" slurred Carter.

"The last toaster you had set off the fire alarm," said Serenity.

"More like a sniffer," laughed Carter.

The women looked at her. "Sniffer?"

"A toothbrush then?" She giggled, then crashed into a deep snore.

As Dolly left for the elusive toaster, Molly turned to Serenity. "She's one of *that* lot, isn't she?"

Serenity nodded.

"I'd better get Don then."

"Tell him to bring the dog," yelled Dolly from the hall.

Chapter Forty-Five

BERYL AND BUNNIE

"They were so old that running their fingers through their hair was a forgotten memory."—Bunnie

Beryl stomped and stormed in the garden.

"Is anyone there?" shouted Bunnie.

Beryl stopped and looked at the shed.

"I said . . . is anyone there?" Bunnie huffed. "I've friggin' had enough of this . . . Don!" she yelled. "*Don!*"

"Just a second," yelled Don. "Mum's on the phone."

Beryl walked into the mess of a shed, a moan on the tip of her tongue. She caught sight of Izzie perched on Bunnie's lap and softened.

Bunnie eyed Beryl's glum face.

"What's eating you?" she said. "You've a face like a smacked arse."

"Mum," Don shouted off-screen. "I can't visit just now. Lockdown, remember?" He appeared on the screen, ear to the phone. "Apparently there's an Alien," he said to Bunnie. Then, catching sight of Beryl, he disappeared again. "Mum, what's the good of me peering in the window . . ."

Beryl slumped at the laptop.

Bunnie recognized that slump. It was a "no one notices me" slump, and it reminded her of the days when, well, she'd stopped getting noticed. When she passed a window and saw not her mum's face but her grandmother's . . .

Poor cow, thought Bunnie. *There is nothing more humiliating than thinking a whistle is for you when it's for the woman half your age behind you.*

She mustered herself for a pick-me-up lecture. Straightening her enormous bust she threw Beryl her "been there, done that, and got the T-shirt" smile, which at best was pretty patronizing.

"There's a point when, well, a woman has to use her noodle rather than her cleavage."

Beryl looked at her. "I've always used my 'noodle,' as you put it, and cleavages don't exist on my planet."

"Yes, but as you said, you don't have men below the age of dribbling there."

"I never said that."

"I think you did, after a rather perky bottle of red."

"I was being funny."

"You were serious. 'Even Legless is a spring chicken there,' you said."

"Pfff—*him*. He has no time for me these days."

"'They are so old they can't remember how to spell *shag*, let alone do it,' you said."

Beryl sulked.

"Less of the *old*," shouted Don.

"So old that sex is just *six* misspelled."

"I never said that," said Beryl.

"I can still spell *sex*," yelled Don. "And there is still a bit of pepper in the shaker."

"Yes, but you can't shake it, can you," Bunnie yelled back.

Beryl almost smiled.

Bunnie almost smiled back.

DJ appeared, his lips set tight. Watching the sparring of two women was not something to interrupt.

"The men on Planet Hy Man are so old," said Bunnie, "that when they were born, *shag* was the name of a bird, queens wore crowns, and fairies had wands." She waited for a smile.

"Even you didn't say that," said Beryl.

"Look, Mum," said Don. He stopped. "All right . . ." He listened. "I'll try and come later . . ." Silence. "This afternoon then?"

Bunnie rolled her eyes.

"Meant to say there is a digger on the couch," said Beryl.

"What?"

"Another from Planet Hy Man," said DJ.

"An Archaeologist," said Beryl.

"I'll kill the Identity who took that Serenity to the meetings," shouted Don. "She does nothing but fire Mum up with all sorts of bullshit."

Izzie jumped off Bunnie's knee and ran to Don.

"Your mother does plenty of her own firing," yelled Bunnie, "on all four cylinders."

Don rolled his eyes. Running a bed and breakfast with Bunnie was not all beer and skittles.

"Just because she was rude about your decor," yelled Don.

"Rude? She said it was too good for a skip."

"That's her sense of humor."

"Too good for a bonfire."

"I think you'll find that was her friend Serenity."

"It is a bit dated," muttered Beryl.

Bunnie glared at her. "Here's me trying to help you."

"A pep talk about cleavages isn't really helping," said Beryl. "More know-it-all, boarding on insult."

"Well, that's your department," said Bunnie.

"Legless is in touch with Mandy's mother," burst in Beryl.

"Her? I heard she was a real ball-breaker." DJ looked at Beryl. "Practically castrated the poor fella. Legless couldn't get away quick enough, and now she wants alimony."

Don shivered. "Poor bastard." He turned to Bunnie "Mum says, 'There's trouble at the mill.'"

"She's always saying that."

"There is another Alien."

"Howard," said Beryl with a "who cares?" look. "The digger. The Archaeologist."

"What's eating her?" Don said to Bunnie.

"I told you, Legless was Skyping Karen."

"FaceTiming," said Beryl.

Bunnie looked at her. "She's a bit upset."

"Or was it Carter?" Beryl mumbled to herself.

"Howard Carter? An Archaeologist?" Don looked at Bunnie. "Is she trying to be funny?"

Verruca, tired, disillusioned, and feeling a bit of a failure, left the tent. Spying the two Archaeologists by the fire, she joined them.

The Rubik's Cube, now pulsating a glow like a lighthouse, was sitting on a log all by itself, everyone too afraid to touch it.

Prudence, still blowing on her hands, turned to Verruca. "Just as well I'm made of Teflon." She forced a smile.

"What?" said Verruca.

"My hands." She shook them. "That thing is as hot as lava."

Verruca looked at her. "Lava?"

"Yes, like on Earth."

"There's nothing that hot on this planet," said Zelia. "Well, apart from a kettle . . ."

"There is now," said Prudence.

The three women looked at the Rubik's Cube, which was now pulsating different colors like a disco light.

"Best ignore it," said Prudence.

"You can't ignore it," said Verruca.

"Yes, you can. Like the birds." She waved at the trees.

"You can't ignore them either," said Howard.

"They'll go away—eventually," said Prudence with a hum.

The three women looked at each other, then at Prudence now finger-drawing a bird on the tent wall.

"She had it in her hands for quite some time," said Zelia.

Alice was inside the tent.

Replaying all to H2 and DBO, they could hear the conversation outside, see the intense light, pulsating stronger by the minute, through the tent wall.

"Alice, see what's happening outside."

Alice flew through the flap, and with her wide-angle lens, she filmed a garden lit up like a rave party, the three women shielding their eyes from the glare, and Prudence now skipping in and out of the line of packer robots.

"What's that?" said Alice gesturing to the Rubik's Cube.

"A mere toy," giggled Prudence.

"Nothing is ever a mere toy," muttered H2. "Toss a sack or a blanket over it," she ordered.

Howard looked at Zelia. "You do it."

"No, you."

"We need to do more than that," said Verruca. "We need to move it, hide it, get rid of it—destroy it."

"But where? How? We can't touch it. We'll end up like her."

They stared at Prudence wrapping a daisy chain around a packer robot.

"This is a job for Cyborg," muttered Verruca.

Chapter Forty-Six

DIGGING UNDERNEATH

"You'll be laughing on the other side of your face."–Every parent that ever existed

A bit of glowing never put a hippie off. They knew a thing or two about effluents, and what they couldn't recycle was nobody's business.

They loved to get their hands dirty, and as the glow of the Rubik's Cube glared through the tent wall, they, unlike the other women, had a good idea what to do next.

"We need to lift the statue," said the cook.

No one said anything.

"Dig underneath."

"I'm not digging under the likes of that," said the lead sportswoman.

The others nodded.

"You can shove that up your arse."

"Unearth . . ." said the cook.

"Unearth? All that glowing stuff? Why not hang a noose around our necks?"

"We need to collect, analyze, and test," said the cook.

"And film," said the Alterationist.

"Redirect . . ." said the cook.

"Or upcycle," said the Alterationist.

"You can't upcycle all this shit," said the militant one with a dismissive gesture. She stopped; her fingers felt hot.

"Prudence is excellent at recycling." The cook turned to the Alterationist. "Isn't she?"

The Alterationist's face reddened. "I think you'll find that is me."

"What do we need?" the cook shouted to Prudence.

"Prudence is more an acting-on-orders sort of robot . . ." She stopped as Prudence appeared through the tent flap with a vampish sway.

Prudence was feeling hot, flushed, and a little sexy, although being a robot, she had no idea that was what she felt.

"How about we start with the Helmet?" said Pete.

A few groaned.

"Or a sweeper . . ."

Prudence winked at him.

". . . with a camera attached?"

"Filming—like the idea of that," swooned Prudence.

The militant one looked around at the other lab assistants, catching sight of the studious lab assistant flicking through the cook's book.

Was that a glow on her fingertips?

"It says here," said the studious lab assistant, "when in the midst of glowing, neutralizing is required . . ."

"What's that mean?" said a voice from the back.

". . . of the acid," she read.

"Acid," automated Cyborg, "promotes chemical reactions."

"Bit late for that," cackled Prudence. "That toy out there is so high on acid it's tripping."

"Tripping," automated Cyborg. "Perhaps over, sometimes under . . . more than a skid."

"We are talking more than acid," said the militant one, blowing on her fingers.

"No we're not," said the cook.

"I think you'll find we are. That stuff is radiation personified."

"Hardly radiation. Just because it's glowing doesn't mean it's—"

The lead sportswoman stopped. Her gloves were glowing like a takeaway neon light.

She pulled them off in a panic.

The lab assistants looked at their hands, which were now glowing like the robot appendages.

They gasped.

"Get your makeup on, luvs," shouted Prudence.

"What's happening?" shouted one.

"Great pickling testicles," yelled another who had spent time in the fertilizing shed.

The studious lad assistant giggled; her best buddy followed.

"My hands!" shouted the shot-putter. Then she burst out laughing.

The Alterationist ordered them to remove their gloves.

Gloves flew into the air with a "hip, hip, hooray!"

"And bag 'em," shouted the cook.

Sending the assistants into a volley of laughter.

Prudence looked at her hands red and raw. "I guess Teflon is not so heatproof after all. Oh, well—who wants a massage?"

She chuckled, circled, then stopped in a dizzy-like fashion.

"I feel sick . . ." She staggered. "All hot and fluffy."

"Try a fan," yelled the cook. "Always works for me."

"Just put her by the bins for the collection," laughed the voice from the back.

Prudence crumbled to the floor.

"Up we come," muttered Pete.

"Don't touch her," shouted the Alterationist.

Verruca and the two Archaeologists, still outside, listened to the commotion in the tent. None wanted to go in. Having tossed every hemp sack they could lay their hands on over the Rubik's Cube, they now watched as the glow deepened, making the hemp sacks as transparent as silk.

They had no idea what to do.

"What's that noise," said H2 to Alice, "inside the tent?"

Alice sighed. "Where do you want me now?"

H2 was about to issue an order, tell her to "go inside," when she caught sight of something that had even the hair on her armpits standing at attention.

"Is that the Rubik's Cube?"

Alice spun around to see, levitating over the bonfire, the mound of hemp sacks. The three women were routed to the spot—speechless.

"Shit," muttered Vegas.

Alice flew into the tent. "Danger, danger."

Prudence belched. "Who's for a back rub?"

"Me first," said the militant one.

"No, me," said the studious lab assistant.

Her best buddy roared with laughter.

The cook glared.

The Alterationist nudged her to look at the tent flap.

"What so funny?" said Woody.

"That," said the best buddy, pointing to the hemp sacks floating through the tent flap like a horror film ghost.

The packer robots jumped to alert. The sweeper robots circled like dogs chasing their tails.

"Danger, danger," automated Cyborg. "Isolate, isolate . . ."

The sweeper robots circled. "Acid reflux, acid reflux."

"Acid . . ." automated Cyborg. He stopped. *Is that steam from the mound of hemp sacks?*

The three statue workers were in Verruca's makeshift kitchen, having spent several hours on the search for biscuits.

Dozy had finally rustled some up in an oven as old as the quarry and, feeling pleased with herself, was just pulling out a tray when she heard screeches from the tent.

She slid the tray onto the bench. "What was that?"

"Nothing a bit of tea won't sort," said the third statue worker. She stopped. "See, they're laughing now."

"Maniac laughing," muttered the ambitious statue worker. Having just watched the rising of the Rubik's Cube, she had her doubts about tea and biscuits sorting things.

She stared into the dark as the Rubik's Cube entered the tent, its silhouette pulsating a glow like a cartoon pimple.

What we need is water, she thought. She turned to see the two setting up a beverage tray. "How about a jug of water to go with that?"

"You'll be laughing on the other side of your face," boomed the cook.

"Make that two."

The statue workers, clutching trays, entered the tent to mayhem.

Lab assistants were screaming, then laughing, while Alice circled uselessly like a mother dog trying to herd her puppies.

The mound of hemp sacks was steaming like a barbecued chicken. Woody was talking of a "fire extinguisher," which confused the hippies, while Pete was trying to keep Prudence from touching it without touching her.

The ambitious statue worker grabbed the jugs and took aim . . .

The Rubik's Cube dodged. Prudence didn't.

She sizzled with an "arrrgh, that's better."

Dozy ran outside and whistled to the parked flying platform. "Here, boy!"

It jumped to attention and scooted to her side, and she did what she always dreamed of: jumped on.

The platform obeyed her every whistled command, circling into the tent, diving behind desks, sneaking around, and pursuing the mound of hemp sack.

Inches from its back, Dozy threw herself off.

The flying platform scooped, contained the Rubik's Cube, and—before the cube had a chance to balance—zoomed like a kamikaze pilot straight for the statue's thigh.

Piff, puff, poof!

Sending the infected women into a frenzy of cheering.

Without even thinking, H2 messaged Beryl: "Another is coming your way, and it's as contagious as a coronavirus sneeze."

The women raced outside and stared at the smoke settling around the arse of Legless's statue.

"We need to contain," yelled the Alterationist with authority.

The infected women laughed.

"Take them to the kitchen." She caught sight of a smirk. "And lock that pickling door."

"I'll do it," said the third statue worker. "Could do with a good laugh." She moved to shove.

"Without touching," boomed the Alterationist. "You have no idea what that stuff does to your brain."

The flying platform appeared upright like a mini monolithic standing stone from the cushions of the couch.

Pulsating at its tip was the Rubik's Cube under the hemp sack.

The Rubik's Cube made several "floating free" attempts, but as the hemp sack was tucked into the couch, the Rubik's Cube eventually flopped into "give up" mode.

Serenity was carrying a milky tea for Carter, who was on her bed taking a power nap. She was restless, aroused, her joint pains as forgotten as her last orgasm. She was on the cusp of a big adventure, possibly saving the world, and she could hardly breathe for excitement.

She passed the TV room, catching sight of a glow on the couch. She stopped. *Is that a fairy light? Or from above?*

Chapter Forty-Seven

THE ESCAPE

"The life of a Rubik's Cube champion could be written on a matchbox."–Serenity

Deidre stared at the door. It was tantalizing ajar.

The cupboard was more than a cupboard; it was a small room lined with shelves of upturned trolleys, oiling implements, and the occasional mechanical mop or broom thrown in by a cleaner who couldn't be arsed to walk down the end of the corridor to the cleaner cupboard to put it away.

Situated on the same floor as the room with a view, it had been easy for the leadership team to shoggle her there, and Deidre figured it would be just as easy for her to shoggle back.

All she needed was something to win over those so-called leaders.

She could hear panic in the corridors, footmen shuffling . . . H2 demanding extra caffeine.

With no idea about the Rubik's Cube, Deidre had quickly come up with a plan that could wangle her a place in the room with a view.

She smiled to herself. Let someone else take over the reporting; she had an inside look into Earth and planned to use it.

She, with her pencil in her mouth, attempted a tied-to-the-chair jump . . .

She moved . . . sparking a clattering of brooms and mop buckets.

She stopped.

A footman shuffled past.

She waited . . .

Silence.

She jumped again.

Pushed the door open with her head.

She heard a rush of feet.

She let it shut.

Silence.

She pushed the door open, shoggled into the passageway. *Just a few more jumps,* she thought, *and I'll be there in the pickling room with a view.*

Using sticks, Pete, the third statue worker, and Verruca shepherded the infected women into Verruca's kitchen to cackle themselves stupid.

The crows settled on the trees, watching like they were expecting the worst, occasionally circling like they'd like to join in the herding.

It wasn't easy. In fact, it took several hours.

The infected women staggered and laughed like drunks, taking it in turns to steady Prudence, then scattering at a whim.

It was like rounding up a set of playful pandas, chickens, cats even.

Prudence, cornering Pete to explain how sorry she was, was eventually lassoed by Verruca, which sent the others into hysterics.

"Ride 'em, cowboy!" shouted the militant one, who had a thing for ancient Earth Westerns.

Verruca locked the door and walked away, her confidence restored, until she realized the window was still open and the shot-putter, with one leg out, was trying to escape.

"Abandon ship," she shouted.

Verruca reached for her lasso. She flicked it through the window above the shot-putter's head and straight for the fan switch. It was an impressive move that silenced the women for several minutes.

The fan revved into action and, like all annoying desk fans, swiveled from left to right.

"Arrrrgh," sighed the lead sportswoman.

The shot-putter jumped in front, soon moaning in a pornographic fashion.

"Oooh . . ."

"Arrrrh . . ."

"Yes, yes, yes!"

"Who's for a back rub?" said Prudence, rallying around with a stagger.

No one answered. They were too busy pushing and shoving for a bit of cool wind.

After much discussion, a camera was attached to a sweeper robot rather than the Helmet, most agreeing that watching the Helmet ride through a portal would be way too boring.

With a quick test to check connections to the hippie's H-Pad and the room with a view, the sweeper robot was ushered to the tiny space underneath the statue's armpit. He skidded and circled, backing off several times, until finally, with a "get on with it" shove, the sweeper robot attempted an entry. He stopped with a squeal of breaks as the space closed in under the crumbly soil.

"I'll get my toothbrush," yelled Howard.

Cyborg pulled her back. "This is robot's work," he said, quickly putting together a set of levers with sticks and ropes to maneuver the statue up from the soil.

"It's up to us, lads," he yelled at the packer robots, motioning for them to follow.

The packer robots, with no idea what he meant, lined up to obey.

"Let's put the kettle on," said Prudence.

The infected women looked at her like she was an idiot. *Kettle, in this heat?*

Apart from the lead sportswoman, who burst into her favorite Wham! song—a song inspired by Pete's first arrival on Earth, found on

YouTube by Woody and replayed many times on their H-Pads. It was the only song she knew the words to.

"*Jitter bug . . .*"

She moved to the window.

"*Wake me up . . .*" she yelled, then stopped, catching sight of the robots preparing for lifting maneuvers. "Don't start without a warm-up," she shouted.

The packer robots stopped.

The cook cursed the "idiots in the kitchen" with a glare.

"You need to do at least ten stretches."

The packer robots looked at each other.

"Don't forget the jumping jacks," said one.

"And some squats," yelled another.

The cook finally snapped. With a string of curses a mile long, she barked at the robots like a sergeant major.

The robots stalled.

Verruca, thinking with her stomach, grabbed the cook's bag, raced to the kitchen window, and handed a toffee to the lead sportswoman.

She slid it into her mouth. "Hmmm," she sighed as her teeth cemented together . . .

Tossing a few soya-toms and a vibrator aside, Cyborg pushed a long stick under the statue. The packer robots gingerly followed.

Lifting the statue from a distance, they peered beneath to a bubbling mash of vegetable roots and effluent.

They gasped, holding their noses . . .

The sweeper edged closer.

It stopped.

"Warning, warning."

The cook prodded it with a stick.

"Danger, danger."

It began to reverse.

The infected women, mid cheer, stopped as Verruca handed out toffee. Ignoring the lead sportswoman's "can't speak" mime, they slid handfuls of the stuff into their mouths—even Prudence with an "oooh, yes please."

"Evacuate, evacuate," automated the sweeper robot.

"Evacu—"

Piff, puff, poof . . .

A cloud of smoke appeared, covering the sweeper robot.

Silence.

The hippies and their entourage waited . . .

The smoke evaporated.

They stared at the empty space where the sweeper robot had been, then headed back to the tent, the hippies practically dusting their hands on their thighs with a satisfied "job done."

The sweeper plunged head deep into a cavern, passing florescent scrabbling rodents that looked dangerously hungry.

He stopped at a cave the size of a gigantic turtle footstep, inch deep in effluent, and riddled with rodents.

One coughed; another sneezed, sparking a wheezing fit.

The Alterationist stared at the image on the tent wall.

"It's not as bad as we thought," she said, trying to put a positive spin on things.

The others stared at a floating turtle torso illuminating the darkness.

"Bad? It's worse than bad—that glow could light a whole street," said Woody.

The effluent began to bubble . . . and everything went red. Then the red began to swirl, twisting into a kaleidoscope of shades and shapes.

The women in the tent and the room with a view waited . . .

The shapes turned to a tunnel, colors shooting forth like fire-crackers.

Bump, crash, silence.

The colors cleared . . .

Under the statue, a glow appeared.

The best buddy, fed up with the whole push-and-shove in front of the fan, leaned out the window, breathed in the cool air, and stopped.

Two eyes appeared at the statue's armpit, followed by its rodent-like body. It sniffed a rodent-like sniff, its long whiskers twitching . . . just like a mechanical rat . . .

The best buddy, her teeth cemented tight with fudge, nudged the shot-putter, who, mid sucking, nudged her back—until they both caught a glimpse of a freakishly glowing rat.

It crawled toward the packer robots, coughing and wheezing.

The packer robots jumped onto a log with a squeal.

The rat stopped and cleaned its nose, then keeled over with a dribble.

A few packer robots jumped off the log.

Whew!

Another rat appeared, spluttering and gasping.

The packer robots jumped back onto the log.

More followed, sneezing like they had dust up their breathing apparatuses, which the robots suddenly realized were not breathing apparatuses at all but real, breathing *noses*.

"The rats are alive," automated one, sparking a frenzy of panic circling—an impressive feat while balancing on a log.

The rats, sourcing the kitchen, began to croak and pant their way to the back door, sparking a mimed panic in the women.

They slammed everything they could think of shut.

A rat squeezed under the door, wriggled to its feet, circled like it was stoned, then collapsed by the shot-putter's shoe, spit bubbling from its mouth.

"Run for it," the shot-putter mimed, sparking a hysteria of silent door pushing.

They broke out like scared mute children, dodging the stream of sickly-looking rats like footballers heading for a goal. They charged into the tent, catching the tail end of the sort of argument no amount of yelling could interrupt, let alone miming.

No one noticed the infected women.

Chapter Forty-Eight

MIMING AND SILENCE

"Robots have orifices too."–Cyborg

The tent, now a virtual reality auditorium, was a hive of panicked discussion.

Alice, circling with agitation, was projecting the room with a view onto one wall of the tent while the video from the sweeper's camera was on the other.

The two hippies and the two "diggers" (which the hippies had taken to calling them in frustration) were arguing with each other. Woody and Pete were doing their best to be positive, while H_2, looking a tad agitated, wasn't getting a word in.

The hippies felt that with a little tweaking, a connection could be made.

The others, seeing various flaws in such a theory, argued.

"We just need some gears and a dial or two," said the Alterationist.

"Are you kidding? That thing is fifth dimensional at least," said Howard. "Way past dials and the like."

"Perhaps a lever then?"

"Pfff—levers are way out of its league."

"Will you stop being so negative?" jumped in Woody.

"I'm just being realistic. The chances of setting up a 'viable connection,' as you put it, are as slim as Cyborg over there procreating."

Cyborg jumped to respond.

Woody interrupted. "Why don't we ask the operations room?"

"And start a panic?" screeched H2 and the hippies in unison.

"I think that has already started," said Howard.

"Well, what do you suggest then?" someone said.

"Sell tickets to Earth," muttered Alice. "Buy one, get one free."

The lead sportswoman jumped in front of Woody and gestured to outside with a panicky look. "Earth rats are coming from the portal," she mimed—not exactly the easiest thing to mime, especially when high and in a state of panic.

The hippies looked at her like she was stupid.

The lead sportswoman jumped up and down with her best silent "we're in danger" gesture.

"That glowing stuff must be stronger than we thought," said the Alterationist.

The militant one attempted a mime of mass destruction.

"She's trying to say something," shouted H2.

Prudence, now fully sober, began to crawl on her knees like a rat. The unaffected stared at her blankly.

"A four-legged creature?" said Verruca.

She stood up, nodding vigorously, then mimed a smaller version with her hands.

"A ball?" said the cook.

The militant lab assistant, huffing with impatience, flapped her hands around like an orchestra conductor.

"A fly?" said Woody. "No, wait—a minute mosquito?"

The shot-putter, hot with frustration, pulled the tent flap wide with great drama followed by an "out there" gesture.

A rat scurried past with a wheeze; a packing robot fainted; another trumpeted a loud fart, startling a crow nearby.

The women gasped.

"Rats!" yelled the militant lab assistant, finally swallowing her toffee.

"Rats?" sprayed the lead sportswoman with way too much spit.

"What are they?" said the voice from the back.

"Bit like mice," said Cyborg, "but not so cute."

"No need to panic," said the cook. "We are prepared," she lied.

Which no one took with even a pinch of salt.

Carter's power nap in Serenity's room ended abruptly as Serenity shut the TV room door in a panic and flew down the corridor.

Dolly and Molly were keeping watch outside Serenity's bedroom door, as excited as a six-year-old waiting for Santa. They had spent their days waiting for the next meal, for the next visitor, for their turn in the shower, for their meds, for the tea trolley to come round, their bodies motionless with pain, and suddenly they were in the thick of something neither they nor those who had told them what to do had any idea about.

It was like they were in the middle of an Enid Blyton book and they were the Famous Five, calling the friggin' shots.

Molly, her Zimmer frame forgotten, was pacing like a military general while Dolly talked of sandwiches for the new arrivals.

"We need to be quiet," said Serenity.

Molly rolled her eyes. "Well, that's a given."

Deidre shoggled her chair toward the door. "I heard that," she lied.

H2, Vegas, Mex, and DBO looked at each other.

Vegas opened the door.

Deidre chair-jumped into the room with a view. "I heard everything!"

They dragged the chair fully inside the room and shut the door behind Dierdre.

"Keep it down," snapped Vegas.

Deidre took in the distressed faces and quickly assessed that the remains of the leadership had no idea what to do. *Why else would they have Mex there? Total last resort.*

Perhaps things were finally going her way . . .

"I've a plan," she jumped in. "The portal could be a real money spinner. You could sell tickets, make enough to do up the friggin' road."

She stopped and looked at the screen, which was split with a view of inside the tent and outside, where large rodents staggered from the Legless statue's groin.

"We think the rats are from Earth," said Vegas.

The rat coughed, spat, then simultaneously collapsed.

"Full of that Earth virus, by the look of it," said Deidre.

Silence . . .

The women in the tent looked at each other.

Woody looked at Pete.

H2, with no idea who to look at, put on her best I'm-in-charge face.

DBO eyed Deidre with suspicion. *Her motives are as fishy as her idiotic plan.* "How do you know there's a virus?" she said.

"It's my job."

Another rat appeared, wrenching himself up like he'd just been hit with a sledgehammer. With a gag, he collapsed.

"She *is* a journalist," said Mex.

"With excellent sources," said Deidre. "And from what I've heard, that virus is as contagious as fear itself."

The three elderly women and Carter stood outside the TV room, ears to the door . . .

Squeak, squawk, flutter . . .

Carter made to open when Serenity pushed her aside.

"I'm the oldest," she said, "and if there is anything dangerous, it's me that should take the bullet."

Molly huffed. "For Pete's sake, just get in before the carers hear."

They opened the door . . . to a room lit up like fairground.

"Shit," said Carter.

"Oh, my," said Dolly.

On the floor was the Rubik's Cube, hemp sack free and lit up like a lighthouse. Precariously balanced on the tip of the flying platform was the sweeper robot. It looked painful.

Carter lifted the sweeper robot with care.

Dolly walked over to the Rubik's Cube. "Well, well, what have we here?" she whispered. She bent to pick it up.

"Don't," hissed Carter.

"Come to Mama," purred Dolly.

"I said don't . . ."

Dolly worked the cube like a master, turning each side a single color in seconds, rendering the cube powerless—a mere Earth Rubik's Cube.

Dolly slid it into her pocket.

"How the hell did she do that?" said Carter.

To say the leader and her team were panicked would be an understatement. They had little idea of any Earth virus, let alone a lockdown.

Beryl had been too preoccupied to inform them.

"This whole Legless thing has grown arms and legs," said H2. "I mean how was I to know that his statue would unearth some sort of portal?"

"You did cover up a quarry," shouted Howard.

"I can't take credit for that," said H2.

"How about a bomb?" said Deidre, who considered herself on a roll.

"What?" said everyone at once.

"Yes, they use them all the time on Earth. Lock the rats in Verruca's house and blow the bastards to smithereens."

"Bit messy," muttered Vegas.

"It could work," said Mex, who, having been on Earth, knew a thing or two about destruction.

"You'll spread the virus even farther," shouted the cook. "A virus is as indestructible as . . . that pickling effluent in the pickling quarry."

"We need to stop the rats, plug up the portal," said Verruca.

"With what?" said DBO.

Verruca looked around . . . "I don't know."

It was then that Deidre came up with an idea she would brag about for the rest of her life. "Why not make a passageway to your kitchen—funnel them until we block things up?"

No one said anything. Complimenting a smug face is not an easy thing to do, even when sugared up on toffee.

Chapter Forty-Nine

STRAINED SILENCE

"A good journalist is as suspicious as a conspiracy theorist."– Deidre

Beryl's Nokia rumbled. She pulled it out.

"Just a quick word," messaged H2, "about that virus on Earth . . ."

The camper van was silent; no one knew what to say. Beryl's suppressed anger had put a strain on all.

"Beryl's not so bad," Hilda finally said.

"She'll come around," said Archie.

Legless nodded.

DJ had his doubts. He had just spent the better part of an hour with Beryl, who had misunderstood the whole concept of a ball-breaker.

She thought it was a compliment.

"Beryl will take some time," he muttered, and was about to expand when Beryl charged in.

"Apparently, rats in space are not just carriers," she said.

"I didn't know," said Legless.

"Well, they are more," said Beryl. "And they are currently rampaging via the portal to Planet Hy Man like, well . . ."

"Rats," suggested Legless.

"Not only full of that virus but coughing and dying like, well."

"The plague?" said Legless.

"Told you," muttered Archie.

Which the rest chose to ignore.

"They want us to do something," said Beryl.

"Blocking them is the only answer," said Legless. "On our end."

"Obviously," snapped Beryl.

"We could dump the couch," said DJ.

Hilda shook her head. "We need to destroy it."

"Burn it," said Legless, a man for bonfires.

Hilda nodded.

"We're going in," said Archie to DJ. "We'll bring it back here and burn the bastard."

"You're going to raid a nursing home?" said Mandy. "How are you going to do that without getting caught?"

"We'll figure that out when we get there," said Archie. "Call Don," he said to DJ. "We'll rendezvous under the window."

"We could wire you up," said Mandy, "keep connected with earpieces, let you know if we see anything."

Legless looked at Beryl. She looked away.

"Well, I'll just go and rig up a bonfire then, shall I?"

"Do what you want. You always do," muttered Beryl.

Legless glared at Beryl. Then, with a slam of the door, he headed out.

Beryl, eyes on the camper van door, said little.

Hilda's face softened.

Chapter Fifty

THE LIST

"I guess there's nothing new under the Milky Way after all."– Verruca

Don appeared at the care home's back window to find Archie already there with DJ. "What are you doing here?"

"Saving the world—you?"

Don smiled, a manly joke on the tip of his tongue. Then Molly appeared with a wave, followed by Dolly and Serenity.

"Did you bring Izzie?" mouthed Dolly through the glass.

"Shhhh," hissed Serenity. "There's a couch that needs capturing."

"Capturing?" Her eyes widened. "A couch?"

"Must you talk in riddles?" snapped Molly.

Serenity, tight-lipped, opened the window.

The Identities crept in.

"There's more," whispered Serenity. "A robot with brushes—"

Molly glared at her.

"Well, there is," said Serenity. "Not to mention that other thing."

"Pfff—I'm not taking in robots from some godforsaken planet," said Don. "Bunnie would have a fit."

"Shhhh," hissed Molly.

"You never know what they've got," he whispered to DJ. "And we've a B&B to run."

"I said quiet," snapped Molly.

The women led the Identities into a corridor lined with black-and-white photos of Dunoon in the "days of ole" and way too many pot plants.

Someone snored.

Archie stared into the corridor dimly lit with night-lights and several green fire exit signs.

"Out for the count," he muttered.

"Shhhh," said Molly. "Old McFadden's a light sleeper."

"He can't walk," said Dolly.

"He'll call a nurse."

"I've sorted that," said Serenity.

Molly stopped. "You've what?"

"A little sleeping pill—in their hot chocolate."

"Jesus, where did you get that?" said Don.

"Shhhh."

"It's McFadden's."

"So he'll wake up then," said Molly.

"I've hidden his wheelchair," said Serenity with pride.

Archie looked at Don and DJ. "In and out, no mucking about. The last thing we need is a full-scale . . ." He stopped.

"Shep!" croaked a confused elderly voice.

"I'll see to him," said Dolly, pulling a hip flask from her pocket.

"Where did you get that?" said Molly.

She tapped her nose. "The kitchen."

"The kitchen?" Molly hissed a shriek.

"Won't they find out?" said DJ.

"Not before we're done," said Archie. He looked at Don. "We should be out by midnight."

Don nodded. "A simple lift-and-drive job—piece of piss."

Molly looked at her son. She didn't have the heart to tell him about the other arrivals.

Hilda and Mandy, on the edges of their seats, looked at the blank screen.

Having read Hilda's mind several times and asked her many questions, Mandy had a vision of Hilda's home—and she could not wait to see it.

Beryl, sitting by the window, peered out.

Legless was piling wood for a bonfire in that irritating way of his, while Charlton Heston followed like he was helping.

Beryl huffed. *Only a dog would follow that,* she grumbled to herself.

"Just go out and talk to him, hear what he has to say," tutted Mandy.

Beryl said nothing. The last person she was going to listen to was *her*.

"You could even give him a hand."

"Pfff—*him*. As if," said Beryl, her eyes never leaving Legless.

Hilda twiddled with the remote.

Mandy peered in expectation.

H2's face appeared—then the screen panned out to the leadership team crowded around the small table in the room with a view, which without the view and the chandeliers was pretty unimpressive.

A doddery footman in the corner staggered, clutching at the wall.

"You weren't exaggerating when you said ancient," Mandy muttered to Hilda.

The footman, with the hearing of a sheepdog, threw her a "less of the old" glare, and he continued to glare as Deidre brought him a chair and ushered him to sit.

"This is Mandy," said Hilda to the leadership team.

Mandy waved a comradely wave.

They gingerly waved back. They had heard of Earth men, but they'd never seen one dressed as a woman.

"She's an Identity," said Hilda.

"Oh." They nodded like that explained the wig, expansive shoulders, and square, masculine jaw.

"She's here to help," said Hilda with a look of admiration that had the leadership team stunned. "Aren't you, Mandy?"

Mandy coughed uncomfortably.

H2 was about to interrupt, talk of urgency and collaboration, when the camper van rattled and Bunnie, with a jangle of beads, thrust open the door. Clutching Izzie with an under-the-breast hold, she bounded in, jostling the camper van like an earthquake.

Hilda steadied the TV.

One week into lockdown and Bunnie was as bored as a "grounded" teenager. She couldn't wait to head over to Legless's place, meet Hilda and Mandy (whom she had met on FaceTime), see those on Planet Hy Man Beryl had talked of over the past year (some she had even spoken to) and . . . maybe even get a glimpse of this so-called Planet Hy Man.

She beamed, pulling up a chair. "Have they touched down yet?"

Hilda and Mandy nodded, watching Bunnie squeeze herself into position. Bunnie in the flesh was way more expansive. She had the sort of voluptuous body a man could drown in.

Bunnie waved at the screen.

"Hi, I am Bunnie, I run a B&B . . ."

"No time for introductions," said DBO.

"She's awful young," said Bunnie, "for running a planet."

DBO gestured to H2. "She's the leader."

"We work as a team," said H2.

"You look even younger," said Bunnie.

H2 blushed and was about to mutter a "thank you" when she caught sight of the ex-leader cooing to what looked like a *real* four-legged creature.

Bunnie dumped Izzie onto Beryl's lap.

Izzy nestled in.

Beryl patted with bliss.

The leadership team watched, speechless. To them, four-legged creatures were large, mythical creatures the size of a horse or a cow, or small scurrying rodents. They had never seen anything alive before let alone a living, breathing, cute-as-fuck puffball of white fur like Lizzie.

"It's a pet," said Deidre with authority.

Izzie looked up and blinked her best cute look, like she knew she was the center of attention.

The TV room in the care home appeared on-screen in both the room with a view and the camper van.

The sweeper robot, perched on the coffee table, was holding up a leg as Carter, on her knees, was oiling the "lubricant intake" opening with a yellow substance from a tub called Stork.

Carter had no idea she was on a screen, or even what an Identity was, let alone that they were marching down the corridor with the three women.

When the Identities walked in, she stopped and looked up.

The Identities stared at the apparition on the couch. "And what the hell is that?" said Don.

"It's a cleaner robot," said Dolly to the Identities. "Be great for your B&B."

"B&B?" said Vegas.

"Bit like a hotel, but with fewer facilities and a better breakfast," said Deidre.

"Not really," said Mandy.

"*That* is a cleaner robot? What the hell does that clean?" said Don.

"That," said Serenity with authority, "is a flying platform." She gestured to the sweeper robot. "And that is the cleaning robot."

Don walked around the couch, surveying it. "And just how the frig are we gonna move *that*?"

Chapter Fifty-One

SPLIT SCREEN

"There is nothing 'mere' about a toy"—Serenity

The screen split into three as cook's plump, round face appeared—panning out to a tent full of anxious-looking women and robots struggling to remain at attention.

"There's more?" said Bunnie.

"Of course there is more. It is another planet," said Hilda, "not some cockamamie Earth sci-fi film."

A few waved, until they spied Izzie. They stopped . . .

"It's a pet," yelled Deidre.

"There's no time for introductions," said H2.

"I'm the cook," said the cook.

"The cook?" said Bunnie.

"And according to my books, we've a few things to put into place before plugging that portal."

Bunnie looked at her comrades. "What's a cook to do with things?"

"Cooks are very different over there." Hilda looked at Beryl. "Aren't they?"

Beryl turned, and for the first time, she noticed a softness in Hilda. She nodded.

Hilda smiled back.

The Alterationist appeared on-screen. "We need a few things."

"Who's she then, the dishwasher?" said Bunnie.

"Alterationist," shouted a voice from the tent.

"What's that when it's at home—an upholsterer?" she joked.

The Alterationist glared at Bunnie. She glared back.

"We could just blow them up," said Deidre.

"Who's that?" Bunnie stopped. "Wait a minute—is she talking of a bomb? Here?"

"We're not blowing anything up," snapped H2.

"You can't detonate a bomb on our planet," said Bunnie.

"Well, you all do," said Deidre.

"That's different," said Bunnie.

Mandy turned to Bunnie. "How?"

"I said we're not using bombs," snapped H2.

Izzie jumped off Beryl's lap and scratched at the door with an "I need a pee" urgency.

Beryl took her outside, and with a long glance at Legless still busy bonfire setting, she headed as far as possible from him.

"We're plugging up the portal," said Hilda. "Archie is there now with DJ removing the couch . . ."

"And Legless is setting up a bonfire," said Mandy.

The cook spluttered her sparkly water. "You need to stop!"

"Stop!" yelled several more from the tent.

"Tell them to wait," said H2.

Hilda yelled into her phone to Archie and DJ.

"Did you hear that?"

Archie, mid couch lifting, looked up. "Hear? I am in the middle of friggin' couch stealing, I don't have time to listen to you lot."

"You need to stop!" shouted Mandy.

"What?" said Archie.

"Stop."

He dropped the couch, jolting the flying platform loose. "What's she talking about?"

"We're to stop?" said DJ. He listened. "The cook says so."

"The cook?" Archie looked at Don.

Don dropped his end. "What's a friggin' cook got to do with things?"

The flying platform inched away from the cushions.

"We need a few things before the plugging commences," said the cook.

"They need a few things before plugging," yelled Hilda.

"We *can* hear," whispered DJ.

"Once we start, we don't stop," whispered Archie, grabbing the couch again.

Don nodded.

They lifted.

"It's *your* rats," said the Alterationist.

"Our rats?" said Bunnie.

"Rats," said DJ.

"Rats, here?" Don dropped the couch, which landed with a shudder.

Archie followed with a "thanks for the warning."

The flying platform tumbled to the floor. It slid behind the couch in ready mode.

"We need *Earth* stuff to clean it up—stop the spread."

"You've robots for that," said Hilda.

"Yes, but without the Earth chemicals, we'll have to block the site off for who knows how long."

"We need real Earth garlic," shouted the cook.

DJ looked at Archie. "Hardly a chemical."

"What?" said Don.

Archie handed him an earpiece.

"For us," snapped DBO. "So we're not infected when cleaning up."

"What's garlic?" said a voice from the tent.

"Bit like onions but smaller," Deidre shouted. "And smellier."

"Not really," said Mex.

"Protection," said Mandy, nodding and jotting it down.

"Plus a shitload of vitamin C, and some lubricant . . . water soluble."

"Piece of piss," muttered Hilda.

Beryl almost smiled.

"And some stoppers, a bagful, and plastic bottles—preferably Coke."

"Another piece of piss," said Hilda.

"Oh, and a bottle of Dettol—make that several."

Hilda looked at Mandy quizzically.

"I've some," said Bunnie, finally getting into the spirit of things.

"And it must be Dettol," said the cook. She threw a look at Bunnie. "None of your cheap no-name-brand stuff."

"What sort of establishment do you think I run?"

"I'm just saying."

"Cotton buds, a bottle of beer—for yeast purposes—and some wet wipes, while you're at it, of the makeup removal kind . . . and oh yes, toilet paper," said Woody.

"Toilet paper? You'll be lucky," muttered DJ.

"Oh, and could you get me a yoga mat while you're at it . . . and a McDonald's?" said Pete.

Woody looked at him. "Seriously?"

Bunnie and Mandy jumped up to collect.

"Oh, and there is one other thing," said H2.

Silence.

"We need a plastic protector. The cook predicts a melting issue if there is no wrapping around the Coke bottles."

"And before you say anything, ice won't work," said the cook. "Must be something with a pulse. Perhaps a person—a dog at a push."

"Not my Izzie again," snapped Bunnie.

Legless, outside mid log hauling, stopped. He looked up to catch Beryl at the end of the yard looking at him.

She turned away.

Legless thought about Karen and her threats, Beryl and her tantrums.

Maybe it's time, he thought, *to go home.*

Archie, Don, and DJ stared at the sweeper robot perched on the coffee table as Carter continued to oil. Waiting was not something they had planned to do.

The sweeper robot shifted from leg to leg with a squeak.

"Perhaps we could shove him under something," muttered Archie. "Keep it quiet."

Carter glared at him. "You'd be squeaking too if you had that thing shoved up your whatever."

The three Identities stared at the wild-haired Alien.

"I thought it was a robot," muttered Don.

Carter huffed. "Robots have feelings too, you know."

DJ turned to the glass cabinet. The bottom doors were wood—perfect for hiding things.

They could fit, he thought.

The flying platform, however, had other ideas.

Chapter Fifty-Two

THE BIG SULK

"Brushing up on one's techniques has little to do with a brush."– Archie

Beryl, with no idea about the latest discussion in the camper van, remained outside stewing about all she had done for Legless.

Her mind was a rush of illogical thoughts, raging jealousy, and drama—feelings she had never felt before. She watched Legless leave the bonfire to begin collecting things. *Looking,* Beryl told herself, *pickling happy.*

"How could he throw it all away for some loudmouth, alimony-obsessed woman?" she said to Izzie.

Izzie, bored and hungry, began to whine.

Beryl, with an "OK, poppet," took her into the kitchen. She began to rummage for food.

What the hell is wrong with me? I should be thinking about saving the planet, not obsessing about Legless. Maybe I should jump on the couch, head home—leave him with Mandy and that pickling ex.

Hilda raced in. "Any garlic here?"

Beryl looked up. "Tons." She gestured to a bowl.

Hilda picked up a bulb and inspected it. "That's garlic?"

Beryl nodded.

"It's nothing like an onion."

Beryl, with a sad look, let out a long sigh.

Hilda stopped. A feeling of warmth filled her. She wanted to help Beryl, tell her how wrong she was, that Karen was the last thing Legless wanted, but she couldn't find the words.

She thought of the notebook, her plans to use it to her own ends, and before she had time to stop herself, she'd pulled it out. "Read this," she said.

Beryl turned it in her hands.

"It will help you understand."

Beryl threw her a distrustful look.

Hilda smiled with a warmth that startled Beryl. And Beryl felt something—a sort of "kindness connection."

She stared at the cover. "I thought I'd seen everything he had written, all the crazy books with stupid names: *The Spark Plug Odyssey*, *Sugar Is the Noose around the Universe* . . ."

"He wrote about you too."

"I can imagine."

"But not as you think."

Beryl ran her fingers over the "memoir" scribbled across the cover.

"Trust me," said Hilda.

Beryl looked at Hilda's warm eyes, and for some weird reason, she did.

She opened it, and soon she was reading about the heartache of an Alien on Earth, never feeling at home, never understood.

It didn't take long to collect things. Legless's home was that sort of place—it was full of stuff. They even found a yoga mat. In fact, the only thing they couldn't pack was a McDonald's; the nearest was a ferry trip away.

"Let's get a fish supper," said Bunnie, shoving several packets of Hilda's pilfered crisps into a backpack.

Mandy, busy strapping an empty plastic Coke bottle to Legless's torso, didn't hear.

Strapping Coke bottles to a torso is not as easy as it sounds. It had taken several attempts, several swear words, and two rather sore nipples to get it right.

She looked up at her father. "You sure about this?"

Legless skulled the remains of a Coke bottle and handed it to her with a belch. "Someone's got to do it," he said.

"You've only just met Mandy," said Bunnie, emptying another Coke bottle into the dog bowl. She hated the stuff, even with a vodka.

Charlton Heston sniffed, jolted, then looked at Bunnie with a "what the fuck?" expression.

Legless looked at his daughter. "We'll keep in contact."

She nodded with a rip of tape.

"It's time. I want to go back, be with my own kind. Reminisce."

"Going back home isn't all it's cracked up to be," said Bunnie. "It will have changed."

Mandy strapped another bottle. "What about Beryl?"

Legless belched.

Charlton Heston jumped.

"So you told her then?" said Bunnie.

"Of course," lied Legless. "She's all for it."

The bottom of the glass cabinet was full of good old-fashioned pre-digital games that had been stashed inside with a "shove it in and slam the door" philosophy.

DJ had no idea.

He opened it.

Monopoly money, dice of several sizes, cards, a Snakes and Ladders board, a Ker Plunk funnel, marbles, chess figures, dominoes, and more marbles all tumbled onto the carpet without a sound.

"Shit," muttered DJ.

The sweeper robot swept into motion with a hushed hover until it came across a marble.

"Shut it off," hissed Don with panic.

Archie grabbed the robot. "How? Where?" He turned and shoved it at Don.

Don juggled it.

Archie opened the window with a "quick."

Carter slid her hand underneath Don's armpit and, with a smug look, pressed the robot's off switch.

While Beryl was in the kitchen discovering Legless's true feelings about Karen and her, Legless, looking a bit like a turtle on two legs, was waddling to his car. With a crackle of plastic, he attempted to slide behind the driver's wheel. Then he looked at Mandy and gave up.

"Just as well you can drive," he said, easing himself into the passenger seat.

Mandy jumped behind the wheel.

Bunnie dumped the backpacks in the back. "You sure Beryl knows?" she said.

"Of course," muttered Legless.

The car sped off, and Beryl, with visions of making peace with a "letting down of her beehive" maneuver, had no idea. She charged outside.

When Bunnie was done waving them off, she turned to find Beryl looking confused.

"Where's he going?" Beryl said.

Bunnie looked at her. "I thought you knew."

Carter, who'd had years of packing training, lurched into action, tidying with a meticulousness that stopped not only the Identities in their tracks but also Dolly and Molly—two "shove it in and slam the door" sort of women.

They watched as Carter filled the Ker Plunk funnel with not only its marbles but any stray ones as well, along with all the Chest and Monopoly figures, the deck of cards, and several dice. She casually piled boards around the funnel from largest to smallest to support it upright.

Dolly and Molly were spellbound. *Why didn't we think of that?*

"There is room for the sweeper here," she said, standing it on its side and sharply closing the door on any protest by the sweeper robot.

As Carter dusted her hands off with more than a hint of smugness, Legless crashed through the window, knocking over a large Swiss cheese plant and a black-and-white photo of Dunoon pier behind it.

The two-night shift carers sitting in the common room at the end of the corridor, hot chocolate poised, groaned. *Love Island* was about to start.

Carer Two turned down the TV.

Carer One peered into the corridor.

Ol' McFadden bolted upright, wide awake.

"Shep, Shep!" he yelled. "Here boy!" He whistled.

"Who's that?" said Don.

Dolly and Molly looked at each other. "McFadden."

No one noticed the flying platform, designed to obey the call of a whistle, light up behind the couch.

It didn't need a second calling. With the silence of a weasel, it flew through the door inches from the ground.

DJ felt a brush against his leg. He stopped, then turned with a "what was that?"

As ol' McFadden, silent and petrified, watched the flying platform circle his bed like a menacing shark.

He hurled his clock at it.

Crash!

Bunnie, the sort of woman who loves not only a romantic challenge but a good car chase, jumped into action.

After arguing over who should drive, Hilda, taking both by surprise with a "get in," shoved Beryl into the back of the hatchback.

Beryl, clasping Izzie, stumbled into the seat behind Bunnie, catching her beehive on the way. Hairpins clattered to the seat, and for the first time ever, Beryl didn't notice let alone try to adjust.

"Text them to wait," said Bunnie, revving up the engine, and with a crunch of gears, she sped off in her Fiat 500.

Heart pounding, knees under her chin, and beehive squashed to a bun, Beryl scrabbled with her phone.

"Tell them we'll pick up the takeaway, that should slow them," said Hilda.

"Ask for a battered sausage," said Bunnie, negotiating a roundabout.

"A battered what?" said Hilda

"To temp the stray rats," said Bunnie. "They love 'em."

Beryl turned to Hilda in panic. "I can't get a signal."

"No worries. It only takes ten minutes," said Bunnie.

"Yes, but Mandy's driving."

"Shit!" said Bunnie, wrenching into fifth. The car jolted, Hilda lurched forward, and Izzie flew from Beryl's arms with a yelp.

The phone clattered to the floor.

Hilda grabbed it. "H2, are you there?"

"Of course," said H2.

"You need to stall Legless. Can you do that?"

"Leave it to me," said H2, finally getting the chance to make someone happy.

The carers thumped down the corridor.

The flying platform slid under the bed.

"Quick," hissed Serenity, pushing Legless and Mandy into her room. She shoved them into her bathroom, slid the door tight, and climbed into bed.

They could hear the carers seeing to ol' McFadden in the next room.

"Up we come," said Carer One.

"I'm being stalked," he stuttered.

"Let's get you comfortable," said Carer Two.

"How can I be comfortable when they are after me?"

"It's just a dream."

"Oh," said ol' McFadden, trumpeting the sort of fart that would shame a dog.

"Jesus," said Carer Two. "What did you have for dinner?"

"Chicken," he said. "I think it was a bit off."

Mandy started to laugh.

Legless started to chuckle.

Their minds met . . .

Meeting you is something I'll never forget, thought Mandy.

We are more alike than not, thought Legless.

She nodded, her eyes welling.

I've only just found you, and you're leaving? she thought.

But we've met—that's more than most, he thought.

They came close to hugging. In fact, if it wasn't for the disabled toilet between them, they would have. Instead, as ol' McFadden ranted about the previous night's "rancid-as-my-bleeding-underpants dinner" giving him nightmares, they looked at each other, their hands touching over the heated towel rail.

We'll keep in contact, thought Legless.

Mandy nodded. Then her mind strayed to Beryl. *Did you really tell her you're leaving?*

Of course, thought Legless with a gentle grip of her hand.

Mandy looked at her mobile. A message from H2.

She read it and texted back: *Stalling Legless? A piece of piss.*

Chapter Fifty-Three

INFILTRATION

"He was so old that everything drooped, even his balls; they hung so low he could polish his shoes with them." DJ's blog, The Secret Life of a Stand-Up

Getting ol' McFadden settled took some time—enough time for the two carers to become exasperated.

By the time the coast was clear, Bunnie was pulling up at the back of the care home. And by the time Legless and Mandy had made it to the TV room, Beryl was staggering out of Bunnie's Fiat 500, and Bunnie was so excited she needed the loo.

Legless, impatient as a child on Christmas morning, raced to the TV room and charged to the couch. He wanted to escape before he had time to change his mind, think of Beryl.

Forgetting Mandy was holding one of the backpacks, he began to lie back.

Mandy wrenched him off the couch.

"Wait," she whispered. "We need to fit your camera."

Hilda poked her head in the window; the corridor was clear. "All systems go," she whispered.

Bunnie, Izzie in her arms, motioned for Beryl to "run." For a moment, Beryl stopped, looking from Izzy to Bunnie.

"Go on," said Bunnie with a warm look.

Beryl's beehive, now more a half-arsed bun, flopped to the side; a whisper of hair fell to her cheek, and Bunnie brushed it away.

"Izzie will miss you," she said. "But I friggin' won't."

Hilda shoved Legless's memoir into Beryl's arms, then tugged her to hurry. "Go."

Beryl hesitated, not sure how to say thank you.

"Go on." Hilda shoved her. "Mandy can't stall forever."

Clutching Legless's memoir, Beryl sprinted off, surprising even herself. Then she skidded with a muffled "shit!"

Carer One, reheating their hot chocolate for the second time, stopped. "What was that?"

Carer Two turned the TV down with a sigh.

Beryl hid behind a bedroom door.

Carer Two peered down the corridor. "It's nothing," she whispered.

"Thank frig for that," said Carer One, turning up *Love Island*.

"It's now or never," said Legless.

"Wait," whispered Archie and DJ.

"Not yet," added Don.

Legless threw them a look.

"There is a problem," said Serenity. "The flying platform has disappeared."

Ol' McFadden stared at the beauty behind his door, her hair tumbling about her shoulders. He wolf-whistled her.

The flying platform lit up.

Beryl turned to see an old man eyeing her up like she was a beauty.

He slid his leg out of the bed.

She motioned a "shhhh" and tiptoed out into the corridor.

The flying platform slid out from underneath the bed and hovered under his foot.

Hellbent on following such a rare beauty, he slid his other foot out of the bed with a "hey, come back" yell, and when that didn't work, he whistled again.

The flying platform lifted him into the air.

"Jesus wept," hissed Ol' McFadden, tugging at his pajamas for decency.

Beryl tiptoed past the carer's common room.

Carer One, washing their hot chocolate down the sink under a tap on full, didn't hear. "This stuff is as off as your ex's jokes," she shouted to her colleague in the loo, who, mid flush, missed her joke completely.

Beryl hightailed it into the room, skidding through the door to find Mandy adjusting Legless's camera, the Identities giving useless advice, and Carter sniffing about the couch like a detective.

The Identities stopped, Legless glared, and Mandy dropped Legless's camera. No one had ever seen Beryl without her cement-like beehive before.

"Her hair is real?" muttered Don.

"I always thought it was a wig," whispered Archie.

"You can't go without me," said Beryl.

"Oh yes I can," Legless hissed back. He made for the couch.

"Wait—Dad."

"We need two cameras," lied DJ.

Legless looked confused, "two?" on the tip of his tongue, when a crash and a clutter stopped him.

Ol' McFadden, poised on the flying platform grimly holding the front of his pajamas together, filled the doorway.

"Get me off?" he whispered.

"Jesus Christ," muttered Archie.

"I don't know how to fly."

Carer Two thought she heard something: a swish, a clutter, perhaps a skid, or was it a moan?

She peered into the corridor and flicked on the lights.

Archie pulled Ol' McFadden in.

"It's nothing," muttered Carer Two. She flicked off the lights.

"Help me," said Ol' McFadden.

The flying platform wrenched itself from Archie's hands and began to circle the room, bumping into the cabinet.

"Shut the door," someone hissed.

The bottom cupboard door swung wide, a game board toppled to the floor like a ramp, and the sweeper robot cluttered out like a tank down a plank with a momentum that was hard to stop . . .

Serenity, who already had spite against Ol' McFadden, grabbed her Queenie and hurled it at him rather than the platform with a "take that!"

The flying platform swerved.

Ol' McFadden tumbled off.

The doll landed on the ground; its head rolled off into the corridor.

"Told you to shut the door," snapped Molly.

"What the hell was that?" shouted Carer Two.

The corridor lights flicked on.

"Help!" shouted Ol' McFadden as the sweeper robot began to climb his leg. "I'm being attacked . . . in the TV room."

Carer Two turned to Carer One. "What's he doing out of bed?"

Carer Two peered into the corridor and spotted Queenie's head, its eyes menacingly glaring like the dead.

She turned back to her colleague. "He's been at Queenie again—the old bugger."

The sweeper robot, like a shark on the scent of blood, headed toward Ol' McFadden . . .

The flying platform circled.

"I said help," yelled Ol' McFadden. "There's a friggin' tank!" He looked above his head. "And a flying torpedo thing."

"Aye right," said Carer One. She turned to her comrade. "Hallucinating again. Told them those pills are no good, but will they listen?"

"Doctors," muttered Carer Two. "Like to see them do a shift, change a pad or two."

"Come on, let's get him back to bed," said Carer One.

They headed down the corridor.

Ol' McFadden made to yell again.

Don shoved a hand over his face.

Archie and Don tackled the platform to the ground . . .

Serenity shuffled into the corridor with her best insane face. "I'm looking for my Queenie." She blinked.

The carers stopped.

Carer Two smiled. "You need a hand, luv?"

Serenity, muttering something about her wardrobe, gestured for them to follow.

Carer Two took her by the arm back to her room.

Carer One stopped at the TV room and made to go in when Molly appeared.

"That man has made a right mess in my room," Molly said.

"For heaven's sake," snapped Carer One.

Molly dragged her up the corridor.

"Quick," Archie hissed.

Legless jumped onto the couch.

Beryl followed.

Ol' McFadden, now on the floor, reached out like a drowning man, clasping the nearest thing he could find.

He grabbed Beryl's leg.

She tried to kick free.

Legless hit Ol' McFadden with his memoir.

Ol' McFadden wrenched it from his hand.

"Nooooo," yelled Legless . . .

Piff, puff, poof . . . they disappeared under a haze.

DJ, thinking on his feet, grabbed the memoir from the old boy and tossed it at the couch.

Piff, puff, poof . . .

It was gone.

They stared.

The haze cleared.

No one said anything.

It was like the end of a wedding—after seeing the couple ride off into the sunset.

"Guess they'll be all right," muttered DJ as Carer Two approached the room.

"Quick!" Don grabbed the flying platform and threw it at Archie; Archie tossed it at DJ; Dolly intervened and with an "I'll take that" slid the platform under her extra-large dressing gown.

"What the hell?" Gasped Ol' McFadden.

Carter threw herself onto the sweeper robot, dragging it behind the couch.

The Identities followed, hiding anywhere they could as the two carers entered.

The carers looked down at the carnage, too stunned to swear.

Carter's meticulous packing had unraveled into a 1970s Christmas-morning floor, a sea of marbles and figurines, and in the middle, sprawled out like a starfish and clutching a Monopoly boot, was Ol' McFadden.

"It just disappeared," he muttered to himself. "One poof and gone."

Carer Two, acutely aware that *Love Island* was halfway through, quickly administered her best "shove it in and slam the door" maneuver, causing Carter to have a silent panic attack.

"He tried to suffocate me," said Dolly, looking like she had a hot water bottle under her dressing gown.

"Typical," tutted Carer One, lifting the Ker Plunk funnel and sliding in a few marbles.

"Piff, puff, poof, and gone," mumbled ol' McFadden. A half bottle clattered from his pocket.

"Have you've been drinking?" said Carer One.

He gestured to Dolly. "She gave it to me."

"I gave you my best whisky and that's the thanks I get."

"Grouse? Hardly the best," huffed ol' McFadden

"You gave him whisky?" Carer Two turned to Dolly. "With his medication?"

"Oh, I took them off him," said Serenity, appearing from behind.

The carers turned to Serenity, her "lunatic look" having no effect whatsoever.

Chapter Fifty-Four

PORTAL TIPPING

"A trip in a portal is anything but a trip abroad."–Carter

There was a swirl of red shades, a crash of a landing, and a splash, followed by the sort of smell that led to nose-holding and gagging, as Legless and Beryl landed in the cave.

A rat snarled.

Legless jumped.

Beryl clocked it with the battered sausage.

Legless threw her a look. "Show-off."

The memoir dropped from above—smack straight onto Legless's head.

He rubbed.

Beryl picked it up.

"Gimme that," he said.

"I have read it, you know."

He looked at her with a "really?"

Another rat appeared.

Legless jumped.

Beryl whacked it with the same battered sausage; its teeth sunk into the batter. She tried to flick it off, but the rat stuck like toffee.

Legless administered a flick and kick.

The rat flew into the air.

"Show-off." Beryl almost smiled.

Another rat appeared and jumped on Legless's shoulder.

He wrestled it to the ground.

As Beryl kicked it into the air, her hair finally fell completely to her shoulders.

The carers returned to their room confused, hungry, and, with only coffee machine coffee to drink, pissed off.

The highlight of the night was a hot chocolate—a deluxe triple shot with caffeine, caramel, and cream. Neither could work out how such a delicacy had "gone off," but with *Love Island* over and done and just a *Murder, She Wrote* rerun to pass the so-called quiet hour, they worked on their report of events.

They had walked into the TV room with no idea that four Identities, one in transition, plus an Alien were hiding—but then why would they? They saw what they expected to see: elderly folk behaving irrationally, one hallucinating under the influence of seventies board games. A half bottle had been drunk between the three of them, and now they were arguing over the second.

"Well, at least it passed the night," said Carer One with a look at her limp lettuce-and-cheese sandwich.

"Exactly," muttered Carer Two, flicking open a low-fat yogurt with a splatter.

Both agreed to overlook the bottle. Instead, Ol' McFadden's hallucinations would be the main theme of their shift report, along with a recommendation to "review his medication."

"We'll just say we found him on the floor and fudge over the rest," said Carer One, still staring at her sandwiches.

Carer Two nodded, glad for once not only that she was not in charge but that she didn't have to eat yesterday's past-their-best lettuce-and-cheese sandwiches.

When all was clear and *Murder, She Wrote* could be heard down the corridor, the Identities came out from their hiding places.

The sweeper robot, on full sniffer alert, remained behind the couch. He was picking up something not of Earth origin.

He sniffed around the back.

Carter pulled her emergency toothbrush from her breast pocket. *That robot doesn't go sniffing around for nothing.*

The sweeper robot slid his sweeper underneath and, with a tug and a pull, retrieved the foreign "something."

"What's this?" said Carter.

"A dog collar," whispered Archie in the dim light.

"An heirloom," said Don.

Carter turned the collar in her hands. It was black and lined with gold studs, and attached to one of them was a wire.

She pulled it off and turned it in her fingers. She had seen one of these on her planet before; they were usually attached to old robots in the tunnels.

She blew on it.

"Useless when dry," she said. "But with just a mere dribble, it becomes, well . . . a connector of unspeakable strength. We'll need to leave this in the sun for days—months—to destabilize. Perhaps a greenhouse?"

Piff, puff, poof . . .

Beryl and Legless appeared between the legs of the Legless statue, Beryl clutching Legless's memoirs and Legless a battered sausage.

He looked around at his statue, saw the large groin bag, and, coming to completely the wrong conclusion, sighed. *If only it were true.*

Beryl read his face. "It is but a bag," she said.

"I know that," he lied and waited for an insult.

Those in the room with a view breathed a sigh of relief, even

Deidre, who for once agreed to the "what happens in the room with a view stays in the room with a view" pact.

"I will write a piece to keep the peace," she said, and for the first time, those in the room with a view believed her.

Within a week of Beryl's arrival, the rat funnel was obsolete due to a good spring cleaning and portal disconnecting. The wiry thing—now drying out in Bunnie's airing cupboard—was as obsolete as a Ker Plunk funnel.

It was Woody who had come up with the idea for a good old-fashion scrub.

While the arrival of Beryl and Legless had the women clamoring for a look, Woody read the cook's books and couldn't wait to share his knowledge.

He stood in the tent watching the cook and Cyborg unpack Legless's backpacks—the cook with the occasional tut and Cyborg with a running commentary—while Verruca, ignoring both, lined the makeshift shelves with bottles of Dettol and packets of wet wipes.

Pete had just charged off with his almost-new yoga mat (Prudence at his heels) when Woody spied the book and couldn't help but look. He opened it to the "Cleaning Is Not a Dirty Word" chapter, right in the middle of the book.

He read it aloud, causing more tutting from the cook and almost silencing Cyborg.

"'Many would call a good scrub an archaic system handed down from the days of old, back when the planet was run by men and scrubbing the likes of piggeries and hen sheds was a given.'"

"Everyone is aware of such things," huffed Cyborg.

"'A job for women until it was handed down to the Mae West robots,'" continued Woody.

"And we all know what happened to them," snapped the cook. She pulled out a stray bottle of bleach with a sniff, then tossed it in the "do not use" bin.

"'With the sort of mop that requires a wrestler's arm to wield.'"

Woody looked up. "A Colt 45 is mentioned here," he said, pointing to the passage.

"They are as out-of-date as Hilda's short back and sides," said Cyborg, surprising everyone with his wit.

"'They took mopping to a new level, not like the automatic,'" read Woody. "'Their cleaning raised the bar.'"

The shelves full, Verruca looked outside at the elongated see-through tunnel winding its way through the mess that was now her garden. Her home was full of rat droppings and dirty dishes—care of the out-of-it sportswomen. It was going to take her forever to get it in some sort of order.

Not that Cyborg was much help. He, having proven he knew a thing or two about things, had been snapped up by the hippies.

"We've plenty of greenhouses that could do with your kind of expertise," said the Alterationist.

Verruca could hardly argue. Her greenhouse was as buggered as her shed.

She looked at Beryl and Legless; they were almost unrecognizable.

He, old and wrinkly, had the look of a stunned mechanical fish and she like she'd won a free cup of caffeine. Her hair was all over the place, the "post making love" mess—not that Verruca knew about such looks. Sex was as rare on Planet Hy Man as a young man.

The couple were surrounded by women—the whole let's-save-the-planet team—claiming that getting her and him to the Building of Opulence was a "priority."

Truth was, they just wanted to get out of cleaning up.

The mess, it seems, was all Verruca's.

"Who was going to help?" she muttered to herself.

"The robots, of course," said the cook.

"What pickling robots?" she said. "They're off to do something with Coke bottles."

Chapter Fifty-Five

PRUDENCE

"There is more to cleaning than a scrubber."—The cook

Pete and Prudence, with a bag of toffee sat on a yoga mat under the veranda.

Pot and Pope were in the greenhouse sorting out a few spliffs for reconciliation purposes. All of four of the robots had smoked enough to find the mechanical birds funny and chucking toffee at them even funnier, and for Pete to not only enthuse over the scarecrows but try to have a conversation with them.

It was Prudence's idea to take Pete back to the commune to meet and talk with the others.

Pete had agreed, as long as there were no more comments about his outfit.

Prudence apologized for "the past," even gave Pope and Pot a telling-off when they made snide comments about Pete's underwire.

Which, by the time they said it, Pete—on his third spliff—actually thought was funny. "Let's build a bonfire," he said, "and burn it."

At which point Woody arrived to take him home.

With the wiry thing drying out in Bunnie's airing cupboard, the couch was now a mere couch again, as forgotten as yesterday's takeaway. With no visitors thanks to lockdown, it sat in the TV room, its cushions fading from the sun streaming through the window.

No one used it, no one knew of its past, and Molly, Serenity, and Dolly liked it that way.

Ol' McFadden did attempt to spill the beans once, until the "dementia" word was mentioned—apparently, seeing flying platforms is a sure sign of it—and as Molly, Serenity, and Dolly denied all knowledge, he decided to keep schtum.

The last thing he wanted was to be talked to like folk often did to Dolly.

Instead, he started sitting at the same table as Dolly, Molly, and Serenity for meals, making innuendos about "that night" over mince in various guises and "custard" over various puddings.

It made "dining," as the carers called it, fun.

Sometimes they'd sit in the TV room and, with a hidden half bottle, toast the couch and their adventures in the dark until a visiting consultant did the rounds.

Ignoring the "don't" from Carer One, he, with a jovial twinkle, a coffee in one hand, and his notes in the other, collapsed into the couch.

His jovial twinkle turned to a barked "shit" as he sunk into the soft cushions of the couch, half his coffee on his notes.

After several "hauling out" attempts from Carers One and Two, he, finally standing, pronounced the couch a death trap and ordered an immediate removal. And before the carers could object, he shouted, "Fuck the social distancing."

Don roped in Archie and DJ.

Donned in plastic aprons, masks, and gloves, they rustled up the empty corridor. There was not a soul in sight, no one to make any Identity eye contact. Everyone was ordered to their rooms.

They stripped the cushions, stacked them in the van, and marched back to find Ol' McFadden poised at his door.

"You need a hand?" he said.

The three Identities looked at him in his wheelchair, unsure what to say.

He ushered them closer. "I've just the thing," he whispered, "but don't tell anyone." He looked about and lowered his voice. "Don't lift the couch, just wait until you hear a whistle."

Archie and Don, poised at either end of the couch, made to bend when they heard a whistle, and before they could say "What the fuck?" the flying platform appeared and shot under the couch.

No one saw as it eased the couch into the van, and as Archie slammed the van door shut, the Identities looked up to see Ol' McFadden watching from his window.

They raised a thumbs-up, and the old man beamed the sort of beam that would make anyone feel good inside.

Carter, feet up in front of the telly, was having a good old chuckle at *The Flying Archaeologist* on BBC iPlayer when Archie's van reversed into the yard, causing Charlton Heston to race to the window.

Carter had been staying at Legless's place. There had been talk of her telespraying back, but she was taking her time, holding out till lockdown had finished. There were so many documentaries to watch, and she had heard of museums to visit, many apparently free.

Besides, she liked living at Legless's place. It was the sort of place you could rummage around in forever; all she had to do was ignore Hilda and that bossy Mandy.

She headed outside. Perhaps they had found the Rubik's Cube or the flying platform.

Archie and Don jumped into the back of the van.

She turned to DJ with an "any luck?" look.

"No sign," he said.

The other men nodded.

"That's weird," said Carter. "Flying platforms don't disappear—they're like homing pigeons. What about my Rubik's Cube?"

"No luck," said DJ.

Carter sighed. "Oh. Guess it's all different on Earth."

The Identities slid the couch onto the ground. It looked small and less impressive in the sun.

Sophia jumped up on the couch and started to parade, and DJ stroked her. "It'll make a good bonfire," he said.

Sophia purred.

"We could collect more rubbish," said Mandy. "Have a right good clear-out."

Carter inspected the back of the couch, running her fingers along the dark patch where the wiry thing had been. "Perhaps we could take some samples first, see if there's anything to learn."

Mandy rolled her eyes. "Well, we're not leaving it here."

Carter looked up. "Could we put it in the shed for a few weeks, just so I can do a bit of digging about?"

Mandy huffed. Legless's shed was crammed with stuff; finding space was as easy as peeling Carter from the TV. "The last thing we need is more crap," she snapped.

"Just a few weeks."

Mandy opened the shed; a paint tin clattered out. "We really should sort this out," said Mandy.

"I have offered," said Hilda.

"Yes, but we're not using it for vibrator making," she snapped.

Hilda threw a comradely look at Carter. "Look there—a space over there. Just need to move that old lawn mower."

A shelf came crashing down.

DJ stopped, spying something in the corner. He pulled it out, then, with a beaming face, handed it to Carter.

"It's a metal detector," he said.

"A what?"

DJ ran it across the floor of the shed. It went mental . . . He stopped and looked at her. "You take it across fields to see if you can find anything to, well, dig up."

Carter's face lit up, Rubik's Cube and flying platform forgotten. She took it outside. "How wonderful!" she shouted.

"At least it will keep her from under my feet," said Mandy.

It took some time to wedge the couch into position, and once there, it soon became a home for Sophia and the hens.

A week later, Mandy walked out, caught sight of Legless's menagerie cozy in the shed, and thought, *Bugger the bonfire—a full shed will keep that Hilda from her friggin' vibrator dream.*

Chapter Fifty-Six

COKE BOTTLES

"To be a hero is any Identity's dream, but none more so than Archie and DJ."—Don

A year later, Verruca, clutching a tin of organic pseudo-gold paint, was heading back to her tent, shooing mechanical birds with a resignation that no one would witness.

She lived alone, minus Hilda and Cyborg, waiting for the all clear—virus wise.

She was nearly there.

The funnel was now dismantled, the ground was almost normal, acid-wise, and her kitchen—clear of dead rats—was, on a scale of one to ten, a promising three when it came to virus infestation. Hopefully she would still be alive when it was a zero, when the virus had died off, but she wasn't holding her breath . . .

Her garden was now a shrine in the making.

The statue, care of some decent rope and Planet Hy Man's best tug-of-war team, had been rolled off the quarry.

It took the better part of a day and was such hard work that the powers that be, taking pity on the tug-of-war team, lined up the footman for foot rubs and brow wiping and even joined in the pulling themselves.

"Let's leave it there," H2 finally said, "on its side, like the golden reclining Buddha of Phuket."

H2 had been prepared for such an event.

She assigned Deidre to search Earth via the internet for great statues, even downloaded a picture of the golden reclining Buddha of Phuket to inspire. She was determined to make it work, celebrating the pulling of the Legless statue to its new home with one of Earths' much-talked-about picnics.

"It's the bee's knees," said Beryl. "Takes a sandwich to a different level altogether."

"And we could bring a footy," muttered Legless, which most chose to ignore.

Everyone went home happy, cheerful in the knowledge that they now had a picnic area. Finally, a sandwich made sense.

The last thing Verruca cared about was a pickling sandwich.

As she watched her garden empty, the sun set on the statue's rump, she realized that not only was it covered in effluent, but if she didn't scrub it off soon, it would dry to the sort of hard crust that even scraping wouldn't cure and she was assigned to "deal with it."

Like she didn't have enough to get on with. Hadn't she retired? Wasn't she entitled to, well, putting her feet up?

Painting the damn thing gold was the last straw. It had taken her almost as long as her kitchen took to "de-viral," and no one seemed to care.

Beryl and Legless did visit from time to time, usually with advice and suggestions all unasked for and as stupid as Legless's "footy" comments.

The day of their arrival, they were taken to the room with a view for debriefing, which took months of "collating," as H2 called it.

Legless's memory was not what it used to be. Matching up his memoirs with his memory was as easy as moving his statue, and Beryl wasn't much better.

It seems the transition from Earth to Planet Hy Man was not without its side effects.

The robot's glowing appendages were encased in Coke bottles and strung up on the trees that lined the rocky road from the city to the outlands.

The Coke bottles rendered the appendages harmless and gave a sort of festive feel to an otherwise pretty grim dirt track road.

Sometimes the women spent their happy hour under the lights, camped under the trees. Some even danced, until one broke her ankle in a pothole, sparking a "let's sort this pickling road" campaign.

Which is still in the planning stage—pending funds.

Archie held a meeting for the Identities on Zoom, calling for the hoodies to stop their "mooning."

Many muttered; some, claiming poor connections, signed off.

After all, it was lockdown. They hadn't had a meeting for a year—what else were they to do?

For a while, it was touch and go with the Identities. They felt abandoned by Legless, some even angry. How could they go on if their so-called father figure had abandoned them to shack up in outer space with some woman with a beehive?

Lockdown had led to pent-up frustrations for the Identities.

Without their meetings, they were frustrated, isolated, paranoid, missing the very essence of their existence: pleasuring women, dancing, laughing, and touching.

Some took to drink, others to eating, baking, and watching reruns of *Star Trek* on Netflix—until, that is, Legless came up with the big-screen meetings and digital tours of Planet Hy Man.

It changed their world. Some became vegans, others environmentalists, some bloggers; they had seen a world without animals and sex and realized they had something to protect.

"There is more to an Identity," said Legless, "than pleasuring women," and for the first time, they listened. Some even called him a mentor.

Chapter Fifty-Seven

COLD QUICHE

A year later

Beryl and Legless had taken a day off from filming the outlands and were picnicking by the statue. They talked of Legless's great spaghetti Bolognese as they tucked into Planet Hy Man's answer—a cold quiche-like affair which, as Legless put it, left them wanting.

He belched.

She laughed.

"A little indigestion," he said, "care of Planet Hy Man's soya."

She laughed again, then filled the air with the sort of belch that had birds fluttering from their nest.

Legless roared with laughter, ending with a sort of rolling-on-top-of plop that Beryl didn't resist.

She pulled him down hard onto her, and as the sun rose in the sky, they moaned like it was the first time.

Verruca heard something, but having never been in such a position, she had no idea what it could be. She, leaving her new state-of-the-art greenhouse with a handful of extra-juicy soya-toms, headed back to her tent.

Legless rolled off with an "arrrgh," falling asleep by the big yin, as they liked to call the statue, his hand in Beryl's. Making love in the sun can do that to a person, especially at the age when you hardly expect it to happen.

They had surprised themselves; it was the sort of lovemaking they often reminisced about, Legless wrote about, and Beryl dreamed about.

Legless started to snore, and before Beryl could turn and roll him on his side, he stopped. She, with no idea he was gone, snuggled into his chest.

She leaned her cheek against his nipple, and without even wondering why there was no heartbeat, she closed her eyes.

The next morning, H2 discovered the two of them, twirled about each other like a vine about a tree. They were still warm, with the sort of happy look anyone would want to die with.

She left them there long enough to dry her eyes and call Verruca.

When Hilda heard, she was in Legless's garden tossing leftovers to Gina, Lolla, Bridget, and Bardo.

Mandy appeared and looked at her best pal; Hilda stopped, and before Mandy could hold her, Charlton Heston was there, his head under her hands.

EPILOGUE

When it was OK to meet outside again, Archie, Don, and DJ piled the couch on top of the pile of rubbish for a bonfire.

A great day was planned with dancing, singing, and stories of Legless and Beryl.

All the Identities came, each reading their favorite passage from one of Legless's books, and those that couldn't be there could join online. They even hooked up with Planet Hy Man.

Don arrived at the care home to take Serenity, Molly, Dolly, and ol' McFadden. "You lot ready?" he said to Molly.

Serenity appeared with ol' McFadden, shouting for Dolly.

Dolly was in her room. "I'll be there," she said and turned to her window. She lifted the Rubik's Cube from the sill and twirled it in her hands. For a moment it lit up; then it died.

She pulled a shoebox from her wardrobe, placed it inside, hid the box away, and headed to the others.

She was right about the sun: it charged up the Rubik's Cube, no worries. It would just take time, and she was happy to wait.

Would you like to read more? **_The Other Side Of Planet Hy Man-
Book Five_** will is on sale at your favourite store.
If you would like a sneak preview, then please keep reading.

THE OTHER SIDE OF PLANET HY MAN CHAPTER ONE-WOODY

"Being right is not always welcome" – Pete

"Are you sure there are no other cities? Not even one?" said Woody.

Pete, scrolling through his latest-just-out-of-its-box H-Pad (Planet Hy Man's iPad equivalent, with bells on) didn't look up. Woody waffling on about how the rest of the planet could not *possibly* be empty was nothing new. The first time Woody asked such questions Pete was stumped, now he didn't bat an eyelid.

"There really *is* no one else?" said Woody.

Pete, engrossed in photos of Earth's street performers, said nothing.

"No other cities, or towns?"

Pete sighed, flicking onto pictures of male performers dressed as females.

"You can't just be the only inhabitants? Not even a village shop?"

"There is no such thing as a village on planet Hy Man," said Pete. "Nor a shop."

"What about the market place?"

"That's different," said Pete. "The market is, well..." He stopped, lost for words.

———

Pete had been a PA robot for Mex, an ex-Man Spy, Planet Hy Man's elite. All that changed when he landed on Earth and, well, virtually saved Planet Hy Man, before returning with his new best mate, Woody.

Woody a real live male dwarf from Earth had elevated Pete's status to more than a robot. There had been no male babies for decades and decades on planet Hy Man and the only men left were tall, *anorexic-*lean, ancient, doddery retired footmen. They were so old they looked mummified, which made touching them as attractive as having your teeth pulled with no anaesthetic. Woody, a young man in his twenties, changed all that.

The women watching Earth on their H-pads, swooned like teenage girls when Woody appeared on their screens and almost fainted when he, along with Pete, 'saved their planet'. And when his fresh wrinkle-free smile bounced onto the planet itself, the women were swept off their feet, proclaiming their undying gratitude to Pete for, 'making such a gift possible'.

Woody had been brought up in a family that laughed at him, with a mother who talked about his chances of finding love being as small as his height. Yet here on Planet Hy Man he was a god. Women stopped to admire, watch him walk by. They hung on his every word, like he was the next Buddha. But Woody, unlike Pete, was embarrassed about the whole thing.

And now he was driving Pete insane with his 'there must be others on the planet' questions.

Woody had no plans to live on another planet, in fact he had no plans for anything and was as aimless as misspent sperm, dreaming his life away in coffee shops, pen poised. He dreamt of being Scotland's Terry Pratchett, of his books flying off the shelves at Waterstones, of fans lining up for his signature. All he needed was to finish, well, *start* a book. Now on Planet Hy Man everything was in front of him, he only had to write down what he saw, but one thing niggled him: this planet...there just had to be more than one city, more than one race of women.

Of course *they* maintained they were the only ones, there was none but them living on the planet. They said their ancestors had landed, discovered and civilised the planet, albeit said ancestors killed all the four-legged creatures, all the water creatures, and just about everything that breathed. The women were so sure of this, they didn't even have a name for the city, just called it 'the city' or 'our place.'

But how could they truly know, thought Woody. *When they didn't even have a map, let alone a history of exploration.*

———

"Still the market is a shop of sorts, it still sells things," said Woody.

"It's not a shop…and we would know if there was another."

"How?" said Woody

"We just would."

"What about the emporium, then?" said Woody.

"The emporium is but a mere memory." Pete sighed again. He flicked onto pictures of burlesque performers. He couldn't care less about other cities and people, he had enough on his plate, he had his fame to uphold.

Earth had changed Pete, made him all squidgy with human feelings, tough with ambition, addicted to attention, and sometimes a little jealous.

He loved to entertain the Planet Hy Man women with his Earth stories, such as his 'Edinburgh Festival adventure', what a flapjack tasted like, and the joys of patting a real dog, and Pete loved to do it dressed as an Earth woman. Dressing as a woman was how he blended in on earth and he hadn't stopped since. He was addicted to the swish of nylon, the tightness of a bra and the clip of a heel. As for lipstick, he had a drawer full.

Pete could rustle up an outfits quicker than a robot could pant 'where's my lubricant?', which was just as well because the other robots looked up to him. Within months of his arrival back from Earth they all wanted to look like him. Bras were soon all the rage and it wasn't long before Pete's spare time was spent giving advice on underwire. Spurred on by such success he acquired a small shed, filled it with robotic tailors and started his 'finding the woman in robots' venture: feminine outfits for robots of any shape, any size. They sold off-the-peg outfits at the market, and took measurements in a wobbly tent behind the stall for those of unusual shapes. Nothing was too much trouble for Pete and his tailors and soon he had a following. With good old- fashion marketing he doubled that following.

He wrote books on the subject, and held meetings, claiming that he liberated the robot to 'almost woman status' with a bra, a corset and a wig. And it wasn't long before the city was full of metallic strutting androids done up like drag queens and cheering most women up, even the leader H2 and her sidekicks DBO and Vegas.

Thanks to Pete the city was now a colourful, prettier place – and Pete had more plans.

He wanted to retire from his official role of supporting the leadership team, retire from his work in the scientific shed 'investigating things', and devote all his time to his passion, the 'finding the woman in robots' venture. He wanted to elevate the dress code, create better outfits, dresses for every occasion, clothes befitting his status. To create the corset to end all corsets, maybe even create a troupe of performers and impress not just the robots but the women too.

"What do you think of this?" He shoved a picture of Dita Von Tease under Woody's nose.

It silenced Woody for a least a few days.

Book Five ***The Other Side Of Planet Hy Man*** is out at your favourite store....

A NOTE FROM THE AUTHOR

I hope you enjoyed my homage to corona virus. The world will never
be the same, and I guess neither will Planet Hy Man.
Over the years, I have told many stories, some to a paid audience,
but never have I worn a mask...
until now.
Of course masks have come and gone since the start of the pandemic.
But I can't help thinking we haven't seen the end of them.
You can find me and my groovy blogs at
www.kerrienoor.com
And

 facebook.com/planetHyman

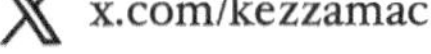 x.com/kezzamac

 instagram.com/kerrienoor

OTHER BOOKS BY KERRIE A NOOR

Planet Hy Man Series
Book 1 Rebel Without A Clue
Book 2 Rebel Without A Bra
Book 3 Rebel Without A Crew
Book4 Rebel Without A Mask
Book 5 The Other Side Of Planet Hy Man
Prequels
Prequel 1 The Rise Of Manifesto The Great
Prequel 2 The Downfall Of Manifesto The Great
Prequel 3 The Legacy Of Manifesto The Great

And Finally
If you love **Rebel without a Mask**. I would really appreciate a short
review., in fact my gratitude would hold no bounds.
Regards and Cheers
Kerrie A Noor